FROZEN DESIRES

Jessie Donovan

This book is a work of fiction. Names, characters, places, and incidents are either the product of the writer's imagination or are used fictitiously, and any resemblance to actual persons, living or dead, business establishments, events, or locales is entirely coincidental.

To Grandma Betty
Your love and influence will remain with me always.

Other Books by Jessie Donovan

Asylums for Magical Threats
Blaze of Secrets
Frozen Desires
Shadow of Temptation

Stonefire Dragons
Sacrificed to the Dragon: Parts 1-4
Seducing the Dragon (forthcoming)

Cascade Shifters
Convincing the Cougar
Reclaiming the Wolf
Cougar's First Christmas (Nov 2014)

The *Feiru*

The Feiru *(FEY-roo) are a race similar in appearance to humans, but with slight genetic differences...First-born children of* Feiru *mothers have the ability to manipulate elemental energy particles, which, until recently, had been undetectable to human scientists. What type of element they can control—fire, earth, water, or wind— and whether their ability is aggressive or healing in nature is determined by genetics. These* Feiru-*specific abilities are commonly referred to as "elemental magic" amongst their kind.*

...As long as the Feiru *continue to uphold the rules and regulations set forth in The Agreement, and hide their unique abilities and existence from humans, they will be allowed to govern over their own kind. If they violate The Agreement, the* Feiru *liaison offices of the various world governments will meet and devise a plan on how to handle the* Feiru *failures...The primary function of the* Feiru *liaison office is to prevent worldwide paranoia, no matter the cost.*

—Excerpt from the *Feiru* Liaison Training Guide, US Edition

CHAPTER ONE

"In 1953, the first-born children of Feiru (FEY-roo) mothers were deemed dangerous by the Feiru High Council. Because these first-born children have the ability to control fire, earth, water, or wind, the council passed a law requiring them to be imprisoned at the age of magical maturity. The council's aim was to keep the Feiru secret of elemental magic from humans...One of DEFEND's primary goals is to dismantle the Asylums for Magical Threats' prison system and to integrate elemental magic users back into our society."
—Excerpt from *DEFEND Rules and Regulations*

After what had happened four years ago, Camilla Melini had never expected to be back in Merida, Mexico.

But DEFEND had sent her here to find one of the Four Talents—legendary elemental magic users who could both heal and destroy—and she wasn't about to let memories of that day from four years ago ruin her chances of success. As long as she kept her eyes open, and was careful, she should be able to get in and out of Merida before anyone from her old life could find her.

And if they did, well, she had a few extra tricks up her sleeves these days that she could use to try to defeat them.

Cam looked over at Zalika, one of two people that made up her team, and asked, "Are we finally on the right street?"

Zalika offered Cam the map in her hands. "You try reading a map in Spanish and see how far you get."

"All I care about is reaching our contact's shop. The sooner we get there, the sooner I can take off this stupid straw thing on my head."

Zalika smiled. "But since the real Cam would never be caught dead in that hat, it's a good disguise."

"I'd rather take my chances if it means I can see properly."

Zalika laughed as they turned the corner. "Jacek is watching our backs, and he'll let us know if he sees anything suspicious."

Jacek was the other half of Cam's team. "He's a good enough lookout, but that's not what I'm worried about."

"You haven't seen your asshole ex or any of the other psychos from your past, have you?"

"No, but that doesn't mean they're not here."

Zalika nodded to the right. "Well, there's the stall. If everything goes to plan, then we should be out of Merida by this evening, and you'll have one less thing to worry about."

She only hoped it would be that easy. "Let's try to be out of here by this afternoon."

Doing the best she could with the brim of her hat hanging partially in front of her face, Cam did a sweep of the area. But nothing seemed out of the ordinary—just street vendors selling food, salespeople trying to entice tourists into their shops, and friends chatting on the street.

Confident that no one was following them, she nodded the all clear to Zalika, and they approached the vendor stall filled with Mexican handicrafts.

Cam glanced over the brightly colored tablecloths, place mats, and purses until she found the section of hand-painted nothing more than a token rank. It was time for Marco to realize she was more than just bark.

She wrenched his shoulders back as far as she could before they would dislocate and said, "Try to pull a fast one on me, and I won't be so gentle next time. Are we clear?"

"Ma'am, yes, ma'am."

Wishing she had someone as straightforward as Jaxton Ward here in Marco's place, she released his arms and stood back. But she wasn't a fool, so she kept her claws extended as a precaution. "What happened to my team patrolling the area?"

Marco rotated his shoulders and nodded behind him. "Jacek's over there, tucked up in a tree. And Zalika, well, let's just say that she isn't as resistant to my smiles and compliments as you are, beauty, and I convinced her to let me try to sneak up on you. She swore it was impossible, and that I couldn't do it. Too bad I didn't make a bet with her, or I'd have some extra fun time money right now."

Cam narrowed her eyes, but managed to keep from making a snarky comment since Marco still had information she might need. "And the danger?"

He gave a half-shrug. "A man was tailing you in Merida."

Dread gathered in the pit of her stomach. She didn't want it to be *him*. "What did he look like?"

"A man with some sort of local indigenous descent, but not much taller than me. Sound familiar?"

She shook her head, her heart calming a little. Marco's description could fit any number of people from her past, but the only person she wanted to avoid at all costs was taller, with different features. "What happened to him?"

"Well, first off, the 'him' in question turned out to be a Shadow-Shifter." He raised an eyebrow. "Do you have any idea why first the female Shadow-Shifter back in the States, and now this man, could be following you?"

Shadow-Shifters were rare, which made this all the more interesting—and dangerous. "No, but what happened to the shifter?"

~~*

Marco was good at reading people. He'd learned it at an early age out of necessity—his special first-born training as a teenager down in Colombia had required it.

So he wondered why Cam had seemed to relax upon hearing that the Shadow-Shifter back in Merida had been of Hispanic descent.

Part of him wanted to bargain, giving information about the shifter in exchange for the information Cam had received from the vendor back in Merida. But if he was going to work with her—and he was, whether she wanted his help or not—then he needed to start earning her trust.

He knew that charming her would only irritate her further, but he needed to keep up appearances to protect his fellow first-born trainees. Not even Jaxton Ward knew the extent of Marco's skills.

After all, Elemental Masters weren't supposed to exist.

He took a few steps toward her. "I chased the shifter to an abandoned shop, but he managed to slip away."

"Somehow, that doesn't surprise me."

He forced himself to keep smiling. Telling her that he could best just about anyone with his elemental magic was out of the question. Instead, he leaned in close and said, "Tsk, tsk, so dismissive. Give me a chance to pin you to the ground, and then maybe you'll revise that statement."

Cam rolled her eyes. "Spare me the flirting. You know you don't have a chance in hell with me." She moved toward her pack and said over her shoulder, "Unless you have something else to share, you can be on your way. I'm sure there are dozens of half-clad girls in bikinis on vacation somewhere in Mexico just waiting to drool all over you."

"I'm afraid I can't do that, Camilla. I'm going to stick around and help you."

Cam paused in tightening up her pack and looked at him. "This is my mission, Marco, not yours. You don't get to tell me what to do."

"Ah, but you see"—he moved toward her until he was close enough that he could grab her if she tried to bolt—"DEFEND sent me here to make sure your mission is a success."

Cam went still, and he tried to figure out what was going through her head. But for once, he had no idea. She wasn't happy, that much was clear.

Then she hoisted up her pack and strapped it on as if she hadn't heard him. She started walking, and Marco gripped her wrist. "Ignoring me is only going to waste time that could be better spent combining our resources and devising a plan."

Cam turned her face toward him, her eyes like ice. "If you'd cared to ask, then I would've told you that I already have a plan." She glanced to his grip on her arm and back again. "You have five seconds to release me before I grab your balls with my claws. Five...four...three..."

He tightened his grip. "You didn't notice the Shadow-Shifter tailing you back in Merida, Camilla. No doubt there are things you've missed or overlooked, and I can help with that."

Cam's eyes went cold, and Marco knew that he'd said the wrong thing.

CHAPTER THREE

Cam clenched her fist, her claws biting into her palm. Marco, like most every other male member of DEFEND, was playing the 'I have a penis so I know better' card.

If he'd approached her in a normal fashion, and had asked about her plans, she would've told him and seen what he had to offer. But she knew from experience that working with men who couldn't see a woman soldier as an equal, let alone a superior, always ended badly. And every moment she spent fighting it out with Marco was time that could be better spent hunting down the Talents.

The rules of DEFEND prevented her from just knocking him unconscious and leaving, so Cam took a deep breath through her nose and hoped explaining things would convince the man to leave her the hell alone. "First off, Jacek would've gone after the man harassing my contact's son if he hadn't seen you do it first. And second, you know nothing about my plans or what intelligence I've gathered. Who the hell are you to judge me? I may be a woman, but I have more experience with missions than you."

"This has nothing to do with you being a woman, Camilla."

"Oh, really? Then do enlighten me, oh 'Great One'."

Marco was no longer smiling. "I have knowledge you need. Most *Feiru* don't know Shadow-Shifters exist, let alone how to deal with them. There's a reason they used to be assassins-for-hire."

Cam watched him closely as she said, "Did you conveniently forget how I took one down in the States? You claim that you want to help, yet you dismiss me without a thought." Explaining had done nothing, so she dug the claws of her free hand into his arm, but the bastard still didn't let go. "If this is your idea of 'help', then I don't need it. Besides, I only work with those I trust, and you're not one of those people, especially since you get distracted at the first sign of cleavage."

He yanked her arm until her face was inches from his. The smile was gone from both his eyes and mouth. "I'm not letting you go until you accept my help. Jaxton Ward sent me here for a reason, and I'm not about to let him down."

Cam shook her head. "You can say that the President of the United States sent you, but I still won't believe you. More than that, we both know this—us working together—would never work."

Marco's expression was dark, but she'd dealt with far worse.

She raised an eyebrow. "Well, are you ready to put aside this silly notion and let me get on with my mission? I have a list of things to do, and standing in the forest with a disreputable man-whore isn't high on that list."

He let go of her and stepped back. But before she could walk away, a whoosh sounded behind her. In the blink of an eye, a stream of ice came around her and continued to circle first around her legs, and then around her torso. She tried to push her way through, but the ice nicked her skin and forced her to stand in the middle of the two twirling rings. With the pack strapped to her back, it was going to take finesse to get out of this situation.

Frozen Desires

Despite his showboating, Marco was a member of DEFEND, and wouldn't hurt her.

Or would he?

The ice stopped moving, but remained suspended in mid-air. She kept her face expressionless as he walked up to her, until only a few inches separated them again, his gaze intent. "If I can help break into an AMT compound and escape alive, I'm more than qualified to watch your back and help search a bunch of Mayan ruins for clues." The upper circle of ice moved, maneuvering under her chin and gently lifting her head up. "Have I made myself clear?"

~~*

Marco kept his mind partitioned; one side focused on maneuvering the elemental water particles in the air, while the other side focused on the reactions of the woman in front of him. Like any well-trained member of DEFEND, Cam was keeping her cool under pressure. But as he tipped her chin up with his frozen ring of elemental water, he saw something he hadn't expected when uncertainty flashed across her face.

Uncertain about what? He'd never hurt her, unless she was an actual threat to his life. He was here to help her.

However, she didn't know that, did she? *Hell of a way to convince a woman you're on her side, Marco.*

While he understood that Cam respected strength, her taunting had stoked his temper, and he'd displayed more of his power than he ever should have let someone see. Despite his childhood vow and all of the years of training with his grandfather, he'd let this woman get to him. In short, he'd fucked up big time.

He couldn't let it happen again.

Few elemental water first-borns could do what he was doing with the rings. But while he couldn't change what he'd shown her in terms of his powers, he could at least wipe the uncertain look from Cam's eyes. If he didn't get in her good graces, he'd never be able to complete the first part of his mission.

And DEFEND needed to be the first to find the Talents.

Determined not to fail, he stepped back and melted the ice before allowing the water to fall to the ground. "I wouldn't have hurt you. I just wanted to make my point. Things will go a whole lot smoother if you just forget my reputation and start taking me seriously."

Even though Cam was now free of his ice cage, she remained in place, watching him with piercing brown eyes. Marco's mother or sisters would be yelling at him by now, or at least they'd be lecturing him on manners, but apparently not this woman. Her look alone said he was nothing but a hotheaded young recruit, unworthy of her time.

Her opinion of him shouldn't matter, but he barely prevented himself from clenching his fist and saying something he'd regret later. Jaxton had trusted Marco enough to send him here, and he wouldn't let his friend and former boss down.

Just as he opened his mouth to try to smooth things over, Cam turned away and started walking. *I don't think so, Camilla.* Marco reached for her, but she tossed her pack at him, throwing him off-balance. She rushed low and tackled him to the ground. She was faster than he'd anticipated, and between one blink and the next, she'd managed to wrestle herself on top of him, the tips of her claws pressed against his neck.

24

FROZEN DESIRES

Cam leaned down and her braid brushed his chest as her claws dug a little deeper into his skin. "I don't trust you, and your parlor tricks won't change that." A drop of warm blood trickled down his neck. "Your bullshit is a waste of my time. This is me being lenient, so unless you want me to take off the kid gloves and show you what I can really do, stay away from me and mine. You'll just slow us down."

Marco wasn't afraid of her threats, or even her claws. He knew an offensive scare tactic when he saw it, and overkill-mode Cam was nothing he couldn't handle. She was going to accept his help one way or another.

If he wiggled his right hand a little, it would face west and allow him to draw on his elemental water. Cam would notice the movement, so he needed to distract her.

She'd accused him of being a man-whore, so he decided to act the part. He had a feeling his attentions would make her uncomfortable long enough to call on his elemental water.

He gazed down at the opening of her tank top and stared at her breasts. They were sheathed in a plain cotton bra, but were full and round, big enough to fill his palms. His hand itched to cup one and feel her nipple bead at his touch, but he pushed that thought away, knowing full well he'd never get the chance.

No, best to stick to his plan of making her uncomfortable, so he growled in appreciation, "At least I'd die a happy man."

Her breath hitched and he took advantage, moving his hand to the west and drawing the elemental energy he needed to hit Cam with enough water to push her off his chest. He rolled on top of her and used his weight to pin her lower body to the ground while he pinned her hands over her head. He then secured them in place with bands of ice.

Cam tugged her arms, her muscles straining in an attempt to break free. She tried to buck her legs to throw him off, but all she succeeded in doing was rubbing her lean body against his. A picture of her naked, toned thighs wrapped around his waist flashed into his mind, but he quickly pushed it away. He wouldn't let this woman use her body to distract him and regain the upper hand.

Marco let his full weight pin her down, the scent of earth and female filling his nose as he whispered into her ear, "If I were really out to get you, you'd be dead by now, Camilla." She moved again, and between the friction and the musky female scent of her skin, it took every bit of control he had to prevent his cock from hardening.

He leaned in closer, hoping the proximity would make her feel more uncomfortable, and said, "You don't trust me? Fine. But you will."

~~*

Cam lay restrained on the ground, the ice around her wrists like cold steel. She tried not to think of how Marco had bested her. It'd been nearly four years since anyone had managed it, and Neena had only succeeded because of her foresight ability.

She needed to concentrate and find an opening to make a move, but she was finding it hard to notice anything apart from the one-hundred-and-eighty pounds of hard muscle cradled between her thighs. She remembered how he'd rubbed up against her when she'd first struggled, and combined with his heat currently surrounding her, she felt feminine in a way she hadn't in a long time.

FROZEN DESIRES

What am I doing? Marco Alvarez was known for his way with women. And somehow, he'd managed to weave his spell over her. Thankfully, he stood up, and with Marco's heavy male body no longer touching hers, the rational part of Cam's mind was back in control. She needed to find a way to shift the situation back into her favor. If she could break his concentration, he might not be able to keep the ice around her wrists in place, and she could get free.

She looked up at him, and waited. The man liked to talk, and whether it was the silence or something else, he finally said, "Whether you accept my help or not, I'll be watching you, Camilla, just as you should be watching out for the shifter." He gave a mock bow, and she prevented herself from striking—it wasn't the right moment. "I know you're going to the ruins tomorrow, beauty, so keep an eye out for me. I'll let you know if I see or hear anything that could help you."

Even though she wanted to yell at him for dismissing her wishes and intelligence yet again, she stayed still and said nothing. She would stick to her plan.

Marco frowned down at her. "While I'm happy you've stopped resisting my help, I find it hard to believe you have nothing to say."

She remained silent, and as he shrugged and turned away, she knew her tactic had worked. She tugged at her ice restraints to maximize her range, and then she lifted her leg back and kicked him with everything she had. As her foot made contact with the back of his knee, she felt a sense of satisfaction at surprising the bastard.

He cursed as he lost his balance. But even as he tumbled to the ground, he must have maintained his concentration, because no matter how hard she tugged, the ice restraints stayed in place.

Shit. That should've worked. Between the twirling ice rings and the restraints, she started to wonder if there was something more to this man than his charm and muscles. His elemental magic was like nothing she'd ever seen.

Marco jumped up and faced her with a satisfied smile, almost as if he was pleased that she'd failed. Again.

Cam decided it was time to ask him point blank about his abilities. "That fall should've broken your concentration long enough for me to get free. Are you going to tell me why it didn't work?"

"Are you going to ask nicely? Considering you tried to slit my throat, and then bust my knee, I think that's a fair exchange."

She made a noise of frustration. "If you think I'm going to be nice to you after what you've done, then you're insane."

He shrugged. "Then I'm not going to tell you anything." He turned and raised a hand. "See you tomorrow, beauty."

Cam watched him fade into the jungle and decided that Marco Alvarez had just been added to her shit list.

CHAPTER FOUR

As Marco rode his motorcycle toward the village of Pistè, his mind kept replaying the fight he'd had with Cam. He was more than a little irritated that she wouldn't accept his help, but a part of him had enjoyed the challenge. He couldn't remember the last time he'd been able to show the extent of his powers. It'd been even longer since his temper had affected his playboy persona act, to show the man he was beneath the façade.

Of course, he needed to be careful. She'd proven to be both smart and observant with her little silence and kick-him-in-the-knee move. He couldn't risk her finding out about the Elemental Masters.

If she knew about Shadow-Shifters, she might just know more of the old, outlawed *Feiru* legends. Maybe even those about him and his friends. He'd adopted his playboy routine to keep anyone from guessing the true extent of his powers. And no matter how much he enjoyed tossing aside that routine, he would never put his fellow Elemental Masters in danger. If that much power fell into the wrong hands, bad things would happen.

He finally entered the village of Pistè, and focused on finding the correct street. He parked his motorcycle, and started walking.

As he passed the restaurants and small shops full of customers, he couldn't help but notice all of the people talking and laughing with one another. They were living their lives unaware that any of them could be the next victim of the attacks he was here to investigate.

A group of unknown arsonists was targeting *Feiru* houses and businesses. All of the *Feiru* victims had one key thing in common, namely that they all had concrete connections to AMT compounds. Until recently, the fires had been amateurish and riddled with mistakes that had ended in innocent casualties, including the death of at least eight children so far.

Marco clenched his fist. *Who fucking killed children?* Just like his cousin Isa, those other children's lives had been stolen, leaving behind only grief for their families.

Anyone who targeted the weak was weak themselves, and since he couldn't rush down to Colombia to help his family find Isa's killer, he could at least find the people responsible for the deaths of the children here.

He flexed his hand and pushed down his anger. He needed to question a witness about a fire that had happened here in Pistè, and it was easier to get people talking if you didn't look like you wanted to rip off their heads.

By the time he reached the restaurant he was looking for, his face and demeanor were once again calm, or at least would appear that way to strangers.

He headed around the back of the building to where the family who owned the restaurant lived. He stopped and knocked on the screen door before saying in Spanish, "I'm looking for my dog, have you seen him?"

CHAPTER FIVE

Five year-old Millie Ward ran after her two older brothers, her little legs unable to keep up. Sometimes she hated being so much younger. "Jax! Gary! Wait for me. I want to see the fishies too."

Garrett, her eldest brother, paused, but Jaxton tugged on his arm. "We can't use the boat if she comes. Leave her."

Millie tried to move her short little legs faster, but she stumbled and let out a shout, sliding on her hands and knees across the grass, her skin scraping against the rocks. The scrapes hurt so much. She couldn't hold back her tears and her nose started running. Then she felt a hand on her cheek and she looked up to see Garrett. He crouched down, pulled her into a hug, and said, "Your crying will scare away the fish."

She leaned back and sniffled. "I can go with you?"

A tissue appeared in front of her face and Jaxton said, "If you stay quiet and listen to everything we say."

Garrett gave her a serious look, but then smiled. "And no wandering without us. Adventure is something to share."

Millie nodded, wiping her tears with the tissue. "I promise."

Garrett stood, pulled her up by her hand, and said, "Then let's go."

The three of them reached the lake, and as her brothers set up their fishing poles, Millie crawled on top of a big rock next to the water and looked down. A baby fish swam by and she touched the surface. The fish darted away, but she saw another and reached for that one. She stretched her arm to the water underneath the rock, but she lost her balance and fell into the lake.

The water was like ice, and she couldn't swim. She sank further down, and panic caused her to take a breath, but instead of air, she breathed in freezing water. Unable to breathe, she tried to scream.

Millie jolted awake, but as she drew in deep gulps of air and not water, she realized that she'd been dreaming about her childhood vacation to the Lake District. She couldn't remember the last time she'd dreamed of that particular near-death experience. Over the years, she'd had too many of them.

She rubbed her face in an effort to wake up and erase the last vestiges of panic from her dream. Millie didn't remember going to sleep, and with a quick glance around the room, she acknowledged that she was some place unknown. After years of working private security, waking up in strange places—while not exactly common—wasn't too much of a surprise. If she could just calm the pounding in her head, she could start figuring out what she needed to do next.

Her symptoms of headache, slight nausea, and dehydration all pointed to a hangover. But she was one of those unfortunate people who remembered everything when she was drunk, and right now, she had no bloody idea how she'd got here, meaning the only explanation for her current state was that she'd been drugged.

Drugged. The word triggered a memory, and the face of Kiarra Melini's brother danced in front of her eyes, showing him right before he'd emptied the syringe of rowanberry juice into her arm.

Despite incredible odds, the man had told her the truth and hadn't killed her with an overdose after all. She wondered where Kiarra's posh younger brother had learned that little trick.

FROZEN DESIRES

Millie rubbed her face again, and tried to clear her mind. She'd worry about the play of events later, after she'd escaped and found a way to contact her brother Jaxton and let him know that she was okay. She only hoped that he hadn't done something daft, like storm into an AMT compound and demand answers. From what she'd seen, Kiarra Melini might've been able to drill some sense into Jaxton's thick head and stop him.

Unsure of how much time she had remaining until someone came to check on her, Millie lowered her hands from her face and looked around the unfamiliar room that smelled faintly of dust and brine. There was a bed, a small table, and a chair. The wall was bare except for a square window no more than a foot across, covered by a dark blue curtain.

Gritting her teeth against the pain in her head, she threw the blankets off and walked to the window. Just in case there was a guard posted outside, she moved the curtain just a fraction to peek out.

To her right, there were jagged mountains in the distance, framed by a bright blue sky, but as she looked up, she saw that her room was only a few feet from a rock face that went up past her line of sight. To the left, she spotted low-lying vegetation and a few scattered trees. Everything on the ground was a bright shade of green.

She let go of the curtain and plopped back down onto the bed. Through the process of elimination, Millie knew she was no longer in Scotland, or anywhere in the UK for that matter—the mountains and vegetation were all wrong. The shape of the mountains, the vegetation, the faint smell of the sea, and the coolness in the air despite it being summer meant she was probably somewhere in Scandinavia, either near the coast or on a small island.

But how? The last thing she remembered was being interrogated and strapped to a table. She raised a hand to her face, but the tenderness and swelling from her earlier beating was nearly gone, which meant she'd been unconscious for at least a few days.

Remembering Mr. Fist-Bastard, her first interrogator, brought back other memories, specifically of Kiarra's nameless brother.

He was the one who'd drugged her with diluted rowanberry juice, or so he'd claimed. He'd tried to tell her via small bits of masking tape on the syringe to pretend the stuff was real since the amount, in full strength, would've caused an overdose and her death. His words had hinted at her freedom, but while she was no longer in the research facility, this was not quite her idea of freedom.

She'd broken out of impossible situations before, and she could do it again. All she needed to do was find out who or what was guarding her, before formulating the next steps in her plan—namely finding a weapon and some money. A fake or stolen EU driver's license would also make crossing the UK border easier.

Looking down at her clothes, she added less conspicuous clothing to her list of items to find. The sweatpants and oversized thermal shirt she wore were more suited to a Sunday staying in than to a woman rambling the countryside. The rambler cover story would allow her to dress practically and be able to hide weapons in the various pockets of her trousers, or under a loose top.

She heard a door open somewhere not far from her room, and Millie searched for something to use as a weapon, but nothing was handy. If she smashed the chair, she could use a chair

FROZEN DESIRES

The tour guide motioned to his watch and told them that they had fifteen minutes to explore the nearby buildings before they moved to the next section of the ruins. Right as the group started to disperse, she had the feeling she was being watched. Her phone was silent in her pocket, so neither Zalika nor Jacek had spotted anything of concern, but Cam's gut had never failed her before. She did a sweep until her eyes landed on Marco Alavarez, who was standing near the trees along the left side of the rectangular stone platform.

He smiled when their eyes met, but she looked away and started for the stairs. In broad daylight amongst the humans, he couldn't use his elemental water tricks to stop her.

CHAPTER SIX

Cam looked up at the top of the observatory building and decided that even if the inner staircase was too dilapidated to use, they should be able to find a way to climb up to the small windows and slip inside. The jungle behind the building would provide all the cover they'd need.

She walked around the outside of the building, searching for an alternate route to reach the top of the platform without using the stairs. She soon ran into a dead end, where the outer wall fused with the observatory building. The wall surrounding the observatory wasn't falling apart like most of the other sections of the ruins, and with the cover of the jungle behind it, should be easy enough to scale without being seen. This was how they were going to get in later tonight.

Cam turned and started to head back toward the stairs to rejoin her tour group when she heard a scuffling sound coming from behind the wall. She extended her claws on one hand and took a few steps back in case she needed to attack and possibly tackle someone to the ground. There were no other tourists in this corner, so she could use her latent ability if either the Shadow-Shifter or the people from her past had found her.

Two beats later, a deeply tanned hand reached up and grabbed the top of the wall, followed by another. She reached with her claw-free hand for the knife hidden under her top just as a man's head popped up into view.

Cam let out a curse. "Why don't you use the stairs like a normal person? We can't afford to draw unwanted attention."

Marco grinned as he pulled himself up and over the wall with a grace that belied his strength. He jumped and landed three feet away from her. "We?" He dusted off his hands. "I was hoping you'd recognize my talents and invite me to join your team. I'd be delighted; although, you might want to ask directly next time, to avoid confusion."

She narrowed her eyes. "You left me restrained on the ground in the middle of a jungle." She took a step closer and raised a claw. "You were supposedly sent to help me, but team members don't leave each other behind, especially when there's a possible danger lurking in the shadows."

Marco shrugged. "I kept watch over you. It was quite a show, watching you writhe on the ground in your wet tank top. I was too far away to tell, but I swear I saw the outline of your bra from where I was perched."

Cam growled. "I don't have time to deal with you and your skeevy comments right now. I'm trying to do some reconnaissance work, so go annoy someone else."

The sudden sound of distant voices prevented Marco from replying, but they gave her the out she needed. If she could reach the safety of the tourists approaching them, Marco would have to leave her alone, unless he wanted her to scream and draw attention. Having him carted away by the police would make tonight's operation easier. Too bad she was required to help and protect other DEFEND members unless they tried to hurt or betray her. And so far, he hadn't done either.

She turned, but when she tried to move her legs to walk, they wouldn't budge. She looked down and saw that her boots were encased in ice. When had that happened?

She looked over her shoulder and said, "You're risking a hell of a lot to get my attention. So say what you have to say, and quickly."

Marco came up behind her, and despite it being at least ninety degrees outside, the heat of his body permeated her tank top and thin cotton skirt. His head was facing her cheek and his breath tickled her skin as he said, "Why do you have to be in overkill-mode twenty-four/seven? I already know you're a badass, but your hot badass self could use my help. I know the area, the language, and how to charm information out of people." He leaned his head around further until it was facing her, his lips a scant few inches away from hers. "You're the only one who seems immune."

His dark chocolate eyes were heavy lidded, and between the heat of his body and his spicy male scent, Cam's pulse sped up. This was a man used to getting what he wanted.

Then she remembered the rumors of Marco's conquests. She would not be one of them.

She cleared her throat and got her heart rate under control. "The simple answer is that I just don't trust you. I've been burned in the past, and with something as important as finding the Talents, I'm trying to avoid any risk that might cause me to fail."

His leg brushed the back of hers, but Cam was no longer under the spell of his magnetism. She kept her posture stiff and unresponsive, hoping he'd take the hint and leave.

Unfortunately, it didn't work and, if anything, he leaned in closer than before. "Then give me a trial period, or some kind of test. If I deliver and prove myself, you promise to stop fighting me at every turn and allow me to help you. If I fail, you can tell me to fuck off and I'll comply."

She was tempted, but she didn't want to make a decision like this lightly.

The sound of a giggling couple drew closer and she poked Marco's arm with a claw. "People are coming, and if they notice the ice around my feet, they'll ask too many questions. You need to melt the ice. Now."

"Not until you give me an answer."

As they stared at one another, the giggling drew closer. Cam couldn't afford to be caught with a first-born right now, leaving her only a few seconds to decide what to do.

He did know the language and probably had more contacts in this part of the world than she did. Playing a clueless tourist only went so far. If she did find something inside the observatory later tonight, the clue could lead her anywhere, maybe even to a remote village deep in the jungle. DEFEND had an extensive web of contacts, but she knew little about their reputations outside of the US or Europe. In the ever-changing *Feiru* world of political allegiances, too many former trusted allies could be acting as double agents.

Her boss, Neena, was one of the few people Cam trusted with her life, and while she hadn't fully endorsed Marco, she hadn't warned Cam to stay away either.

The giggling people would see them any second, so she decided to trust Neena on the issue of Marco, at least for now. "Fine, I'll give you a series of tests. Now, hurry up and release me."

Marco laid a hand on her lower back, sending a jolt through her body at the contact, and the ice melted away. He leaned in close and whispered. "Pretend that you adore me for the next thirty seconds."

~~*

Marco had made a mistake.

It wasn't the fact that Cam was still resisting him, or that he'd had to use his elemental magic in public. No, his mistake had been donning his fake playboy routine. Because trying to be suave and charming around Cam had forced him to touch her again, to lean in and smell the wildness of the jungle mixed with her own womanly scent, to notice the way her shirt clung to her breasts. In other words, he was starting to notice her more as a woman than a fellow DEFEND soldier.

Attachments were dangerous enough for someone like him, with a secret to hide, but on top of that, she wasn't just any soldier—she was one of the few who would never see him as anything more than a young, smooth-talking recruit.

However, he'd been out of options when he'd heard the giggling couple approach, leaving him with the choice of either letting Cam run away from him or pulling her up against his side and treating her as his lover. Getting her to stay put and actually talk to him was difficult, and he needed to know exactly what sort of "tests" she had in mind for him, so he decided to go with the latter option.

He moved his hand from Cam's lower back to her waist, and he hauled her against his side. From a distance, Cam could be intimidating to strangers, but with her frame pressed up against his muscular one, she almost appeared small.

He barely had time to move his hand to Cam's hip to get a better grip before a man and woman in their mid-twenties came around the corner of the building. Cam tucked her head against his side—probably to hide her pissed off looking face—so he smiled at the couple and said in Spanish, "Sorry, friends, my girlfriend and I were just trying to steal a few moments alone."

The man laughed. "No worries. We kind of had the same idea."

The man looked at the woman at his side, and Marco felt a pang of jealousy at their obvious affection. Good thing he had lots of experience hiding his emotions. "My girl and I were just leaving. But if you know of any other little secluded spots we can take advantage of, I'd love to hear them."

Cam chose that moment to lift her head and peek at the couple opposite them. The woman winked at Cam, and unaware that Cam didn't speak Spanish, she said, "Get your boyfriend to take you to a secluded cenote at night. You haven't tried anything until you've been naked in a sunken waterhole with the moonlight streaming down on you."

Marco nearly choked. A naked Cam, floating on her back with the moonlight caressing her breasts, was not the image he needed right now.

When Cam merely stared at the couple, the other man saved him from sputtering some half-assed reply. "Ah, she doesn't understand us. That might work in your favor, my friend, because now you can surprise her. No doubt the sudden 'romance' will score you some extra points."

Marco forced a grin and wink. "Thanks for the tip. I think it's time for me to go look up cenotes and plan a big evening."

The pair laughed and walked past them.

~~*

JESSIE DONOVAN

Cam hated not understanding what had just happened. The man and woman had been laughing with Marco, and her inner control freak desperately wanted to know why.

Still, the experience had only reinforced her decision to accept Marco's help. She loathed admitting it, but his language skills alone would no doubt make her mission easier, provided he was honest with her.

When the couple finally left, she'd expected Marco to let go, but if anything, he tightened his grip on her hip. She gave a quick check to make sure the couple was gone before she hissed, "Let me go."

He merely smiled down at her, which only irritated her more. "Not until you tell me what kind of tests you plan to put me through."

"I need some time to think them through, unless you want some half-assed impossible task, like asking you to take out all of the security guards here tonight without getting caught."

"I doubt even you could do that."

"That's the point." She inched her arm toward his, but he saw the movement, and took hold of both of her wrists. She narrowed her eyes. "I may have agreed to give you a try, but that doesn't give you the right to manhandle me."

He raised an eyebrow. "What if that couple came back? I'm just keeping up my role, beauty."

The stupid, meaningless endearment was the last straw. She needed to find a way to get free of Marco's ironclad hold on her body.

While Marco was strong, both physically and magically, he was just a man, and there was more than one way to get out of his hold without letting on that she wasn't human.

Cam reached out her hand and tickled his side. He yelped and she slipped away. She dashed to the top of the stairs before he caught up to her with a grin on his face. "So it does exist."

She spotted Zalika at the foot of the stairs and put on her hat, the signal that everything was okay. "What does?"

"A non-badass version of you."

"Escape doesn't always require violence." When Marco didn't reply, she looked over at him, but he was just staring at her. "What?"

"You're full of surprises, beauty."

Cam raised her eyebrows. "There is more to women than tits and ass, Alvarez."

"Oh, I know that. But I'm starting to think that you're not as harsh as people make you out to be."

He was closer to the truth than she'd ever admit. "I'm starting to regret my decision to give you a chance."

Marco grinned. "Oh, I'm just getting started. Wait until you see what I'm really capable of."

While she knew deep down that she needed his help on this mission, she was going to make his tests difficult on purpose. The man was too confident by half.

Cam looked away from him and said, "I'm going to finish scouting the location. Meet us three kilometers west of the main entrance at 8 p.m."

She didn't wait for a reply, but started down the stairs.

"Wait, I know how to sneak in. Some of the peddlers told me about the holes in the security."

Chichen Itza was filled with locals selling everything from carved Mayan gods to t-shirts. Since there was a chance Marco was telling the truth, she turned around and went to stand on the same stair as him. "And?"

51

"Your meeting spot is close to where they sneak in and out sometimes. I'll see you there at 8 p.m."

Marco flew down the stairs before she could ask for any more specifics.

Just in case he was wrong, Cam headed down the stairs and rejoined the tour group. She'd learned a long time ago to always have a contingency plan because you never knew when someone would betray you, as her ex-boyfriend had taught her.

CHAPTER SEVEN

Marco stood in the pouring rain and looked up at the observatory, the outline of the building barely visible in the darkness. Cam and Zalika were inside, and while Marco wanted to be there with them, the first stage of his "test" had been to keep the security cameras fogged up.

While directing a few chilled drops of rain against three security cameras every few seconds was mundane, the thin ice shield at his back kept his mind occupied. It'd been more than twenty-four hours since he'd last seen the Shadow-Shifter, which meant that he had to keep up his guard or risk having the shifter creep up on him undetected.

Maybe the shifter had been merely a coincidence and wasn't after Cam or her information, but Marco didn't count on it.

He'd warned Cam to be careful before she left, but she'd dismissed him with a wave of her hand, informing him that she wasn't an idiot. If he hadn't been the recipient of her tickling earlier, he wouldn't believe she'd had it in her.

Playing the part of Cam's lover had been a little too easy. He'd had to charm and flirt his way through the world to keep his true self hidden and protect the others who shared his secret, but as he'd pulled Cam up against his side and breathed in her earthy female scent, he'd wanted to charm her into bed for real.

He could still remember the feel of her hip under his hand, strong and toned. Even now, he wondered what it'd be like to dominate her when she was naked. He wouldn't have to worry about being too rough with Camilla—he had a feeling she would fight it as long as possible, before handing control over to him and enjoying it.

Marco realized where his thoughts were heading, and he focused back on the cameras. Due to his reputation, he was the last person Camilla would sleep with. His reputation had never bothered him before since it had kept people from guessing the truth about his elemental powers, but right now, he was tired of living two lives.

The sooner he put distance between him and Cam, the sooner he could go back to his two-faced existence and forget about getting her naked.

A security guard came into view, and Marco created an icicle in the doorway of the observatory—the sign to stay out of sight.

The guard reached the foot of the stairs and looked up toward the observatory. Cam hadn't mentioned any sensors or internal security cameras, but as the guard started to ascend the stairs to investigate, he had a feeling that Cam had overlooked something.

Not even badass Cam was perfect.

The guard was only a few steps from the bottom of the stairs, so he iced the small pool of water on the next step up. The guard slipped and fell back onto the muddy ground, and while he remained on his back, he was squirming and clearly conscious. Marco needed to create a diversion so that Cam and Zalika could get the hell out of there.

Jacek was standing guard behind the stone platforms that held up the observatory. Marco sent him a text, and quickly checked his phone before brushing his drenched hair over his face, and grinding his knees into the mud.

He made his way to the stone platform, careful to keep to the trees until he was next to the bottom of the structure. He jumped, grabbed the edge, and pulled himself up. He staggered out into the guard's line of sight and sung one of the hit songs he'd heard in Merida, deliberately slurring his words. He stumbled down the stairs, making sure to trip on the last one, and landed on his hands and knees in the mud next to the security guard. Marco swayed a little for extra effect.

The guard reached for something at his side, so Marco quickly said in Spanish, "Can you believe Mexico lost to Brazil in the Confederation Cup?" Marco rolled none too gently until his ass plopped into the mud. "Don't get me wrong, Mexico is strong this year and would kick Colombia's ass in a rematch. But just once, I'd like to see Brazil lose."

The guard visibly relaxed. "The ruins closed hours ago and you shouldn't be here."

Marco gave a one-shoulder shrug. "I remember drinking at one of the eateries on the road into Chichen Itza, stepping out for a smoke, and somehow ending up here." He attempted to get up, but fell back onto his ass. "Are you going to call the cops on me?"

The guard sat up slowly, trying not to wince and show weakness. Marco finally stumbled to his feet and put out a hand. The guard took it, and Marco stumbled backward enough to get the guard on his feet. "No," the guard said. "I probably would've tried to drink away the loss to Brazil too, if I hadn't been on duty. I'll escort you to the entrance and call you a taxi."

"Thanks, friend." Marco followed the guard, careful to wobble on his feet as if he were drunk, and drew the guard into a

Brazilian soccer trash talk competition all the way to the front entrance.

~~*

Cam held herself up on the window's ledge with her arms and watched as Marco drew the guard away. From the way he was stumbling and practically yelling at the guard, he played a convincing drunk.

Out of the corner of her eye, she saw the icicle in the doorway splash to the floor. That was their cue to leave.

Except there was a problem. Cam lowered herself from the window and went to where Zalika was slumped against the wall, massaging her ankle. Cam whispered, "Can you walk?"

"I won't be running any marathons, but I can limp pretty well."

Cam nodded, helping Zalika to her feet. "Lean on me."

Between the two of them, Zalika managed to hobble out of the door. She made it as far as the outer wall surrounding the observatory building before she had to lean against it and take the weight off her ankle. "I won't be able to climb down the rope like this."

Cam had been afraid of that. "Then we'll get Jacek to help."

However, before she could take out her phone, she heard an owl hoot and Cam returned the call. Jacek came over the wall, took one look at Zalika, and said, "Couldn't contain your clumsy side, eh?"

Zalika stuck out her tongue. "At least I'm not afraid of moths."

Cam shushed them. "Jacek, can you scale down the wall with Zalika on your back?"

Jacek nodded and moved so his back was toward Zalika. "Climb on."

Zalika put her hands over his shoulders and jumped. Jacek grabbed her thighs and hefted her up. "Squeeze with your thighs because I won't be able to hold you as I climb down."

Jacek took the rope, maneuvered over the wall, and slowly walked down the side of the first wall, and then the other. Only once the pair had reached the bottom did Cam follow. When her feet touched the ground, she swung the rope upwards a few times until the grapple came lose. She gathered it up and disappeared into the jungle.

She ran and only caught up to Jacek's long legged stride because of Zalika's extra weight. As soon as they were deep enough in the forest and far enough away from the site, Jacek broke the silence. "Not only did Marco save your asses back there, but he also let me know that you two might need some help. I think it's safe to say he's on our side, and we should start to trust him."

Cam probably could've come up with an alternative escape plan, but with Zalika twisting her ankle on the spiral staircase inside the observatory, Marco's solution had simplified things. "Finding one of the Talents is too important to risk on 'maybe' trusting someone. We have no idea what waits for us at the end of all this clue chasing, and I don't want Marco to fail us at the last minute. He's young, with little experience. Do you remember how long it took me to trust the two of you?"

Jacek frowned. "Yes, but you said Jaxton Ward sent him here. That counts for something."

"Do you want to know my true reason for an additional test?" They nodded. "I need to figure out his strengths and weaknesses so I can use him in the most effective way. If I ask

Marco directly, he'll probably say he's good at everything, so I need a way to find out the truth."

Zalika spoke up from Jacek's back. "Well, that kind of makes sense."

"Of course it does. I've been known to be clever on occasion."

She slowed her pace as they approached the area where they'd stashed their packs up in the trees. As Jacek knelt on the ground to let Zalika down, Cam decided to get them focused again. "Besides, Zalika and I found something inside the observatory, and we need to focus on that."

Jacek stood up and said, "Please tell me it was an address and phone number, complete with the first and last name of the person who left it there."

Zalika shot him a look. "That sounds like something from a B movie, right before the star walks into a trap."

Jacek shrugged. "Hey, not everyone is a creative mastermind."

"Enough," Cam said, aware from experience that their banter could go on for hours. "There was a message, but I need help translating it, so we're heading back to Merida."

Zalika raised an eyebrow. "Was it in Spanish?"

"No, in the old language."

Jacek blinked. "As in the old, punishable by life imprisonment if you're heard speaking it *Feiru* language?" Cam nodded, and Jacek continued. "And you just happen to know someone willing to admit they can read it?"

Cam tapped her temple. "Well, I have an idea of where to start." She slung on her pack and said, "Zalika, if you lean against Jacek, can you walk?"

"Sure, I guess."

"Okay, then let's go. But make sure to tell me when you need a rest, because I don't want you to hurt yourself any more than you already are."

As Jacek and Zalika managed to put on their packs and started walking, Cam brought up the rear. Merida was the last place she wanted to be, but hopefully her good luck would continue, and she'd avoid running into *him*. Neither Zalika nor Jacek knew the full extent of her past, and Cam wanted to keep it that way.

She sent Marco a clue via text message. It was time to see if he was as good of a tracker as he was an actor.

CHAPTER EIGHT

Marco walked with purpose down the crowded streets of Merida. Cam had sent him a text asking him to find her, and thanks to his affinity for technology and his web of contacts, he knew her location. And not only that, he'd lucked out—she should be alone, which meant that he could finally talk with her one-on-one.

She'd claimed to have found something inside the observatory, and he wanted to know what.

He entered the main plaza. Music was coming from near the town hall on the west edge of the square. The glow of twilight gave the maze of food stalls and handicraft vendors in the square an almost magical quality. But he didn't give the scenery more than a cursory glance so that he could keep an eye out for anything suspicious—Shadow-Shifter or otherwise. While there'd been one fire here already, this city had one of the largest *Feiru* populations in the area, and if he were the one wanting to make a statement, then Merida would be the perfect place to do it.

While he didn't know exactly where in the plaza Cam might be, he headed toward the salmon-colored town hall. There was a big crowd in front of a group of musicians. That was as good as any place to start looking.

Zalika had been the last person he'd talked to, and she was the one who'd told him about Cam going out to listen to some live music. While he was grateful that Cam's team was starting to trust him, he wondered yet again about Zalika's odd request. *Show Cam a good time. She deserves it.* Sure, Marco had a reputation for doing just that, but after what had happened between him and Cam in the jungle the day before yesterday, Zalika had to know what Cam thought of him. He wasn't exactly high on her list of people she admired.

But whatever she thought of him with her mind, Cam's body had reacted to his touch at the observatory when he'd climbed over the wall and ended up hauling her against his side. She'd leaned into him at first, before pulling away. When she'd tickled him and escaped his grip, he'd wanted to haul her back and tickle her in return. But his chances with Camilla Melini were about as good as him learning Chinese in the span of a week. In other words, it wasn't going to happen.

He'd tease and challenge her as long as they were working together, but then he'd just have to forget her and move on. He couldn't afford to allow anyone to get close to him. Too many other people's lives depended on his ability to keep mum about the Elemental Masters, and he couldn't risk a relationship, no matter how much he might want one.

As he got closer to the crowd, he spotted an open section in front of the building set aside for dancing, with the musicians set up under the ground-floor veranda. People packed the outer edges of the dancing space. Some bobbed their heads while others swayed in place. If Cam had told her team members the truth, and she'd gone out to enjoy some music, this would be the place to go.

He scanned the crowds, looking for Cam's braid and lighter skin tone. Since she had her fair share of experience with blending in—a necessary trait when it came to working for DEFEND— she wouldn't stand at the front of the crowd. He moved to get a better look at the people standing in the middle or toward the back. He'd nearly reached the veranda before he spotted her.

She was wearing a tight black tank top and a flowing dark blue skirt that swayed as she moved her body to the music. Her braid swung back and forth across her breasts in time with her hips. The harsh look she always had on her face, daring people to cross her, was gone. It had been replaced with a dimple-filled smile and crinkles near the corner of her eyes.

This version of Cam was softer, younger, and almost vulnerable. This was the woman who would tickle people to try to escape their hold.

A man approached her and motioned toward the dancing square, but Cam shook her head as she said something to him. The man nodded and left her, probably to find another woman willing to dance with him.

She resumed swaying to the music. Marco watched her another minute, mesmerized by her movements. He suspected she had a weapon or two strapped to her thigh, but he'd bet his own life that Cam rarely let herself smile, let alone sway and just enjoy herself. This was a rare glimpse of the woman hidden beneath. No doubt, there was a reason for her defensive walls, and he wondered what had caused them.

The music ended and the crowd clapped, Cam included. He drew in a breath as she clapped and let out a whistle before grinning with unadulterated joy on her face. If he didn't have a million other responsibilities resting on his shoulders, he would be tempted to see how long it would take before he could make her grin that way while in his company.

Of course, until he found out what she'd discovered inside the observatory, Cam was one of the reasons he was here. And there was no reason he couldn't try to have a little fun with her before he went back to hiding behind a fake face and an even faker smile.

The music started up again and he made his way toward Cam, careful to stay far enough back in the crowd to blend in and not draw attention to himself. When she was a few feet in front of him, he pushed up behind her and placed his hands on her waist. She froze and quickly placed her hand on his arm, her nails close to his skin, ready to slice him.

He caressed one of his fingers against her side and leaned close to her ear, catching the wild scent of the jungle. He smiled and whispered, "Gotcha."

~~*

Cam had a weakness for live music.

After her sister had been carted off to the Asylum for Magical Threats' prison system, or even when her parents had died in a staged car accident, music had been her sole source of healing. Lyrics in particular had often shown her that she wasn't the only one with painful memories or a difficult life history.

Things were not as dark for her as they'd been five or ten years ago, but music still played a pivotal role in helping her calm down and focus. When she'd heard the music drifting through the window of the bed and breakfast, it had called to her, inviting her to relax for a few minutes and recharge her batteries. Zalika and Jacek had assured her they'd be fine, so after a quick change of clothes, she'd gone to the main plaza where the band was performing in front of the town hall.

The large ensemble was playing some of kind of upbeat Mexican folk song. People were even dancing in the square. A man had asked her to dance, but she'd turned him down. Even if she didn't have to avoid drawing attention to herself, Cam had a reputation to uphold. The only dancing she did was in her kitchen.

For now, she simply swayed and enjoyed the music guilt-free. After finding people to help translate bits of the message she'd found at Chichen Itza—split into sections for security reasons—she'd discovered that she couldn't do anything for her mission until tomorrow at the Sunday market near this plaza. She'd also inquired about the Shadow-Shifter, but no one had spotted him since that first day. She'd decided that if she stayed in the crowds and well-lit areas, she'd be fine, so she had gone out.

The song finished, and she clapped. She could stay for one or two more songs before heading back. The market started bright and early tomorrow morning, and she wanted to double-check her strategy with Jacek and Zalika before going to sleep.

As another song began, two hands circled her waist, and while she should've tensed at the contact, the touch felt familiar. She glanced down without moving her head, and noticed that the hands were a rich mahogany color. That ruled out her ex, but not Marco.

She frowned. She knew of his reputation, but honestly, she'd expected better of him in public.

Since she was in the middle of a crowded area full of humans, all Cam could do was lay her hand on the man's arm with her nails close to the skin, ready to skewer him at the first sign of trouble.

One of the fingers around her waist began gently stroking her lower ribcage. The heat and touch was similar to what she'd felt when she'd been pressed up against Marco's side back at the observatory. Cam tried to turn and break away so she could see if it was him or not, but the man's hands didn't budge.

Her options were limited in this crowded area, but maybe she could stomp on his foot with her shoe and disappear into the crowd. She could easily play it as discouraging a drunken man's unwanted attention.

As she tried to determine the best way to cause maximum pain, the man shifted behind her, his breath warm against her ear. "Gotcha."

Cam narrowed her eyes and decided she'd find a way to make him pay for his manhandling, later when he least expected it. "Marco." She pressed her nails harder against his skin, but not quite breaking it. "You found me."

He snorted. "Wasn't that the point?" He kept one hand on her waist, and while never trying to disengage from her grip on his forearm, he sidled to her side. "What were you translating today?"

She looked askance at him. "Who told you that?"

"Only about five different people." He tugged at her braid with his free hand. "Between your scars and this braid, you're too memorable. You need a better disguise."

She had never been a vain person. But people often commented on how women weren't supposed to have scars on their face, as if she'd had any choice in the matter.

She tried to step away, but Marco's grip was like steel. She clenched her teeth, hating the reminder that Marco would always be physically stronger than she would simply because he was a man.

He tsked. "I saved your ass, yet you repaid me by ditching me in the jungle. You owe me. The least you could do is tell me what you were translating today."

He held her gaze, confidence oozing from every pore. No doubt, he expected her to answer him.

She wanted to wipe that look away just to spite him, but she knew that was childish. Despite how much she wished to forget it, he had helped her back at Chichen Itza. Also, he'd passed her second test, proving he was also a skilled tracker. If that wasn't enough in his favor, his ability to find out information in this neck of the woods was a skill she desperately needed to run a better team.

While she would make him understand that touching her freely in public wasn't an option, she was smart enough to see the value of Marco becoming one of her assets.

To ensure his cooperation in the future, there was no harm in telling him the gist of the message she'd found, especially since she was the only one who knew the entire contents of the message.

She looked around, but everyone in the surrounding crowd was focused on either the dancers or the band. She leaned in toward him and said, "There was a message in the ruins, written in the old *Feiru* language. I don't know enough of the old language to translate it, so I had to get some help."

He pulled her close enough that she could smell the mixture of aftershave and male. She took a deep whiff, but then realized what she was doing and dug her nails a little deeper into his arm.

Before she could think of another way to put distance back between them, Marco whispered into her ear, "Beauty, if you'd bothered to ask, you would've found out that I speak more than just Spanish and English." He tipped up her chin with his finger, his eyes lowering to half-mast. "I have a very talented tongue."

Already relaxed by the music, Cam revised her plans to make him a eunuch and snorted. He was hitting on her or at least attempting to. "Does that line actually work on people?"

Marco blinked. He looked like a deer caught in the headlights, confused and not quite sure what to do. "Usually, yes."

She shook her head and dislodged his grip on her chin. "Pick-up lines don't work on me, so don't even try." Aware that she'd let her guard down temporarily, she leaned away from him to help her focus. For some reason, his nearness always seemed to unsettle her.

After a quick sweep with her eyes to ensure no one was listening to their conversation, she asked, "Where did you learn the old language?"

The band struck up a new song. Marco regained his composure and gave her a lazy smile. "Dance with me and I'll tell you."

"I don't dance in public."

He released his grip on her waist and put out a hand. "I was watching you before, and I know you want to. I can lead you through the steps."

Trying not to think about how he'd snuck up on her a second time—she was going to have to figure out how he did that—Cam tilted her head. "Weren't you saying I'm too memorable and that I needed to blend in more?"

"Then do this." He grabbed her braid, tore off the hair-tie, and tossed it over his shoulder.

She narrowed her eyes. "What is it with you and invading personal boundaries? What if someone comes along and I need to protect myself? I can't have my hair flying into my face. You know that, it's Battle Tactics 101."

He gave a half-shrug. "We're in the middle of a crowded square, full of witnesses. If someone were going to attack, they'd wait until we left."

He had a point, but she still didn't like how he'd just assumed he knew what was best. It'd probably worked for him in the past with other women who'd wanted a dominant male, but not this time. Cam was a high-ranking DEFEND soldier for a reason.

Just as she moved to turn away, Marco grabbed her hand and tugged her toward the square. Cam just barely kept from tripping. "I never said yes."

"But you never said no." He swung around, taking both of her hands in his. "Count to four if it helps, but watch my feet at first until you get a feel for the steps. It's a little fast, so try to keep up."

He started moving, and it took all of her concentration to mimic his steps. There were too many eyes on them, and she needed to avoid drawing any extra attention to her or Marco.

She wouldn't let him make a fool out of her. The next time they were alone, however, she would take him to task.

Once she found the beat and had the hang of it, she looked back up at Marco. He had forced her to dance, but he was trapped with her as much as she was with him. She was determined to get some information out of him. "Now, tell me where you learned the old language."

CHAPTER NINE

Despite her protests, Cam was a quick learner. As she moved to the basic steps of the cumbia, her hair slipped out of her braid and fell into soft waves down to her waist. Between her casual clothes and free-flowing hair, she looked like just another young woman on vacation in Mexico. No one watching them would suspect her of having claws and a way with weapons most soldiers would envy.

Marco could almost like the non-overkill side of Camilla Melini.

She soon looked up with triumph in her eyes at mastering the steps, and he nearly sucked in a breath. Her whole face changed with a smile.

But when she asked about where he'd learned the old language, he remembered that he wasn't here to notice Cam as a woman. His secrets were too dangerous to share with anyone, no matter how much he yearned to be free of the burden.

No, he'd do what he was best at—deflecting.

He tightened his grip on Cam's hands and stuck as close to the truth as he could. "I learned the language, and many other things, from my maternal grandfather. Back in his day, in rural Colombia, it was easier to learn the language and not get caught." Marco added a bit more flair to their dancing. "But what I want to know is why you're out here alone despite my warnings about the shifter."

Cam dug her claws into the back of his hand. "I don't need you to protect me. Unless the shifter is mentally unstable, no one would dare show their abilities in a crowded place like this." She was silent a second, but he knew to hold his tongue. He was rewarded when she added, "I'd thought that since you'd seen me in action in the jungle, you wouldn't second-guess my abilities or skills like every other man I've met, apart from Jacek. But I guess I was wrong."

He tightened his grip on Cam's waist. "How do you know he's not mentally unstable? More and more people have been committing violent acts these days, especially toward our people or the first-borns in general. First, a shifter followed you back in the States, and then another one shows up here. I have a feeling someone wants either you or something you know, and they must want it desperately."

Marco continued the dance steps as he and Cam stared at each other. He couldn't tell what she was thinking, and it pissed him off. The stubborn woman and her pride.

Cam eventually tried to pull away, but he tightened his arm about her waist and never broke eye contact. She had a habit of not wanting to talk, and he wasn't having it.

He wanted some answers.

She tugged again, to try to get away, but Marco didn't let go. Her tone was steel when she said, "I need to get back to my team."

"Why are you so defensive, Camilla? The more you tell me, the more I can ask around for additional information. Whatever you think of me, you know I'm good at tapping contacts."

He nearly stumbled when he felt the heat of her hand under his shirt. When her claws pieced his skin, Marco merely raised an eyebrow. As long as she continued to avoid having a real

70

conversation with him, he was going to make it his mission to irritate her until she started talking. She seemed to let her guard down whenever he made her uncomfortable, so if that was the game he needed play, so be it. He gave her one of his sexy-eyed stares and said in a low voice, "Using your claws on me, huh?" He leaned in. "You should know that I like it a little rough, beauty."

Cam blinked, and as the band finished their song, he used the split second distraction to tug her off the dance area to behind one of the posts of the veranda. When she opened her mouth he held her lips together with his fingers and said, "Were the Shadow-Shifters a coincidence or something else? Do we really need to keep playing these games, Camilla, or will you just tell me if someone is looking for you or not?"

She went utterly still, putting Marco on his guard. He'd been keeping an eye on his surroundings while dancing, but he hadn't seen anything unusual. "What is it?"

She kneed him in the balls and he doubled over at the pain radiating from his groin. After hissing a few breaths through his teeth, he managed to look up and squeak, "What the fuck, Camilla?"

She looked down her nose at him. "Just so we're clear, this is my operation. I'm not one of your floozies, so stop trying to undermine my authority. I don't answer to you, and I never will."

He watched her walked away, and while he admired her for standing up for herself, for some fucked up reason his pride wanted to follow her and issue another challenge.

~~*

71

Millie Ward shoveled another forkful of tinned tuna into her mouth and grimaced. Unless it was covered in batter and deep-fried, she didn't like fish. But after what had happened to her drink back in Edinburgh, she wasn't about to eat anything given to her that could be tampered with. That left her with canned vegetables and meats to keep up her strength.

As she rinsed away the taste with a bottle of unsweetened green tea—also impervious to tampering—Millie looked out of the kitchen window to check on her guard. The red-haired man who'd entered her room yesterday had said no more than a handful of sentences to her since then. He went by Mr. Larsen, which in Norway was about the same thing as calling him Mr. Jones or Mr. Smith. It wasn't his real name, but she hadn't expected him to give it.

But he did know hers.

Larsen had pretty much left her to her own devices and spent his time sitting and reading in front of the house. The only time he left the premises was early in the morning, a few hours after dawn. Checking the clock, she reckoned he was due to go out again any time now.

The last two mornings he'd come back with groceries, meaning that there had to be a village or town nearby.

While the aftereffects of the rowanberry juice had passed, Millie was no closer to escaping than when she'd first woken up. From the Norge addresses on the tins of tuna, she'd learned that she was in Norway. As for her guard, she knew Larsen cleaned and oiled his pair of Glocks in the living room each evening.

She'd once asked him why she was here, but he'd merely shaken his head and said he'd share that information later, when she was ready. Whatever that meant.

Frozen Desires

Millie had tried to come up with a list of people who'd want to capture her, but that list was surprisingly short. Yes, she'd foiled a few blackmail and kidnapping schemes over the last few years, but she'd been very careful about her identity, and where she lived. To date, only one person had located her after the fact, but she'd spotted their clumsy attempt to rig her flat with an explosive straight away.

As much as she wanted to think it was because she was fantastic at her job, more likely people stayed away from her because of the person who gave Millie her non-DEFEND related side jobs. Apparently, whoever was keeping her here either didn't know or didn't care about Mr. B.

She was on her own until she could escape.

Procuring a weapon was her first priority. After searching a little both days, she'd come up empty-handed, not even finding a sharp knife in the kitchen. Even without a weapon, she was hoping to make a move soon. Not only would her family worry about her, she was determined to find out what Kiarra's brother was up to.

She heard steps on the porch, and Millie put on her 'confused and not sure what to think' expression right before the front door opened. Larsen peeked his head in and said, "I'll be back. The person watching you has orders to shoot if they think you're trying to escape."

She gave a weak nod, and Larsen shut the door behind him. She took her time finishing off her tuna and tea before she crept to the front door. She had yet to call Larsen's bluff about someone guarding her whilst he was away, but today she would test it.

There were windows on either side of the door, and Millie leaned over to peek out from the side of the curtain. The chair out front was empty, and no one was in plain sight. Because of the sheer rock face off to the right side of the house, the best place to keep watch would be from the top of the house, on the roof.

Walking out the front door would be useless if she wanted the element of surprise.

Millie eased to the floor and crawled on her hands and knees back to the kitchen, where she'd left the can opener on the edge of the counter. She reached up and eased it down before testing the weight in her hand. It wasn't one of those cheap scraps of metal, but rather a good solid pound of metal and plastic that would do nicely for smacking someone on the back of the head.

With her weapon now in hand, Millie slinked along the floor to the small bathroom across from her bedroom. Once inside, she locked the door and turned on both the fan and the shower. While not usually one to waste water, the noise from the combined shower and fan would cover any noises she made whilst opening the small window and crawling out of it.

She eased the small window open, but when it creaked once, she stilled and waited. After sixty seconds ticked by, she reckoned that it was safe enough to keep going. Most people expected women to take long showers, and she'd use that stereotype to her advantage.

She finally got the window open and used the toilet as a step stool to reach the windowsill. Millie positioned her back facing out and perched her arse on the sill. There was a two-foot space between the house and the rock face, and she leaned until her back touched the solid surface. Looking up, she saw that no one was peeking over the side of the house. They could, of course, be lying in wait. But this was her best chance to plan an escape, and Millie wasn't one to shy away from a little danger.

74

Slowly she managed to get her legs out and place her feet flat against the wall on either side of the window. Keeping a grip on the can opener, she placed her hands against the rock wall behind her, scooted her upper body up a little, and then braced herself as her legs walked up the side of the house. There was a good six feet between the window and the roof, and as she repeated the process, inching her way up, sweat started trailing down her back.

When her head was just shy of the roofline, Millie stopped and listened. The shower and fan droned below her. The wind blew against the house and the few shrubs in the yard. Yet she didn't hear any creaks or movement from the roof. Pushing aside her doubts, she stood by her belief that the roof was the best vantage point for an unknown guard.

Keeping her back against the wall, she reached one hand against the side of the house, and then another. She shimmied up a few inches, ignored the rock scraping against her skin through her thermal t-shirt, and peeked over the top of the roof. Sure enough, there was a woman sitting cross-legged toward the front, watching the front—and only—door.

There was about ten feet between her current location and the woman. Millie was a good sprinter, but not that good. She needed the woman to either leave her post or come closer to Millie's location.

She tried to think of a way to create a diversion for the woman to investigate when the woman moved her head enough that she could see her profile and Millie smiled at her good luck. She knew that fair skin, button nose, and mousy brown ponytail anywhere. It was her sometimes friend, sometimes enemy Petra Brandt.

She remembered spotting Petra and her brother back at the pub in Edinburgh, on the night Millie had been taken. It all seemed too much of a coincidence that Petra would show up here, too. At least Millie knew a little about her adversary.

If Petra was doing this job for money, Millie could easily match it. The real question, however, was whether Petra would wait long enough to listen to her proposition or shoot her on sight.

Larsen would never have left Millie alone and unrestrained if Petra had shared the extent of Millie's skills with him. An average person might think Petra had done it out of compassion, but in her experience, Petra never did anything without a self-serving reason behind it.

Her best option was to approach Petra, keeping the can opener tucked into her waistband, and see how it played out.

It took a few seconds for Millie to hide her would-be weapon under the billowing folds of her shirt. After taking a deep breath, she pulled herself up and said, "Morning, Brandt."

As expected, Petra turned around with her gun pointed straight at her. Petra didn't look the least bit surprised by her sudden appearance. Quite the contrary, she looked as if she'd expected it. She nodded. "Ward."

"Are you here watching me as part of a job or are you doing it as a favor?"

"A favor."

Well, damn, that just made all of this much more delicate. "Then why haven't you told your boss who I am? You knew full well that I'd try something like this."

Petra lowered her gun and said, "Because I need your help."

Millie frowned. "Doing what exactly?"

Petra kept the gun in her hand but took a step toward her. "Something that Dominik can't help me with."

"What could you possibly not entrust to your twin brother?"

"I love my brother, but I can't risk him telling his new boss about the person I want to help."

She was intrigued since the Brandt twins were well known for always working as a team. "I can't do anything until you tell me more about what you're asking, and what's in it for me."

Petra eyed her for a few seconds and finally said, "Tell my brother any of this, and I'll make sure you stay locked up for good." Millie was unimpressed at the threat and merely nodded. Petra continued. "I need to get an old friend of mine out of an AMT research facility, and if you agree to go with me, I'll help you escape Larsen's house."

"But why me?"

"I never thought I'd say this, but you're good at what you do."

"You're nearly as capable as me."

"I'd say better than you, but regardless, I need a second person since I can't let this old friend know I'm behind the rescue."

"Why?"

Petra hesitated and Millie saw a flicker of emotion she couldn't name, but it was gone as quickly as it'd come. What would unsettle a mercenary with a reputation like Petra Brandt?

Petra's face hardened again and she said, "Because he thinks I'm dead and I need it to stay that way."

Millie knew very little of Petra's past before she'd started taking mercenary work, but even so, the request was an odd one. "Let's say that I agree to help you, and you get me away from here, what happens to me after the fact? How do I know you won't give away my location once your rescue mission is complete?"

"If you'll consider my offer, I'll give you an act of good faith tomorrow morning by allowing you to contact your brother Jaxton."

Petra was going to help her escape and contact her brother? Millie narrowed her eyes. Something was up. "Is this facility in the middle of a bloody jungle, with a moat of piranhas that I have to swim across or something?"

The corner of Petra's mouth rose. "I'd like to see you try that, but no, it's not. It's no more dangerous than anything you've done in the past."

Considering she didn't have any other options at the moment, she'd have to take Petra's offer. But not before she'd had some time to think about a detailed list of requirements. "If you hold up your end with the call to Jax, and promise to keep me in the loop with information for the entirety of the assignment, I'll promise to think about it."

"Fine, Ward. Come back here tomorrow morning, fifteen minutes after Larsen leaves."

CHAPTER TEN

The next morning, as Cam reached Santa Lucia Park, she resisted the urge to curse Marco Alvarez for the tenth time.

The message she had translated in pieces said, *"In Merida on Sunday, at the park full of big heads, find the old Spanish coins and ask for the Great-Tailed Grackle."* While she'd put together that the "park full of big heads" was Santa Lucia Park with its collection of busts, she wondered about the rest of the message. Considering she'd done the translating in bits, and not together, she could be following a literal translation when she should be following a figurative one.

If only Marco hadn't crossed the line last night, she would've asked him to take a look at the message and voice his opinion. But shushing her lips had been the last straw, and without thinking, she had sent him to his knees.

Men, in her experience, expected a woman to sooth their hurt ego when needed, but Cam had never been very good at doing that. She held everyone to the same standard as herself, expecting people to buck up and move on. Because most people misunderstood the reasons for her attitude, the rumors within DEFEND had built up her image as a ball-busting ice queen. While it hurt on some level to think that was how people saw her, unless someone spoke directly to her face, she ignored it.

For exactly that reason, it had taken her years to find a team she could work with. Jacek and Zalika understood her brusque manner for what it was—high expectations. She would never ask someone to do something that she wouldn't do. In return for their dedication, Cam would lay down her life for Jacek and Zalika. And deep down, she knew they would do the same.

Marco, on the other hand, was a wild card that she didn't know what to do with. He wasn't her superior, nor was he her subordinate. Colleague might be the closest description, but even that seemed off. Few of her colleagues had ever tried to provoke her, let alone trap her into a situation where she had no choice but to comply, like Marco had done with the dancing last night.

He was far more intelligent than she had initially thought. Maybe she should just refer to him as a nuisance.

Drumbeats started up in the distance, but she ignored their call and focused on the small collection of stalls in Santa Lucia Park. There were handicraft and clothing stalls, secondhand books, and even a blanket full of Mexican antiques. But nothing to do with coins.

Because it was still early, there were a number of empty tables she presumed would be filled later. She decided she had time to head toward the crowded main plaza to check in with Jacek and Zalika before she came back to see which vendors filled the vacant spots. Santa Lucia was the only park she knew of in Merida with "big heads." If one of the empty vendor tables ended up not being a coin booth, she might have to grit her teeth, find Marco, and ask about the correctness of her translation.

She exited the small park and walked out onto one of the streets that were closed to car traffic on Sundays. This section of Merida was part of the historic district, and the old colonial buildings made her wish she could be a tourist for a day. Truth be told, she couldn't remember the last time she'd taken a vacation. DEFEND was her whole life.

Yet she couldn't imagine it being any other way. Her sister was now a member too, which meant she might actually have a chance to get to know Kiarra again.

Cam had made a vow upon joining DEFEND that she would find a way to be reunited with her siblings if it killed her. She'd succeeded with Kiarra, but she wasn't so sure if she could get her brother Giovanni out of James Sinclair's influence.

After their parents had died fourteen years ago, their maternal uncle James Sinclair had adopted her brother Giovanni. James Sinclair had one purpose in life—to accumulate enough power to change the *Feiru* way of life to his liking. Based on the rumors she had heard, Sinclair wanted to find a way to end elemental magic, no matter how far-fetched that idea sounded.

She only hoped that her brother wasn't too indoctrinated with Sinclair's views, and he could still be swayed to Cam—and DEFEND's—way of thinking.

Once she had a minute, she would call Kiarra and check in with her. She'd put off calling her sister for various reasons—mainly because she was afraid Kiarra would believe the rumors inside DEFEND about Cam—but it was time to step up and face her sister's questions.

Cam reached the edge of the main plaza and did a quick scan. Food carts and ad-hoc tent restaurants lined the outer edges, with a maze of vendor stalls in the actual plaza itself. There were some musicians belting out songs, and a few people were even dancing at the edge of the crowd. One couple was dancing steps similar to what Marco had taught her the night before, and she itched to join in.

She nearly started at the thought. She never danced in public. Giving her head a shake, she walked on.

Between deciphering the clue and keeping an eye out for any possible enemies—such as the Shadow-Shifter—Cam needed to push her experiences from last night out of her mind. She wouldn't let Marco distract her. He'd been secretive about learning the old language, and she wondered what else he was hiding from her.

Her cell phone vibrated and she reached into the pocket of her skirt and took it out, only to find a message from Marco: *Look behind you.*

Scowling, she looked over her shoulder and saw Marco waving at her. She was just about to turn back around and ignore him when she noticed a tall, blond man off to the side. Cam's heart skipped a beat, and she froze.

It was *him.*

Four years had passed since she had last seen him, but Cam would recognize Richard Ekstrom anywhere.

Richard caught her eye and a look Cam knew all too well—one of steely determination—came across his face. That look had never bode well for the man's targets in the past, and no doubt, it meant trouble for Cam too.

Richard smiled and moved toward her. However, just as Cam turned to flee, a warm hand cupped her elbow and urged her to go left. She looked over and saw it was Marco.

Marco leaned down to her ear and whispered, "Come with me. I know where we can go."

She was still battling the shock of Richard's appearance, so her usually sharp mind barely said, "Fine," before letting Marco guide her down a side street.

Despite all of her precautions and careful maneuvers over the years, her past had finally caught up with her.

FROZEN DESIRES

~~*

Because Cam had never shared with Marco what she'd found inside the observatory at Chichen Itza, he had spent the morning tailing her through the crowded streets of the Sunday Market, waiting for the most opportune time to approach her. She consistently seemed to restrain her temper in public. He waited for her to exit the most crowded area of the main plaza so that they could have some semblance of privacy.

He'd finally found the perfect location on one of the streets, where a few men were banging out a song on their drums, and he sent her a text message. He upped his charm, grinning and waving when she looked up, signaling that he was far from intimidated by her attitude the night before. She spotted him and made to turn back around when her eyes latched onto something and froze.

He followed her gaze and saw a tall, touristy looking man with a towel tied around his neck. Marco didn't like the look on the man's face, so he turned and weaved his way to Cam's side. When she let him guide her down the street with barely a word, he knew instantly that something was wrong.

Once they were far enough away from the main plaza that Marco could easily keep track of the thinner crowd of people around them, he sent a quick message to Cam's team, put his phone away, and said, "Did you want some ice cream?"

At that, Cam frowned up at him. "Ice cream?"

He nodded toward a nearby stall. "This place has the best in the city, and my *mamá* always said that ice cream helps calm your nerves." Cam opened her mouth, but Marco beat her to it. "You look like someone just walked over your grave, so don't dare say I'm wrong."

Cam dislodged her elbow from his hand. "I was going to say that I don't like sweet things."

He snorted. "Why does that not surprise me?"

Cam had been looking around their surroundings for the man she had seen, but his comment merited a glare. "If you make a crack about how only sweet people eat sweet things, I will punch you in the face."

His aim had been to distract her, and while he had succeeded, Marco decided that he was having too much fun to stop now. He purred, "While sugar is nice now and again, I prefer my food with a little bite."

She rolled her eyes before focusing back on the people around them. "Why do you make everything a joke? The man back there is dangerous, and we should be finding a place to hide."

Interesting. Any person who scared Cam enough to run must be dangerous. He dialed down his smile and raised an eyebrow. "I told you that I know somewhere we can go, but first, who is he and why should I be worried about him?"

She stared at him for a few seconds, but Marco stared right back. She finally let out a sigh of resignation. "If you stop interrogating me long enough to get somewhere safe, I'll tell you all about him."

Cam agreeing to anything was rare, and he wasn't going to give her time to change her mind. "I have two locations of where we can hide, but I need to know if he's human or not."

"He's not."

"Okay, then. Follow me." He started walking and Cam had to jog to catch up. As he weaved through the streets of downtown Merida, he wondered about the man who could scare someone like Camilla Melini, a woman with steel-like claws and a kick that could send any man to his knees.

He had seen a flash of terror on Cam's face before he'd led her away, giving him a glimpse of why she acted the way she did. Something bad must have happened between her and the blond man. Her gruff manner was probably a type of shield she used to avoid getting hurt again.

The thought of that blond man hurting her didn't sit well with him.

While she would never say so, Marco reckoned that Cam needed an ally. He may be impatient to focus on his other mission, but until they had found the underlying cause of the clue from the observatory, he would watch her back and help her in any way that he could. He only hoped that the fires wouldn't claim any more victims in the meantime.

~~*

Cam struggled to keep up with Marco's strides. The man walked with purpose and efficiency. If only he would apply himself the same way to his work.

She didn't like blindly following him through the streets, but Marco knew Merida better than she did. Cam was helpless to do anything but see where he would take her, especially since she couldn't get away from Richard Ekstrom fast enough.

While looking over her shoulder for Richard had become second nature, after four years of working with DEFEND, Cam had thought she'd seen the last of him.

Hell, she didn't even know if he still worked with the Federation League—the old anti-AMT fringe group they'd both worked for in the past—or not. Considering what she knew of

Richard's capabilities, he could be a for-hire assassin. While unlikely, he might even he be here on an assignment to take her out.

No, she didn't think that was it. She did not have any sort of vengeful enemies. Judging from the way he'd looked at her back near the plaza, it left one thing—Richard wanted to use her for something.

Hopefully, she never found out what.

Marco stopped and she had to check herself to keep from smacking into his back. He looked up and down the street, but it was empty. Half of the houses looked dilapidated and unfit for habitation. No doubt, this part of town was a good place to hide.

He looked down at her and said, "Take a hold of my bicep."

She raised an eyebrow. "Care to explain why?"

"So you don't get lost or try to run away. Not that I'd mind if you wanted to admire my muscles while you're at it." He winked. "I'm about to use my god-like powers to save your ass again."

While she was anxious to get away from Richard, she was also curious to see some of Marco's other tricks. She still hadn't figured out why he had such strong control over his elemental water.

Of course, she couldn't pass up warning him. "Any funny business, like back in the jungle, and your dick won't be in any shape to come out and play anytime soon." She ignored his chuckle and wrapped her hand around his bicep, letting her nails graze his skin. His muscles bunched and flexed as he put his hand out in position to the west, and she waited to see what he'd do.

The air around her feet became extremely humid, and warmer, before a sheet of ice started to form a few feet over their heads. As the ice expanded and grew, a fog cloud started to form somewhere in between the ice and the street. She watched as the fog thickened to the point where she could barely make out Marco's form next to her.

She'd seen first-borns use their elemental abilities before, but never anything like this. She couldn't help but whisper, "Are you sure you're not a Talent?"

Marco's arm tensed under her hand, and for once, she wished she could see his face. "No, now shush. I'm trying to concentrate."

She'd allow that comment to pass, only because she needed his help to escape Richard. While she could use her speed or one of her other secret tricks, she much preferred someone else using their abilities. That way she could keep hers a secret for as long as possible. Marco knew some of them, but not all.

When she could see no more than a few inches in front of her face, she felt Marco's hand reach over and push against her hip. "Move behind me and put your hands on my waist."

His hand lingered, his heat soaking into her skin. As she stepped behind him and his hand fell away, she tried not to think about how his touch affected her. But then again, he'd probably perfected the technique with countless other women. That thought kicked her head back into the game.

As soon as she placed her hands around his lean waist, Marco started moving and it took everything she had to let him lead her along rather than just push him aside and blaze a path herself.

Chapter Eleven

As Marco guided Cam out of the second fog trap he'd created, she readjusted her hands on his waist, and he fought the urge to cover her hands with his own. For someone so strong, Cam's touch was light, almost delicate. He wondered what it would feel like to have those deceivingly delicate-feeling hands roam his body before gripping his ass. Then he checked himself, banishing the image. The last thing he needed was for Cam to see him sporting an erection.

Despite what people thought of him, Marco rarely bedded any of the women he flirted with. Even now, his grandfather's words filled his head: *Make people love you so they'll never suspect what you're capable of doing, but remember never to allow them close enough to discover the truth.* While Grandpa Herrera's words had never failed him in the past, Marco wished at times that he could ignore them.

Hell, there were days he wanted to forget everything his grandfather had ever taught him and live life as a normal person.

Of course, that would never happen. The best he could hope for was to find someone who would listen to his biggest secret and understand the need to keep it.

The fog cleared, and like before, Cam removed her hands straight away and moved to walk beside him. Using his elemental abilities was always a risk, but part of him wanted to create more fog so Cam would have to hold onto him again.

Marco took the lead and they weaved through the side streets of Merida in silence. Eventually Marco stilled, cocked his head to the side, and strained his ears. After an hour of zigzagging through the streets, he was pretty confident that the tall blond man was no longer following them. Rather than risk meeting with Cam's teammates and leading the blond man to them, he was going to take her somewhere the man couldn't go. Only then would he be confident they were safe.

He looked to Cam and raised his eyebrows in question. Since they'd done this a number of times on the way, she knew he was asking if she heard anything. Judging from what had happened back in the jungle two nights ago, her hearing was far keener than his, probably due to whatever latent ability she'd inherited. Marco knew some of the old stories and legends, but he had yet to figure out what latent abilities she actually possessed.

Cam squinted her eyes as she looked one way and then the other. Her expression could only be described with a word he'd never thought he'd use for Camilla—adorable—and contrasted greatly with her threat to abuse his cock. Not that he wouldn't mind a little abuse, just not the kind that involved steel-like claws and a temper.

Okay, maybe a little bit of claws and temper.

Whoa, boy, you need to tone that shit down. Hundreds of women had thrown themselves at him over the years, but he'd only been tempted a handful of times. So why was he having such a hard time ignoring the one woman with whom he had no chance?

Careful to keep his expression light to hide his thoughts, he met her gaze again and she shook her head. "I don't hear anything unusual."

He was putting a lot of trust in Cam's words, but the terror he'd seen on her face earlier had been genuine. That was good enough for now. He motioned down the street and said, "Then follow me."

Marco went down one last street, and checking to make sure that Cam was right behind him, entered a fairly nondescript two-story house. The door led into a hallway with another more solid door at the end. Marco knocked out a few beats and a panel slid open. A pair of brown eyes studied both him and Cam.

This wasn't the first time he'd visited this place. He knew nothing would happen until someone gave the correct pass-phrase, so Marco said in Spanish, "Take what I want and never forfeit."

The small panel slid closed, and as the sound of the door being unlocked filled the hallway, he stole a glance at Cam and said, "Follow my lead and try not to say anything."

She opened her mouth but the door opened and cut her off, revealing a stocky, muscular man with close cropped hair. The man nodded them inside and Marco slapped the man on the shoulder. "Thanks, Garcia. If someone comes looking for us, keep them out and I'll buy you a drink later."

Garcia nodded, and Marco pulled Cam inside. A few feet in, he stopped to scan the empty booths. His usual booth in the far corner was empty, but before he guided Cam over, he noticed that she was being unusually quiet. Since she'd never really followed his orders before, he glanced at her face to see if something was wrong, and saw a mixture of curiosity and heat. Following her gaze, he saw the couple in the corner having sex with their clothes mostly still on.

He imagined him and Cam in the couple's place, but quickly pushed the image aside. He had a reputation here, and if he kept standing in the middle of the room, daydreaming, he would blow his cover.

FROZEN DESIRES

He grabbed Cam's hand and yanked her toward the far corner.

~~*

Cam had been about to tell Marco to go fuck himself when the solid door in front of them had swung open, revealing a man who could have been an ex-Marine. Marco seemed to know him, said something to him in Spanish she couldn't understand, and then pulled her inside the building. When he stopped again in the middle of a room to look around, she let her eyes roam over her new surroundings to determine where Marco had brought her.

Men and women were playing poker off to the side, a rowdy bunch of men in soccer jerseys were arguing near the bar, and various couples were necking in the shadows of the booths against the wall. Her eyes stopped on one couple in particular, where the woman was rocking on the man's lap, and Cam swore she saw the undone buckle of his belt glinting off to the side. Would people really have sex like that, out in the open, where anyone could see them?

At first, the thought of doing something like that had mortified her, but as she watched the couple, their exhibitionism started to intrigue her.

While she knew her way around a sniper rifle blindfolded, or could break into most high-security compounds without getting caught, Cam was naive when it came to relationships and sex. She'd focused solely on her work for the last four years, determined to be the best. And before that, she had spent most of her time running from the authorities with the Fed League. She'd missed the experimental years of her early twenties. Instead, she had spent them with her ex, and she couldn't remember him ever looking at her like the man in the corner was looking at the woman rocking against him—like the woman above him was the most desirable woman in the world.

Marco tugged her along again, and she came back to the present. She'd had enough of him always trying to take control.

She barely resisted a growl, and said, "Just because I let you lead me around earlier doesn't mean you have permission to do it whenever you want. From now on, ask me first."

Someone barked something in Spanish, and Marco replied with a grin before he drew her against his side. The other person laughed, and Cam wondered what the hell was going on.

Before she could ask, a damp chill brushed against her neck, and Marco gave a nearly imperceptible shake of his head. In the blink of an eye, his face softened and he looked at her as if she were the most precious thing in the world. "I thought we'd settled our spat, beauty." Marco slid into the most isolated booth, one partially hidden behind a column, and pulled her onto his lap. She squeaked in surprise as she landed, and Marco put his arms around her. "It's time to make up."

She narrowed her eyes. Aware that people were probably watching them, she lowered her head to his ear and hissed, "What do you think you're doing? Something is going on that you're not telling me."

His arms tightened around her and she felt his cheek against hers. She tried to ignore the warmth of his skin and the pleasant smell of his male scent mixed with aftershave, but failed. Marco whispered into her ear, "I'm making sure you stay put long enough to tell me who that man was back there."

She tried to lean back, but Marco's arms didn't budge. "I said I'd tell you, and I will. Now, let me go."

She felt his head shake against hers. "I get a lot of information here, and if I don't keep up my reputation, they'll lose their trust in me. I need you to pretend to be my woman for the night."

His answer surprised her. She'd thought he'd just wanted to cop a feel, not worry about a cover ID. For all she knew, he could be lying. "Out of all the places you could've taken me, you took me to a bar where people are having sex in front of everyone?"

"This is one of the last places that man would look for you, am I right?"

Cam stilled and forced herself to say, "Yes."

Marco chuckled and the vibrations tickled against her skin. "Stop acting so surprised, beauty, and you might finally notice some of my talents."

Maybe she'd judged him too harshly. She still thought he was a flirtatious man-whore, but he seemed to be a man-whore with a brain. "I'm big enough to admit that bringing me here was a smart move. And I can understand hiding your cleverness from strangers, but why do you continue to act as you do around others in DEFEND?"

Marco leaned back and looked her in the eye, his voice low. "Because when you act as people expect you to act, Camilla, it makes you forgettable."

Her brows knitted. "And that's a good thing?"

"It is for someone like me."

"What is that supposed to mean?"

Marco's eyes darted to something behind her and back. "Sorry to ambush you, but I need you to play along."

Before she could reply, he cupped the back of her head and kissed her.

Chapter Twelve

Giovanni Sinclair exited the Austin MTR station in Hong Kong, and headed toward the tallest building in the city—the International Commerce Centre. That was where they were keeping the elemental earth first-born he was here to investigate.

Back in the UK, Dr. Ty Adams had made this visit possible. Even now, Gio was surprised that his adopted father, James Sinclair, had allowed him to come. With Millie Ward pronounced dead and his older sister Kiarra now free and on the run, anyone would question his effectiveness. Gio would just have to be more careful whilst in Hong Kong, especially if he wanted to continue having access to the confidential records of the Asylums for Magical Threats.

While his assignment was to observe and study a particular elemental earth first-born and report the scientists' findings back to his father, Gio had additional goals. From what little research he had done on the subject, he knew that there was a large pediatrics facility hidden in the mountains of mainland China, and he intended to earn access to it. He knew the AMT scientists were breeding first-borns inside their compounds and subsequently shipping off the children to special pediatrics facilities.

However, the records were quiet about how they treated the children once they arrived. He was determined to find out what happened.

FROZEN DESIRES

The tricky part would be keeping the information from his father. James Sinclair hadn't become powerful and influential with the *Feiru* High Council without being careful and overly cautious. No doubt, his father had someone watching his every move. He would have to find a time in private to call his old friend from university and ask him how to lose a tail.

He arrived at the foot of the ICC building and looked up. The building was 118 stories high, and he wondered if the height of the building would affect a first-born's elemental earth magic. He had no idea what it would take to move the earth up ninety stories to the research wing where the first-born was being held. The video clip he had seen earlier, that had shown the first-born using her elemental earth magic without putting her hands in the right direction, had been recorded from her time at a different facility.

Gio entered the lobby. He gave the wide-open space and modern art pieces a cursory glance before he went to the elevator and pushed the button for floor ninety. From what little he'd been told, the AMT Oversight Committee held floors ninety, ninety-one, and ninety-two. The nearest AMT compound was in the Ningxia region, but the facility in Hong Kong served as a special research post. No one had wanted to tell him what they did here exactly, but his visit today should rectify that problem.

The ride to the ninetieth floor was surprisingly short, and when the doors opened, a woman wearing a lab coat greeted him. This woman had to be Dr. Carlie Chan. Gio stepped forward and said, "Dr. Chan."

She nodded. "Mr. Sinclair. Right on time, follow me."

The woman turned, started walking down the hall, and Gio could do nothing but follow. From her tone, he could tell that she thought he was a waste of her time. Good, maybe that meant she would avoid small talk and take him straight to the first-born he'd seen in the video.

Chan stopped at a door, slid a card through a panel, and entered a code. The door slid open, and without looking back, she entered. Gio crossed over to the door. After witnessing the abuse he'd seen at the other facility back in Scotland, he braced himself for whatever lay on the other side.

There was a woman restrained to a bed, her head lolling back and forth. It was obvious that she was under the influence of some kind of drug. Of course, after witnessing what the woman could do—use her elemental earth magic without putting her hand in the direction of elemental earth energy—Gio couldn't fault the researchers for doing it.

The first-born woman's black hair was chopped short, her skin pale, and her almond-shaped eyes half-lidded in a drug stupor. The woman at least looked physically unharmed.

But he'd only recently discovered that all first-born *Feiru* went through some kind of experimentation, and he would have to dig a little deeper to find out if she'd undergone her own set of experiments. The drugs sedating her could be masking the experiments' aftereffects.

No one had wanted to tell him anything over the phone or via email. It was time to find out some information. Gio looked at Dr. Chan and said, "What have you found so far?"

Chan rattled off her report. "E-1655 is a 25-year old female from Thailand. She previously possessed low-level elemental earth abilities. But two weeks ago, during an exercise to try to induce fear and bring out her defensive reflexes, columns of rocks rose from the floor to protect her from a fake surprise attack by AMT guards. She was subsequently sedated, moved to this facility, and tested for abnormalities. But despite extensive testing, her results remain unclear."

"Unclear how?"

Despite the fact that Chan was a good six-inches shorter than he was, she managed to look down her nose at him. "When a *Feiru* first-born's hands are placed in the correct compass direction, regardless if they're conscious or not, particular elements of their DNA will react to elemental particles in the air. So, E-1655's DNA activity should increase when her hands are positioned to the north. However, in this subject's case, sometimes the repositioning of her hands will affect DNA activity, sometimes not. If the subject were lucid, she should be able to draw on elemental earth energy at a moment's notice, regardless of where she puts her hands."

Gio looked to the woman labeled E-1655. "Is there no way to have the subject awake to test that theory?"

"We aren't willing to risk it until enough safeguards are in place."

That delay would work to his advantage, giving him more time to look through the files and locate the pediatrics facility. "Is this an isolated case? Or is it possible that first-born abilities are evolving into something new?"

"That is what we are still trying to determine. Communication between facilities is not what it once was."

He sensed a 'but'. "How about in this facility? Are there any others here with abnormal abilities?"

Chan hesitated, her former arrogance gone, indicating that she didn't want to talk about it. But he'd been given high-level clearance, which he reminded her.

Finally, she said, "A few days ago, one of the scientists here was dissecting a rat, post-experiment, per usual. Partway through, the rat's organs started to heal. When the researcher jumped back, severing contact, the healing stopped. When he picked up the rat again, the flesh knitted completely back together and the rat started to move again."

Gio resisted a blink and kept his face free of emotion. "He brought a dead rat back to life?"

Chan shook her head. "Not exactly. The rat was mostly alive, although I think you're missing the bigger point."

No, he understood the enormity of the situation completely. "Where is this researcher now?"

"He's being kept in quarantine, in an observation room down the hall."

"Right. My clearance should be high enough, so take me to him."

Chan looked like she wanted to tell him to sod off, but she merely nodded. "This way."

As he followed the doctor down the hallway, something niggled at the back of his mind about the healing incident with the rat. It was almost as if he'd heard a story about something similar before, a long time ago.

CHAPTER THIRTEEN

When Marco had seen the waitress watching them, he'd quickly realized that he had one of two choices: either give up coming to this place—*La Noche*—for information, or kiss Cam and deal with her wrath later. He'd opted for the latter.

After mumbling for her to play along, he tilted his head and touched Cam's lips with his. Despite her 'take no shit' attitude, her lips were soft and undeniably feminine. But she continued to be deliberately stiff and unresponsive, unwilling to play along, so he tightened his grip on the back of her head and nibbled her lower lip. Some of the tension eased from Cam's body; but it wasn't enough to convince anyone here that they were both horny, and desperate to be naked, which was what his reputation required.

He decided to play dirty.

He reached a finger to the west and manipulated the water particles under Cam's shirt until they froze, and then swept them across her nipples. As expected, she gasped and Marco took advantage, plunging his tongue inside of her mouth. As he stroked his tongue against hers, he felt Cam's claws lightly scrape against his chest through the thin fabric of his shirt. The light sting felt good, and he wanted more.

He hauled her up against him until her heat and scent surrounded him. The taste of Cam was surprisingly addictive, and it made his cock harder. Not caring that she could feel his desire, and aware that he may never have this chance again, he angled her head and took the kiss deeper.

The tension eased out of Cam's body, but she still refused to participate. Marco resisted a growl and tightened his grip on her hip. He wanted her to kiss him back.

But she didn't. He'd finally found a woman who made him want to act the way his reputation declared, and she wasn't interested.

They'd kissed long enough to suit his cover ID, so before he did something stupid, like straddle her across his cock and rub up against her, Marco reluctantly began to retreat. But then Cam's tongue, although hesitant, lightly brushed against his. He resisted a groan, afraid he might scare her off. Instead, he flicked his tongue against hers again, and retreated. Her response was stronger this time, and it killed him to wonder if she were playing along or responding of her own free will.

Her nails dug deeper into his chest and he was about to see if he could make her engage more when someone said in Spanish, "I was wondering when we'd see you again, Felipe. I'd started to think you'd found a new hangout."

Silently cursing Ynez, the waitress, Marco pulled away from Cam and noticed the flush on her cheeks and the dazed look in her eyes. Clearly, she'd been affected as much as he, although, she was better at hiding it. He winked at Cam to let her know that this was far from over before he pasted a grin on his face, looked at Ynez, and said, "No, my lovely, it would take a thousand horses to drag me away from the stars alight in your eyes." He winked and Ynez giggled. "I had business elsewhere."

While Marco had never said outright that he was part of a drug cartel, everyone inside of *La Noche* assumed it. The cover ID of Felipe Herrera had saved him a time or two in the past.

FROZEN DESIRES

Ynez leaned forward and placed a plate of *panuchos*, his usual, down in front of him. With Cam sitting on his lap, and Marco unsure of whether she was watching him or not, he hesitated to keep up his character and have her believe that he was exactly what his reputation proclaimed. He wasn't exactly sure why it mattered since his reputation kept anyone from suspecting he was an Elemental Master. *I'm being ridiculous.* Of course he would do what was necessary. At least Cam wouldn't understand Spanish. Nevertheless, if she asked him for the truth later, he would give it to her. He had a feeling that if he ever lied to her from this point onward, what tentative trust she'd given him today would vanish irreparably.

And he still needed to hear about that man who'd frightened her in the street.

Pushing aside his reluctance, Marco deliberately stared down Ynez's shirt before meeting her eyes again with another smile. Ynez leaned forward and whispered, "If you want better company later, you know where to find me."

He gave her a heated look. "I'll keep that in mind, lovely."

Ynez gave a slow smile, looked away from his face to something on his right before turning and walking away, her hips swaying in invitation.

~~*

When Marco's lips had touched hers, Cam had gone still, unsure of what to do. Her instinct to avoid drawing attention to herself in public had been too strong to simply push him away. Yet she didn't like being drawn into a cover ID without her consent, if that was indeed what Marco had been doing.

101

But then he'd caressed her nipples with ice, and she couldn't help but gasp. The sensation was oddly stimulating, not that she would admit it to Marco. Especially since the moment her mouth opened, he'd thrust his tongue inside.

She'd started thinking of all of the ways to eviscerate him when he started to stroke her tongue and the action sent a jolt through her body, straight to her core. Her claws lightly scored his chest and the motions of his tongue continued to send heat through her body. The taste of Marco invaded her mouth, making her body scream for more.

It had been years since a man had kissed her; but even then, she'd never felt as hot and bothered as she was now.

His tongue started to retreat, and she barely resisted a sound of protest. She didn't want him to stop. It might be a long time before she was kissed again, and she missed the feeling of a man wanting her. Right here, right now, she didn't care if it was all an act. As she'd done with every other aspect of her life, she would take what she wanted.

She stroked her tongue against his. If Marco was going to use her as a prop for his cover ID, then she would use him too— no strings, no attachment, just an opportunity to appease her desire.

Cam retreated, but Marco tangled his tongue right back with hers, his hand around her waist drawing her closer until her breasts brushed his chest. She resisted a moan at the contact, her nipples already hypersensitive from Marco's icy caress.

Just as she was about to run a hand up Marco's chest and into his hair, she heard a woman's voice. Marco broke the kiss, looked at her face, and smiled. He'd ended the kiss so abruptly that she hadn't had a chance to regain her composure and banish the emotions from her face. When Marco winked at her, she knew she was in trouble.

This is a one-time thing. That's it. There was no way she was going to complicate her mission by sleeping with one of her colleagues, no matter how much he turned her on. Especially since Marco liked to be in control; and she wasn't about to fight him over who was in charge for the entirety of their Talent-searching mission.

Thankfully, Marco looked away, relieving her of his scrutiny, and leaned around her to see who had spoken.

After two deep breaths to regain her composure, Cam turned her head to find a beautiful, curvy woman in her twenties, the plate in her hand identifying her as a waitress. Even though she and Marco were speaking in Spanish, their tone and body language screamed some kind of flirty back and forth. When the woman leaned over more than was necessary, displaying a clear view down her top, Marco's eyes followed. Any lingering heat Cam had from their kiss vanished. What was happening right in front of her was exactly the reason she'd resisted Marco's charm.

Embarrassment for giving in to him in the first place rushed forth. She'd just have to make sure it didn't happen again.

The woman's gaze moved over to Cam, flicking to her scars and simple braid, her eyes telling Cam that she didn't see what Marco saw in her, and that Cam was nothing more than a one-off whim. She willed herself to keep her face calm, not wanting to give the slutty bitch the satisfaction of affecting her.

The waitress's eyes went back to Marco, full of heat, before she walked away, her hips swaying with sexual promise.

Marco's eyes followed.

The humiliation of his obvious rejection of her was too much and she pushed against Marco's arms, wanting to get away from him. The only men who ever seemed to be interested in her were the ones who wanted to use her. She thought she'd learned her lesson with her ex, but apparently not.

Marco's grip remained firm as he whispered, "We'll leave, but wait until we get outside before you start acting out."

His words were cool and even, nothing like his usual lighthearted tone. If she didn't know better, she'd say he was angry.

Like he had any reason to be angry with her. She had done everything he'd asked of her since entering this place. "Then hurry up, because your touch disgusts me."

Marco clenched his jaw, but he kept quiet as he pushed her up off his lap and drew her against his side. He gave her one last look she couldn't read before putting on what she was fast learning was his fake smile. Unable to do the same, Cam tucked her head against his side to hide her expression, which turned out to be a mistake. Despite how he'd hurt her, and how Marco had used her like the others, his scent was warm and oddly comforting, reminding her of how he'd tasted when he'd kissed her.

Am I fucked up or what? He'd just rejected her in plain sight of everyone here, yet she was still attracted to him. Why couldn't a dependable, strong man like Jaxton or Darius be here with her and smell as good?

As they made their way to the door, Cam decided to fall back on what had worked best for her over the last four years— she was going to focus solely on her missions and eschew men completely.

~~*

Cam's words about his touch had stung, and only years of practice had allowed Marco to act the part of Felipe Herrera as he and Cam made their way to the door. He even managed to give Ynez another deliberately heated look before passing by the bouncer and stepping out into the open air.

Cam, thankfully, played along until he turned them down a side street, where she stiffened and tugged to get away. But he kept a grip on her shoulders. "Not yet," he hissed.

Her claws bit into the skin of his ribcage, but he ignored them. She could threaten him all she liked, but he wasn't letting her run off until she understood the truth of his actions back in *La Noche*.

Cam increased the pressure of her claws and said, "There is nothing to justify you touching me. I was your prop inside, but there is no one here to impress." She pressed a little harder. "You're also violating the rules of DEFEND, to never force an innocent to do your will. Maybe working with DEFEND isn't important to you, but it's sure as hell important to me. Maybe us working together isn't such a good idea after all."

He'd had enough of Cam's disdain, and he wasn't going to take her abuse any longer. Gritting his teeth, Marco tugged her inside an abandoned house and lowered his face to hers. "You're quick to judge, Camilla, but it is you who aren't holding up your promise." She opened her mouth, but he placed a hand over it. "No, it's my turn now."

He let his restraint go, showing her the anger he'd been trying so hard to contain. If this was the only way for her to take him seriously, then so be it.

He kept his voice low as he said, "If DEFEND is so important to you, then you'd stop with all your fucking evasion tactics and simply tell me who that man was and how you're connected. Part of my mission is to aid you in looking for Talents, which I will do, but that isn't all." He leaned even closer, his nose a hairbreadth from touching hers. "Every second I spend tracking you down and passing one of your fucking silly little tests, innocent *Feiru* and their families are being murdered by a group who would make even you pause before crossing them."

He forced Cam to take a step back and he cornered her against the wall. "I do what's necessary to make my missions a success, and flirting with someone is the least of it." He narrowed his eyes. "So stop fucking judging me, because you have no idea what I'm capable of when it comes to stopping the murderers of children, especially when one of the bastards killed my cousin."

Cam's eyes widened at his last statement, and he decided she'd had enough. He removed his hand, but didn't step away. Due to Cam's latent abilities, she was fast, but he would be able to stop her at this distance with his own powers.

She held his gaze, her expression unreadable. When she finally replied, he could barely hear her. "Why didn't you just tell me all of this before? I could've helped you."

He growled. She still hadn't answered his fucking question about the man on the street. He put a hand against the wall on either side of her head and leaned forward. "When was I supposed to tell you, Camilla? When you kneed me in the balls? Or how about when you nearly slit my throat? I understand pain. Hell, I understand the need for secrets. But you've done nothing but cut me down since we met, and I don't know if you're aware of it, sweetheart, but trust runs both ways."

CHAPTER FOURTEEN

Cam sucked in a breath. Marco's words were true, but this situation wasn't entirely her fault.

She raised her chin to get a better look at his eyes. "Trust? What do you think just happened in that bar? If I didn't trust you at all, then no matter if it would've blown your cover ID or not, I never would've let you put your tongue in my mouth." She poked him in the chest. "You may let anything with tits kiss you, but it's not that way for the rest of us."

Before she could blink, Marco had grabbed her hands and pinned them to the wall beside her head. She tugged, but his grip didn't budge. "Let's get one thing straight right now, Camilla. Despite whatever the rumors may say, I don't kiss just anyone." He leaned closer and she was surrounded by his intoxicating maleness. "And as I remember it, you were kissing me back."

Cam's heartbeat pounded in her ears. "What does it matter? Two seconds later, you were making sex-eyes at the waitress."

His breath tickled her cheek. "What if she hadn't interrupted? Then what would you have done?"

Her anger had faded to something much hotter. Suddenly, Marco's proximity, and the way he'd kissed her, was all that she could think about. *No.* She wouldn't let anyone hurt her again. "Nothing, because I'm not about to be anyone's whim."

Anger flashed across his face. "Anyone who thinks of you like that isn't worth having. Was it that blond man? What is he to you?"

She jumped at the distraction, anything to put distance between herself and Marco. It wasn't just that his nearness was unsettling, but his fierceness was doing something to her that she didn't want to think about. "First, let me go."

His nearly black eyes pierced hers, but she didn't avert her gaze. She could take any macho bullshit he threw her way.

After a few more heartbeats, Marco loosened his grip and she yanked her hands down to her sides. But Marco kept his hands on either side of her head, not stepping back as she had expected him to do.

"Well, Camilla, who is he?"

She debated telling him the whole truth. He'd said he'd help her locate the Talent or Talents who'd left the message inside the ruins, but after this, he might change his mind.

But he was right—trust ran both ways. If she didn't tell him, he might walk away. And while she could handle the mission aspect herself, the thought of never seeing the fierce man in front of her ever again didn't sit well. It wasn't just that she couldn't keep the information from him any longer, she didn't want to. She was curious to see how he would react.

Ever since they'd left that bar, the charming, flirtatious Marco Alvarez of rumor had disappeared, replaced with an oddly demanding, straightforward man. The same man she'd glimpsed briefly back in the jungle. And while Cam would never admit it to anyone, she was far more intrigued by him than the playboy persona he usually donned.

He kept asking her not to judge him, so maybe, just maybe, he wouldn't judge her like everyone else.

FROZEN DESIRES

"The man from earlier is named Richard Ekstrom." She took a deep breath, risking it all with her next words. "And not only is he my ex-boyfriend, he's a former major with the Federation League."

Marco's face went blank and she waited to see if he'd show the same disgust as the others. Marco was clever, and she didn't doubt for a second he'd make the connection.

~~*

Having Cam all but pinned up against a wall, and trying hard not to notice the rise and fall of her breasts so close to his chest, it took Marco a second to process Cam's words concerning Richard Ekstrom. To be honest, her confession was one of the last things he'd ever expected to hear. Not so much the part about him being her ex-boyfriend, but rather the part dealing with the Federation League—the same group he suspected was setting off the arson fires.

Jaxton's briefing had included a reference to Ekstrom. The man had once been a strong recruiter for the Fed League, slated to take over command, but then he'd all but disappeared into thin air about two years ago. No one had heard from or seen him since.

If Ekstrom had been that high up in the Fed League, then it only stood to reason that Cam had also been a part of the fringe group at one point in her life. Probably in much the same way as DEFEND functioned, the higher ups rarely had free time outside of their duties, and when they did, they couldn't share anything about their work without Neena or Aislinn's approval. Relationships with non-members were, predictably, rare.

Studying Cam's face, he saw her struggling to hide her vulnerability about how he'd respond. While Marco had researched Camilla Melini before coming to Mexico, he hadn't found anything about her involvement with the Fed League, meaning it wasn't public knowledge. But no doubt others had learned the truth and given her hell for it.

He'd see what she had to say before issuing judgment. He wasn't a hypocrite. "You were involved with the Fed League too, weren't you? How?" She hesitated, and Marco decided he didn't like seeing such a strong woman so unsure of herself. "You can tell me, Camilla. Neena let you into DEFEND, and continues to give you important assignments. We both know she wouldn't stand for a double-agent in her ranks."

Cam remained silent, so Marco said, "Please?"

Her mouth parted a little in surprise, and he resisted a smile. Catching Cam off guard was fast becoming one of his favorite pastimes.

Good soldier that she was, Cam recovered quickly and said, "Only if you promise this information won't go any further. I can't do my job if everyone suspects me of being a spy." He nodded, understanding a thing or two about keeping secrets and avoiding unwanted attention.

She continued. "You know from my conversations with Kiarra that our parents were murdered when I was young, by our uncle, James Sinclair." Marco nodded. "After that, I went to live with my Uncle Alex and his two children. They were the best surrogate family I could've hoped for, but my anger at the loss of my sister to the AMT, the loss of my parents, and the loss of my brother Gio to another uncle, grew and festered. By the time I was eighteen, I wanted to make someone pay for all of the pain the AMT had caused in my life."

"And so someone convinced you to join the Fed League."

"Yes." Cam looked away from his gaze to stare out one of the windows. "Richard knew exactly what to say to recruit me. He'd been close to his older sister too, and being as young as we were, we both thought that taking out AMT-related targets would scare the AMT Oversight Committee into making changes. Maybe even convince them to shut down the AMT system for good.

"I trained hard, trying my damnedest to become the best. During the final phase of training, the Fed League conducts tests to pinpoint each person's strengths." She looked back to Marco. "The results told them I was an excellent sharpshooter."

He'd never seen Cam fire a gun, but it wasn't that hard to imagine her doing so with ease. "What did you do after you finished your training?"

"They mostly assigned me to cover members from a distance, watching their backs as they retreated from a target. Unsure of who was working with the AMT or not, I was to incapacitate but never to kill. But as time went on, I became too good at my job, and they decided to make me an assassin."

~~*

Cam watched Marco closely, waiting for the moment when his look would turn to one of revulsion. She rarely revealed her past to anyone—not even her sister Kiarra knew the truth yet—and the few who had heard her case often stopped listening at the word "assassin."

Yet for some reason, she hoped Marco would want to hear all of it, and try to understand her.

When he'd told her about his cousin with such anger and passion, Cam had instinctively known he was telling the truth, and it had made her feel guilty. Her games and outbursts had taken away from Marco's efforts to catch his cousin's murderer. Here she'd thought that he didn't take anything seriously, while all the while he'd been hiding his pain behind fake smiles and flirtatious remarks, balancing the multiple responsibilities DEFEND had thrust upon his shoulders.

Even without considering Marco's elemental water abilities, the man had phenomenal control.

Cam wanted to see more of the real man beneath the facade.

But Marco remained silent, and if Cam didn't do something, she would lose the chance.

Not wanting him to see how much she needed him to listen to the rest of the story, Cam fell back on her usual brusque manner. "I need to know if you want to hear the rest or not because I need to go back to Santa Lucia Park to try to solve the clue I found inside the observatory."

The corner of Marco's mouth ticked up and she felt a small glimmer of hope. "Seeing as it takes intimidating the shit out of you to get you talking, I'm not about to throw away this chance." He cocked his head to the side. "Did you do as they asked and become an assassin?"

Cam blinked. No one had bothered to ask her that question before. "The Fed League didn't allow choice. You either did what they wanted, or they found a way to make you do it."

"And what did they have to do with you, Camilla?"

She forced her voice not to waiver at the memory. "I told them I wasn't interested, but once they took Adella, my cousin-slash-adopted-sister, and started cutting her in front of me, I had no choice but to do what they asked."

CHAPTER FIFTEEN

When Cam's voice cracked, something tugged at Marco's heart, prodding him to reach out and comfort her. While he was hurting from the death of his cousin, he could only imagine how much worse it would be if something had happened to one of his sisters.

He stood up straight and removed his hands from the wall, but just as he was about to cup her cheek, he remembered Cam's words from inside the bar.

Your touch disgusts me.

Marco forced his hands down and took a step back. Touching Cam would probably break the spell of honesty they were having, and he wanted to know more. "Did you kill for them, Camilla?"

She cleared her throat. "Based on my reputation, I'm surprised you'd even bother to ask that."

It seemed that he wasn't the only one who hid behind a reputation. "I don't give a fuck what everyone else says. I want to hear the story from you."

Cam searched his eyes for what seemed like forever before she said, "On one condition."

Of course, the woman would bargain. "Shoot."

Cam put one hand on her waist and pointed a finger at him. "From here on out, I'll only work with the real you. If you use that damn man-whore routine with me again, apart from when you need it for a cover ID, I won't hesitate to use my claws instead of my knee next time. Understood?"

His lips raised in a smile even as warning bells went off in his head. *Never let people close enough to discover the truth.* His grandfather had drilled those words into his head, over and over again. But he knew someone like Cam could keep his secret when she found out.

When? No, it should be "if."

Trying not to focus on the slip, Marco said, "And I expect the same from you. No more overkill-mode Cam."

Judging by the look on her face, she hadn't expected that. She nodded. "Fine." She lowered her finger and said, "To answer your question, no, I didn't kill for the Fed League. I chickened out on my first assignment."

~~*

Even now, Cam remembered that day. She'd had her rifle out and in position, but as soon as her targets—a pregnant *Feiru* woman and her two children—had come into view, Cam had questioned the sincerity of the Fed League's goals. The children had been targeted because of their father. Yet killing them would've done nothing to change the AMT system.

In the end, Cam had put away her gun and run.

Her only mistake had been running to Richard.

"Camilla."

She looked up, unaware that she'd been staring at the floor. Once her eyes met Marco's, he continued. "Since you're standing in front of me, I know you eventually got out. So what does Ekstrom want with you now?"

Good question. "All I know is that he's not hunting me down because of lingering feelings. If he wants me, there's a reason behind it."

Her best guess was that Richard needed her sharpshooting skills. She didn't want to think of the alternative—that he'd learned of her latent abilities.

She needed to finish her assignment in Merida and give Richard the slip. Once she was back at DEFEND's headquarters, there were resources she could use to research the man who'd played such a big part in her past. She knew he'd disappeared a few years ago, and that worried her. Cam knew from working for DEFEND that when people went to such extreme lengths to not be found, it was usually because of some serious skeletons in that person's closet.

Regardless of what they were, she just finally wanted to put that aspect of her past behind her.

She took one step and then another, until she was standing next to Marco. "We can worry about Richard later. Right now, I need to head back to Santa Lucia Park." She raised an eyebrow in question. "Are you going to help me?"

Despite her outer nonchalance, she held her breath and waited. Would he help her despite her past involvement with the Federation League?

Traitor. Murderer. Ignoramus. Those were the names her teammates had called her, back in the early days of DEFEND. And to think she'd called those people her friends. She'd learned to craft a reputation after that, one that would keep the idiots away from her.

She'd put Marco into the idiot category back in the States, but for once, she hoped that she'd been wrong. She was a big enough person to admit that she needed his help more than ever since Richard was back in the picture.

Marco finally grinned, and she let out her breath. Unless he had some sort of hidden cruel nature, he was going to help her.

He wiggled his eyebrows and said, "I've waited a long time to hear those words, Camilla."

So much for the real Marco. Time to shut his bullshit down. Again. "You've known me for less than a week."

"Maybe, but considering I've heard *of* you for years, it makes it that much sweeter."

She resisted an eye roll and poked a claw into his chest. "Marco," she growled in warning. "I thought we'd agreed that you'd drop the act."

"Believe me, Camilla, this isn't an act." He grabbed the hand near his chest and tugged. "Now, tell me what you know and I'll see if I can save your ass again"

Cam growled, but then she told him what she knew about the clue from Chichen Itza. Maybe if she ignored his deliberate attempts to rile her up, he'd once again become the fierce, passionate man she'd glimpsed earlier.

Although, she tried not to think too hard on why she wanted to see that version of Marco again.

Chapter Sixteen

Cam flipped her long hair over her shoulder for the tenth time. Annoyance wasn't the only reason she wished to put it back into a braid. "Stop staring at me."

From the corner of her eye, she saw Marco shrug. "You have pretty hair. Get used to it."

She gave up trying to ignore him and looked him dead in the eye. "If we weren't out in broad daylight, I'd take out my knife and chop it all off if it would help you focus."

"And if my grandmother had wheels, she'd be a bicycle." He grabbed her hand and picked up his pace. "Instead, let's try focusing on the present. You're supposed to be my girlfriend, so act like it."

"I am," Cam muttered, but decided that telling him any girlfriend of his would have to bitch slap him on a regular basis would be counterproductive.

Since Richard had seen them earlier, they'd both changed their clothes and tried to alter their appearances. Marco had slicked his hair back like the American men of the 1950s, and Cam had let her hair down. She'd had it cropped short during her days in the Fed League, and until she could dye it or get a wig, this was the best she could do to disguise herself.

Earlier, she'd sent Zalika and Jacek back to the bed and breakfast since Zalika's ankle had been acting up. While Cam needed her to heal as fast as possible, she was used to looking out for the pair and wished they were here to help.

She just hoped that Marco wouldn't let her down.

Santa Lucia Park came into view and she saw that the empty tables had filled up. The table near the edge of the plaza was stacked with binders.

She hoped they were filled with coins.

They reached the table and Marco squeezed her hand as a reminder—he was to do the talking. She gritted her teeth and pasted a smile on her face. Doing nothing wasn't her style, but she had neither charm nor the ability to speak Spanish, meaning that she was next to useless right now.

She watched as Marco teased and grinned with the people at the table. Even if she didn't understand ninety-nine percent of what they were saying, she could tell he was charming them. The funny thing was that the smiles and humor didn't quite reach his eyes. Most people wouldn't notice it, but Cam had been face to face with the man when he'd been fierce and angry, and right now, his eyes lacked the same depth of emotion.

Marco pinched her hip and winked at her. He'd seen her staring, which meant she'd never hear the end of it later.

But thanks to the years working for the Fed League and DEFEND, Cam kept her cool. Considering he'd stared at her boobs not that long ago, she had nothing to be embarrassed about.

The man sitting at the table made a motion for them to wait a moment and he went riffling inside one of the boxes behind him. She raised an eyebrow in question, and Marco gave a one-shouldered shrug as if to say, "I'm not sure what he's doing."

When Cam turned her head to watch the man behind the table, Marco's hand curled over her hip and tugged her against his side.

Her first reaction was to pull away, but then she stopped. *Remember, you're supposed to be his girlfriend.* She repeated the words inside her head. She'd had assignments in the past when she'd had to act a certain part to get information, but rarely with men, and certainly never with men that smelled as good as Marco.

Stop it, Melini. You've decided to eschew men, remember? It was easy to tell herself that, until she remembered the kiss they'd shared inside the club. She knew it had only been part of Marco's cover ID, but sitting on his muscled thighs while his tongue stroked hers…

Marco poked her in the side and stopped her dangerous thoughts from going any further. He would tease her about staring earlier, and she didn't need to give him more fodder with something worse, like a blush or dilated pupils. Because whether she wanted it to happen or not, she was officially turned on.

More than ever, she needed to find a way to put some space between her and Marco. He may have made some promises, and seemed to be helping her, but she didn't trust him. Not yet.

The man behind the table turned from his box with an envelope in his hand, and she wondered what was inside.

~~*

Marco wasn't entirely sure why he'd pulled Cam up against his side, but he rather liked how she fit. Not only was she the perfect height—only a couple of inches shorter—but the hip under his hand flared just a little, suiting the toned muscles of her body.

He still remembered how those hips had felt cradling his body back in the jungle, when Cam had tried to struggle out of his ice bonds. Contrast that with the hesitant stroke of her tongue back in the club, and he was curious to see what she was like naked in a bed, with no danger or distractions around her. She'd probably be wild, fighting him to be on top until he convinced her to cede control to him. Marco had never had such a partner, and the image made his cock twitch.

But then, the man he'd been chatting with—Jose—turned around and ruined his fantasy. Marco noticed Cam looking the other way, and he poked her in the side to get her attention.

Jose had been surprised to hear him mention the Great-Tailed Grackle. But once he had explained he'd heard of a special coin issued by the Spaniards that featured the bird, the man had turned and started looking through one of his boxes. Since Marco doubted such a coin existed, to ask for it in such detail was the trigger Jose needed to give him the next clue.

He just hoped the clue wouldn't send them on a wild goose chase. He was starting to like helping Cam, but he had his other mission to worry about, too. Until he finished both of them, he'd never be able to go down to Colombia and help his family find his cousin's murderer.

Jose said, "People sell all sorts of trinkets inside Chichen Itza, but if you want a truly unique Mexican souvenir, then this is what you're looking for."

Marco took the proffered envelope. To open it, he released his hold on Cam. When she stepped away, he instantly felt the loss of her heat.

He looked inside the envelope to find a modern-day peso and a letter. *Bingo.* "How much?"

"That one isn't rare, so how about one hundred pesos?"

"Seventy-five."

Jose smiled. "Deal."

Marco paid the man, gave him and his wife a smile, and said, "Thank you. My girlfriend's sister will love this."

He took Cam's hand and led her out of the park, over to a shady spot down one of the empty side streets. When they stopped, Cam removed her hand from his and stepped away. He didn't like it so he pulled her next to his side and said, "This way we can read it at the same time."

She looked askance at him, but rather than push him away, she simply said, "Well, then, stop staring at me and hurry up and open the damn thing."

He grinned and took out the letter, but since it was written in the old language, he leaned down to Cam's ear and whispered the translation:

First the jungle, now off to the ocean. Visit the Bride of the Sea near the old walled city, on Wednesday at twilight. Rosa Elena will have the answers you need.

~~*

Between Marco's heat and his whisperings in her ear, Cam was having a hard time concentrating. She had tried to step away and put at least a foot between Marco and herself, but then the blasted man had pulled her back to his side. The next time they were alone, they were definitely going to have a talk about his demanding nature when they were in public. Just because she had been under the guise of his girlfriend, didn't give him free liberties with touch or demands.

Marco's voice stopped and she focused on the content of the letter. "At least we have until Wednesday to figure out what 'The Bride of the Sea' means."

He folded the paper and placed it back into the envelope. "There's no need. The *Novia del Mar* is a famous statue in Campeche, a city that is about two and a half hours away."

Her previous reasoning that Marco knew the area better than she had been sound. "So does that mean we can leave, Merida as soon as we swing by the bed and breakfast and collect my team?"

Marco turned toward her. "Remember when you said you would've offered to help me find my cousin's murderer? Does that offer still stand?"

He's asking for my help? Cam nodded, curious to see where this was going. "Of course."

"Good, because I need to interview a witness in about an hour and you're coming with me."

He started to walk away, expecting her to follow, but she grabbed his arm and said in a low tone, "I'm not a lackey you can order around. I won't go anywhere until you, A: ask me to go, and B: tell me the details."

Marco turned and raised his eyebrow. "Are you going to give me the same courtesy next time, without me having to pin you up against a wall?"

She remembered being caged by his heat.

Pushing the thought aside, she said, "Fine. First, we put the bullshit aside, and now we treat each other as equals. I wonder what you'll ask for next."

One side of Marco's mouth rose in a half-smile. "I know what I'm betting on."

Cam cleared her throat, not wanting to think of the true meaning of his words. "No man-whore behavior, remember?" She tossed her hair over her shoulder and started walking. "Now, catch up so you can tell me what you know about these murders."

CHAPTER SEVENTEEN

An hour later, Marco stood inside a small house on one of the edges of the city, waiting for his witness to stop crying.

The victim this time had been a twenty-four year old restaurant worker named Fernando Vega. Marco didn't have much information on Vega, which meant he was relying on Vega's widow to determine if this fire was related to the others or not.

And so far, it wasn't going very well.

The sight of the young woman crying only reminded him of what his aunt back in Colombia must be going through after hearing about his cousin Isa's death.

The woman couldn't tell him anything as long as she kept crying—he needed to try a new tactic. In an effort to calm the widow down, Marco softened his voice. "Mrs. Vega, I know this is a difficult time for you, but the more information I get, the greater the chance I can catch the arsonist. So again, I ask you, did your husband's family have any connection with the AMT, either past or present?"

"I—," Mrs. Vega started to sob again and he resisted a sigh. At this rate, they would walk away empty-handed.

Marco had tried to approach this situation in a straightforward manner, but what had worked with the man in Pisté was not going to work here.

He racked his brain, trying to think of a different way to approach the woman, when Cam moved from the corner where she'd been standing and kneeled on the ground next to the woman's chair.

Cam placed a gentle hand on the woman's arm and said in accented Spanish, "What's your name?"

"Ma-maria."

Cam switched back to English. "Maria, can you still understand me?" Maria nodded and she continued. "Maria, I lost my parents when I was eleven. Even now, it's painful to talk about them." She squeezed Maria's arm and the woman looked up. "But every once in a while, I force myself to talk about them because if I always keep silent, and never tell people how kind or loving my parents had been, it would be like the world had forgotten them. And I don't know about you, but I don't want that to ever happen."

Maria had stopped sobbing, but all Marco could do was stare at Cam. Never in a million years would he have pictured her gently comforting a widow. Yet there she was, doing what he should've been doing from the moment they'd walked in the door.

No doubt Cam had hidden her softer side to keep up her reputation within DEFEND. But now he'd seen her empathy, he wondered what else she was hiding. Camilla Melini was fast becoming an enigma he wanted to solve.

Maria Vega lowered her hands from her face, and Cam grasped one of Maria's hands in her own before she continued in a gentle tone. "Maria, help keep your husband's memory alive. Tell me about Fernando."

Fernando. The name Fernando brought up images of Marco's little brother of the same name, one he hadn't seen in years. A little brother who thought he was human, and might never know the truth.

A brother he'd probably never see again.

Focus, Alvarez. Cam's comments about family were bringing up his own memories. He'd had to distance himself from his family to keep them safe. Even if he got the chance to investigate his cousin's murder, his parents probably wouldn't let him anywhere near his siblings.

When Maria finally wiped away her tears with her free hand and nodded, Marco pushed aside thoughts of his family and focused on her answer. "Nando appeared tough on the outside, but inside, he was the most thoughtful man I'd ever met." Maria gave a sad smile. "As soon as I told him I was pregnant, he rushed to the store and bought all of my favorite foods and the best-selling pregnancy book." She placed a hand on her abdomen and looked down. "But he'll never meet our baby—"

Maria let out a sob, and Cam drew the woman into a hug. "Which is why it's so important to keep his memory alive." She released Maria so she could look into the woman's face. "I'm going to try everything in my power to catch the bastards who killed your husband, but to do that, I need you to answer my friend's questions. Can you do that?"

~~*

Cam had broken one of her own rules—never show her soft side in front of a co-worker she didn't trust with her life—but found she didn't care. Maria Vega was hurting, and no matter what people thought of her, Cam wasn't cold-hearted.

She understood grief.

When her own parents had died, she had screamed for two days, calling out for her mom and dad, sobbing herself to sleep each night. Everyone had tiptoed around the issue, unsure of how to handle an eleven-year old girl's grief. Then Uncle Alex—her mother's brother—had come and encouraged her to talk about her parents. As he'd listened, for the first time, Cam hadn't felt completely sad. The happy memories had helped her heal.

And while it'd been some time since she'd spoken about her parents, she hoped that she'd get the chance to reminisce with her sister Kiarra soon.

As she waited for Maria's answer, she was acutely aware of Marco's gaze on her back. She didn't look forward to explaining herself to him later. Right now, Maria was more important, and not just because the woman was grieving.

The arson fires were an old Fed League M.O. If it turned out they were doing them again, Cam had some old contacts that could help stop them.

Even though she'd never killed anyone directly while working for the Fed League, she'd played a part in too many deaths, and that guilt continued to eat at her to this day. While working for DEFEND had helped to make some amends, stopping the fires might just help bring down the Fed League for good, which would nearly atone for her past. She might finally be able to put the Fed League behind her.

Of course, she would only succeed if she found a way to take care of Richard, too.

Maria blew her nose and Cam gave the woman's shoulder a squeeze. "So, what do you say Maria? Do you think you can handle my friend's questions?"

Maria gave a shaky smile. "I will try."

Cam smiled. "All right then, I'll stay right here the whole time." She turned toward Marco, his face softer than before. Whether it was for Maria's sake or because of Cam's revelations, she didn't know, but at least it should encourage Maria more than his 'down to business' face from earlier. "Start again."

~~*

Marco nabbed a spare chair from the dining room table, flipped it around, and sat down with the back facing out. While he wanted to continue in English for Cam's benefit, talking in your native tongue was always easier, so he asked Maria in Spanish, "Do you know if any of Fernando's family ever worked in the AMT compounds?"

Maria wiped her tears away with a tissue and said, "I think his father, but I'm not sure since Nando's dad died long before I'd met him."

"How about Fernando's mother? Is she still alive?"

Maria's eyes widened as she nodded. "Is she in danger?"

"She might be. Once we're done here, reach out to her and maybe visit a relative somewhere far away for a few weeks, just until we can catch the arsonist." Maria gripped Cam's hand, but she squeezed back and gave her arm a pat. Marco pushed on, "Is there anything else you might've seen or heard that could help?"

Maria's brows came together. "It might be nothing, but…" She reached behind her and took her cell phone off the table. She smiled at Cam and removed her hand to fiddle with the screen before offering it to Marco. "My neighbor took this photo and sent it to me, in case I could use it with the police."

He took the phone. The picture showed a few people standing in front of the photographer, with the restaurant on fire in the distance. One of the men in the crowd had blond hair, but he couldn't make out his neck, so he zoomed in and was able to see a grainy scar. Was this the man he was looking for?

Cam put out a hand and he handed her the phone, but as soon as she glanced at the screen, her eyes widened. She recognized someone in that picture. Then she looked up, gave a slight shake with her head, and looked to Maria and back. He got the message—they'd talk about this after they were done here.

Marco took out a card and gave it to Maria. "Could you send that picture to me?" When she nodded, he added, "And feel free to contact me with any other useful information, especially if your mother-in-law can confirm that your father-in-law used to work with the AMT. And if so, which one."

Marco stood up and Cam took Maria's hands in hers again and said, "If you ever need to talk to someone about Fernando, call the number he gave you, leave a message, and I'll get back to you. Okay?"

"Okay, but can I ask you one thing right now?"

Cam smiled. "Of course."

Maria looked from Cam to Marco and back again before she said, "My sister told me you work with a group fighting to bring down the AMT. Was she right?"

Cam glanced at him, but he shrugged and said, "We know people that do. Why do you ask?"

Maria removed her hands from Cam's and placed them over her belly. "This baby will be my first-born, but I don't ever want to give up my child." Maria's eyes started to water. "He or she will be all I have left of Nando. What can I do?"

While Marco's family hadn't known their first-born son would one day have elemental powers, most of the other children he'd trained alongside had told stories of how their families had kept them out of the AMT. "You'll have to go somewhere where no one knows you, preferably to a remote location with others in hiding. If you're truly determined to keep your baby, contact me and I'll see what I can do. But be very sure about it, because if you decide to keep your child, your life will become difficult and stressful. Until things change, you might forever be on the run."

Maria nodded. "I understand. Thank you for giving me hope."

"No, thank you for talking with us. I know it wasn't easy, but that picture might just help us catch the person or persons doing this." He moved to the door. "Take care, Maria."

He looked to Cam, but she shook her head. "Wait for me outside, I'll be there in a moment."

~~*

Gio stood in front of the glass separating him from Dr. William Evans—the man who'd healed a rat with his touch—and waited for an answer.

He'd finally convinced Dr. Chan to let him interview Evans alone, free of camera surveillance, but so far he'd learned nothing from Evans himself.

The man had worked for the AMT Research Division for the last two years, and from all accounts, he had been a dedicated employee, passionate about fixing "the first-born problem." Rumors said his fiancée had been killed by a rogue first-born's elemental magic a few years ago.

When asked if Evans could be a spy who'd hide his abilities to get information, Dr. Chan had rolled her eyes and assured Gio that wasn't possible; other employees had echoed her answer. Between Evans's record of accomplishment and his shock from the event with the rat, Gio reckoned that the event had been unplanned.

First E-1655 being able to control elemental earth at a whim, and now Evans healing a mostly dead rat with his hands. *Feiru* magic was definitely changing, and Gio wanted to know how, especially since the feeling he had heard of such changes before kept nibbling at the back of his mind.

Evans sat with his head bent forward and Gio wondered why he remained silent. Between E-1655 being drugged out of her mind, and Evans not answering his questions, Gio had little to report to his father. News of the rat-healing trick would buy him some time, but not enough to research the pediatrics facilities in mainland China.

He had to do something.

Gio had learned in Scotland that he didn't have the stomach for physical 'persuasion', so instead, he would try perseverance and logic. A scientist might appreciate that approach. "Dr. Evans, until we know how you were able to heal that rat, you'll remain tied up and quarantined. Everyone here has vouched for your character—that isn't an issue. But as a researcher, you know that if your condition is contagious, we need to know as soon as possible so we can try to develop a cure or vaccine."

"It doesn't matter," Evans whispered, never raising his head. "I'm one of them now."

"One of what?"

Evans raised his head with hatred in his eyes. "*Them.*"

Then he remembered about Evans's dead fiancée. "Are you talking about the first-borns?"

"Th-they stole her from me." He paused, lowering his head in shame. "And now, I'm just like them."

Gio needed to try logic again. "But don't you want to keep the others from becoming like you if it's possible? You were working to eradicate elemental magic. Don't you want to try to contain this new strain as well?"

Gio waited. There was nothing else he could say to make his case without pushing too hard. Hopefully, Evans could see past his self-pity and hatred to realize how he could help prevent the same thing from happening to other *Feiru*.

CHAPTER EIGHTEEN

When Cam finally stepped out of Maria Vega's house, Marco put a finger to his lips and motioned with his head down the street. He didn't want to give anyone a reason to believe they were anything more than friends paying a call to a troubled friend. Even though Cam's pale skin made that lie questionable—people of non-Spaniard European descent in Mexico were usually tourists—he could always claim they were a couple that met while she was on vacation. He'd have to tell Cam about their cover story later.

Anxious to get somewhere safe, he started walking. Cam practically had to run in order to catch up. She asked, "Where are we going now? You promised to ask me first, remember, before making decisions?"

He glanced at her and kept his voice low. "We need to talk in private about the man you saw in that picture, not here."

She grabbed his arm and pulled him to a stop. Thankfully, she leaned in and whispered, "We're not going back to that club again, are we?"

Despite the seriousness of the last hour, Marco couldn't help but tease Cam. "Not unless you want to, beauty."

She frowned. "Don't call me that. And if you take me to a place where people are having sex around us, I'm not going to tell you anything about the man I saw in the picture."

He was tempted to tease her some more, but they'd already lingered here too long. "No worries, I know of a place that is both private and sex-free." He offered his hand to Cam. "So, are you going to let me take you there?"

She put her hand in his and he counted that as a small victory toward her starting to trust him.

He wound them through the streets, never letting go of Cam's hand. He was still trying to reconcile the version of her he'd seen comforting the widow with the DEFEND soldier at his side. While he admired Cam's tenacity and strength, a part of him wanted her to let down her guard and tell him more about her past. She cared for her family; that much was clear. Being separated so soon from Kiarra must be killing her, even if Cam didn't show it.

Her walls were as icy as his were, to the point it would take a wrecking ball to break through them.

He glanced at Cam's profile. He knew just about every trick of how to block out others and keep people at a distance. Surely, he could find a way to use that knowledge in reverse and shatter her icy defenses.

Tonight, he decided he was going to try.

He refused to think about why he wanted to know Cam better—the reasons were selfish, and he knew it—so he focused on getting them to the secluded park he'd chosen.

Five minutes later, they arrived. He looked over the small fountain, scattered benches, and trees. It was dimly lit with a few streetlights and, just as he'd hoped, it was empty.

Cam looked around and said, "This isn't exactly private."

Marco gave a slow smile. "Ah, but that's where you're wrong."

He said a silent apology to his grandfather for breaking his vow never to show the true extent of his powers in front of anyone but another Elemental Master. Then he reached a hand to the west and started moving the elemental water particles in the air.

~~*

Cam tried not to let herself be distracted by the quaintness of the park, and kept her ears open for anything unusual, in case someone was following them. If she'd been the one responsible for the arson fires, she would've kept a watch on all of the surviving victims and reported back on any unknown or unusual-looking visitors. Cam definitely fit that category with her pale skin and lack of Spanish.

She wanted to believe Marco was as aware of their surroundings as she was. But since she didn't know all of his surveillance tricks yet, she had a hard time judging what he was doing. Especially since all she could think about was the man she'd seen in the picture that Maria had shown them.

If that man was the one responsible for the fires, then Cam had plenty to worry about. Quite frankly, she was surprised the man with the scarred neck was still alive.

She was just about to ask Marco if they could go somewhere else when she noticed him put a hand to the west, and the air on the outer edges of the park started to become solid. The ice ring slowly rose until the ice came together above them.

Marco had created an ice dome.

She couldn't help but stare at him. Most of the first-borns she had met had weak, barely manageable powers. Even most of the first-borns she'd met who'd never been inside an AMT compound had lacked Marco's control.

Everything pointed to him being a Talent, but he had denied it earlier, and for some reason, she believed him. There was something he wasn't telling her and she was curious to find out what it was.

A far-fetched story from her childhood came to mind, but she pushed it away. The special training academies for elemental magic users had been disbanded decades ago. Like many aspects of *Feiru* history and culture, that information had been lost to time.

She looked up to study his creation better. The light reflecting off the ice was beautiful. Not only that, but the cloudiness of the dome would shield them from anyone who happened to walk past. Then she realized Marco's stupidity.

"Are you crazy?" she hissed. "Ice in southern Mexico is strange enough, but a dome over a park? Melt it so we can leave."

Marco shook his head. "No, beauty, we're safe."

"How do you know that?"

"Because a rainstorm is about to start, and no one's going to come to a park in the middle of the night in a downpour."

She listened, but she didn't hear anything. "There's no rain, Marco. And if you won't melt the ice, I'll just break—" Rain started to patter against the ice dome. She looked up, and despite the streams of water running down the sides of the dome, the ice stayed frozen. She looked back to Marco. "Did you do that?"

He shrugged. "Tell me about the man in the picture, and I'll tell you about the rain." He moved to the nearest bench, sat down, and patted the empty space beside him.

Remember, you promised honesty and to treat him as an equal. Cam moved toward the bench, but hesitated to sit down. Anytime she was that close to Marco, she tended to forget important things and relive the kiss they'd shared earlier.

Then she remembered the man she'd seen in the picture and decided her hatred of him would overpower anything her hormones threw her way.

Cam sat down and said, "The man in the picture Maria showed us is named Harry Watkins. He's a former co-member of the Fed League, and I want to be the one to bring him in."

"Before we start making plans, you need to tell me more about him first."

Even if she didn't like it, if Cam had been in his position, she would've demanded the same thing, so she said, "When I was still with the Fed League, Harry Watkins was the best assassin they had. He did what they asked, every time, without question." She looked up at the dome and watched the water run down the sides. "But in my opinion, he liked his job a little too much.

"He never worried about collateral damage. If he could hurt one person related to the AMT, he'd dismiss ten innocents as part of the process." Cam turned and looked Marco in the eye again. "He's going to difficult to catch, but I might know of a way to find him."

~~*

Marco had been simultaneously listening to Cam's information and staring at her profile. But while his ears perked up at her saying she might know a way to find the man in the photo, he also noted the hatred in Cam's eyes. "Who is Harry Watkins to you?"

She started. "Why would you ask me that?"

He gently tucked her hair behind her ear and was glad she didn't flinch or bat away his hand. "I can see you hate him, Camilla, and I want to know why, especially if it's going to affect your performance." She opened her mouth, but he beat her to it. "This isn't about you being a woman or me trying to be in charge. We both know that during an operation, emotions can end up costing lives."

Cam stared at him a few more seconds before she sighed and said, "You're right. I hate him, but with good reason. He's the one who cut my cousin Adella, to force me to do assassin work."

Marco gripped the edge of the stone bench. Just knowing the man had hurt Cam made him hate the man even more, but he kept his tone even so Cam wouldn't notice. "Tell me how you think we can catch him."

"I have a contact here in Merida who still knows people from our time inside the Fed League."

"Is this person trustworthy?"

"She's been vetted by Neena, so I'd say yes."

Interesting. Despite having worked for DEFEND for three years, Marco learned something new about their leader just about every other day. "How soon can you get in contact with her?"

"Not until tomorrow. There's a specific location this person likes to meet and it's a shop that would be closed by now. I can try to set it up for tomorrow morning."

"That would be fantastic." He noticed Cam was looking at him strangely. "What?"

Cam put her hands behind her on the bench and leaned back, her hair hanging behind her. Right now, she didn't look like a former coerced assassin—just a young woman sitting on a park bench, talking with a friend.

When she rubbed her face against her shoulder to brush her hair out of the way, he started to wonder if this was how she'd been before her life had turned upside down during her childhood. Part of him hoped it was because she felt relaxed enough around him to let down her guard; but more than likely she was just emotionally exhausted from what had happened with Maria Vega.

A corner of her mouth ticked up. "You're starting to convince me that your reputation is unwarranted."

He smiled. "I'd say the same about you." Marco leaned in toward Cam, her scent surrounding him. "And I'm also starting to doubt something else you said earlier."

She raised an eyebrow. "And what would that be?"

He leaned in a little more until only a few inches separated his face from hers. "That my touch disgusts you."

Cam's cheeks flushed. "I—" she looked away for a second and then back. "I was mad at your rejection of me. It hurt."

Marco blinked. He hadn't expected her honesty. He'd been right to worry about what Cam would think of him, and knowing she'd been hurt by his actions stung a little.

But he quickly pushed the feeling aside—he'd only been doing his job—and traced a finger down her cheek, her skin softer than he remembered. "So does that mean you had wanted to keep kissing me back at that club?"

Cam's breathing was fast against his cheek, but she didn't try to push him away or tell him to stop. He took that as a yes, and he leaned in until his lips were a hairbreadth from hers. "I'll let you in on a little secret." He moved to her ear as he cupped her cheek. "I silently cursed that waitress's interruption. And do you know why?"

She let out a breathless, "Why?"

Marco moved to her lips again. The look in her eyes went straight to his cock, and all he could think about was tasting her again.

He pushed his luck further, and nuzzled her cheek. When she placed her hand on his chest and ran her finger against his skin where his shirt met his neck, he took that as the encouragement he needed to say, "Because all I wanted to do was this."

And he kissed her.

CHAPTER NINETEEN

The more Cam saw of Marco in work-mode, the more she started to like him. He was not only intelligent and a more dedicated soldier than she'd originally thought, but he also possessed some powerful elemental magic. She had no doubt he'd created the sudden rain, even if he had yet to admit it.

So when he'd started asking her about Harry Watkins, she'd found herself telling him the truth. By the time she'd told him how his rejection had stung and he'd started tracing a finger down her cheek, she'd wondered if his interest in her was genuine.

However, before she could make up her mind, Marco had whispered in her ear and then kissed her.

His lips touched hers, and the awareness she'd been battling all day came back in full force, sending heat through her body.

Cam decided to stop fighting this pull she felt; the sooner she got it out of her system, the sooner she could focus on other things.

Marco traced the seam of her lips, and Cam decided to accept his tongue. His first stroke only made her hotter, and she wanted to touch him. She shifted her body so she could thread her fingers through his hair as she met him stroke for stroke.

Marco growled as her claws scratched his scalp. Then he gripped her waist and moved her to his lap. She let out a squeak of shock as he bunched her skirt up to mid-thigh, but Marco only took the kiss deeper as he pulled her close enough that she could feel his erection between her legs. He grabbed her ass and rocked her forward. Cam groaned. The combination of her sensitive nipples brushing against his chest as his cock pressed against the thin fabric of her underwear was almost too much.

And yet, she wanted more.

She tugged his head to the side, giving her better access to his mouth. Any hesitation she'd had earlier vanished, and she nibbled and sucked his lower lip. She couldn't get enough of his taste, his heat, his scent. He pulled her tighter up against him, and she loved how his hard body reminded her that she was more than a soldier. She was also a woman.

Cam ran her other hand up his shirt and scraped up his back with her claws, marking him. For now, Marco was hers, and she wasn't about to let him forget it.

As she gripped his shoulder, he rocked her against him again. Hard. Cam cried out, but not wanting to let him control everything, she started moving on her own.

Marco broke the kiss for a second to hiss at the friction before he pressed his lips against her neck. A second later, he started nibbling at the sensitive juncture where her neck met her shoulder.

When he bit hard and then soothed the sting with his tongue, she shivered, wanting him to do it again.

Instead, he pulled away and she instantly felt the loss of his heat. But then he ran his hands down her sides and up to cup her breasts. He started to thrum her nipples with his thumb, using his nail to tease her, and she let out a cry.

So close. If he'd just move his lower body again, she'd come.

He squeezed her right breast and then pulled down her tank top, exposing her taut nipple. He simply stared at her for a moment, making her ache from the tip of her nipple down to her swollen core.

No man had ever treated her like this, as is she were a treasure to be savored. She didn't care if Marco had given the same look to countless others. Right here, right now, it was for her.

He nipped her skin and all thoughts fled her head. She clung to his shoulders as he gave her nipple a slow lick. He continued doing wicked things until he finally sucked her deep and bit down.

She dug her claws into his back, not caring if she drew blood, and groaned. "Marco."

"Camilla," he purred before moving to her other breast. When he bit her harder this time, she wondered if she could come this way.

But then he pulled away and Cam only just prevented herself from whimpering. "Stop teasing me."

Marco ran his hands up her back, under her tank top, before moving them to the front, under her built-in bra. He started playing with her nipples again before he pinched them. The brief flash of pain that followed sent a rush of wetness between her thighs.

She closed her eyes to concentrate on his touch, and he said, "Look at me."

She didn't want to obey him, but he pinched harder and repeated his words. Once Cam met his heavy-lidded gaze he said, "Take what you want from me, Camilla, but let me watch you come."

Marco's accent was thicker now, filled with desire, and his words were less of a command and more of a request.

She grabbed his shoulders under his shirt and maintained eye contact as she moved. He pinched her nipples with each movement, building the pressure to a bursting point. As pleasure started to shoot through her body, she cried out and closed her eyes, but Marco lightly twisted her nipples and said, "Open your eyes."

Somehow, she felt compelled to obey. Cam opened her eyes just as the spasms took over her body. She met Marco's dark gaze filled with desire, the pull too strong to look away. *I think he wants me.*

When her last spasm finished, she went boneless and Marco's hands moved to her back. He kissed her gently on the mouth and forced her head to his shoulder. Even if it wasn't real, Cam wanted to believe for just a moment that she was cradled in the arms of a strong man who accepted her, and didn't want to change her. She nuzzled her head into the side of his neck and wrapped her arms around his torso.

Marco's scent surrounded her, and the image of him naked against her back, warm and protective, entered her mind. But then the enormity of what she'd just done—and of how it might change their working relationship—sank in, and she closed her eyes to think of how she could get out of this and still help Marco with his mission.

~~*

Marco laid his cheek on top of Cam's head as he stroked her back. His cock was still hard and pulsing between their bodies, but with the warmth and weight of Cam against him, he found he could tolerate the pain of his unfulfilled desire. Especially since he didn't know how long this would last. No doubt, any minute Cam would jump up, adjust her skirts, and pretend nothing had happened, much like how she'd acted after their kiss in the club.

He wasn't going to let that happen. If he could just get her to trust him enough to have her naked beneath him, he could convince her that their fierce personalities would clash wonderfully in bed. He still remembered the feel of her claws in his back, and he wondered what it would feel like to have one of her claws delicately trace the underside of his cock.

With Cam, he wouldn't have to hold back either his strength or his powers. That was a first for him, and he realized how desperately he wanted it.

Cam stirred and tried to sit up. He let her lean up, but kept a hold of her hips to keep her from bolting. He tried to catch her eye, but she stubbornly looked off to the side. He squeezed her hips and said, "Why won't you look at me, Camilla? Are you embarrassed? Because I assure you, there is nothing to be embarrassed about—watching your eyes as you came is something I'm going to remember for a long time."

Her cheeks flamed. "This was a mistake, Marco. It can't happen again."

He raised one hand to cup her cheek, and forced her head to face him. She finally met his gaze and he saw uncertainty. "Care to tell me why, beauty?"

Her eyes turned fierce. "That right there—calling me beauty—is why. How do I know this isn't just part of your sweet-talking charm act?" She tried to slide off his lap, but he kept a strong grip on her hips to keep her in place. She poked a claw into his chest. "I accept that your reputation is overinflated, but I won't believe I'm the only woman you've charmed with your elemental powers and rough sex play."

His powers had impressed her? "Camilla, what just happened wasn't an act or some kind of master plan to conquer you. It was passion." He moved his hips so she could feel him. "I'm still rock hard for you. Ever since that first tumble in the jungle, you make me hard whenever you're near. I know I affect you too, so why do you continue to fight it?"

Cam shook her head. "Trust me, it would never work. I'm not going to give up everything I've worked for just so you can feel like a man."

He raised his eyebrows. "I'm not one of those bastards who is going to try to change you just because I've seen you naked. Being a DEFEND soldier is who you are, and I wouldn't take that away from you."

She shook her head. "You say that now, but when the time came for me to give orders, you'd sing a different tune."

He put a finger under her chin. "You've been dealing with the wrong type of men if they couldn't accept an intelligent woman trying to save their asses."

Cam hesitated a second, but then said, "And why should I trust you? You won't even tell me about your powers. I know you're too strong to be a regular first-born, yet you claim you're not a Talent. So what are you, Marco?"

"If I tell you the truth, would you let me kiss you again?"

She searched his eyes. "Maybe."

Her answer caused a flicker of hope in his stomach. For so long, Marco had wanted to be honest with someone, to let someone see the true version of himself. Cam had already seen more of him than he'd allowed anyone else, at least since he'd finished his training. What he said next would either bring them closer, or end up costing him his life.

He only hoped he was right about Camilla Melini's ability to keep a secret.

Marco took a deep breath and said, "Have you ever heard the stories about the Elemental Master training academies?"

Cam stilled, but then smiled and said, "It was far-fetched, but that was one of my theories."

He blinked. "What theory?"

"I've been wondering about it ever since I couldn't break out of your ice bonds. The fog trick and ice dome only convinced me more, and I started to believe you were an Elemental Master." He kept his face blank and her brows came together. "That's what you were going to tell me, right? That somehow, despite the law and forced disbanding of the academies, you went through the training."

~~*

Marco had to be an Elemental Master; there was no other explanation for the control he had over his abilities.

Cam knew the stories. But she had never imagined that the Elemental Masters, or their training academies, were still around. In the past, EMs had been heroes, defending their home territories, or helping to end conflicts. If the academies were still recruiting and training potential EMs, she wondered what they did once their training was complete. Cam had access to a lot of privileged information via DEFEND's resources, so if she'd never heard about their actions, it was a well-kept secret.

Marco tightened his grip on her hips, leaned forward, and said, "How do you know about the Elemental Masters? Even mentioning the term was outlawed nearly a century ago."

Okay. That wasn't the answer she'd been hoping for. "I'm not saying anything until you confirm or deny that you are one."

He narrowed his eyes. "Yes, fine, I'm an Elemental Water Master." He squeezed her hips. "Now, tell me how much you know and where you heard it."

She didn't trust Marco enough to simply take him at his word, especially with something as far-fetched as being an EM. She wanted to see it with her own eyes. "Prove that you're an EM first."

He created a carnation flower out of ice and handed it to her. "Have you ever seen a regular first-born create something like that with barely a thought?"

Cam stared at the ice flower glistening in the faint light from the street lamps. "No."

"Or how about this?"

A second later, snow started to fall, but when she looked up, all she saw was the ice dome—there weren't any clouds.

Marco could control the weather, just like in the stories.

She looked back at him, and he raised his eyebrow. "Good enough for you? I could do this all night."

The ice bonds, the dome, the flower, the snow—all of it pointed to one conclusion. Marco had to be an Elemental Master.

But he'd said Masters with an "s"—as in plural—so there had to be more of them somewhere. The question was how they'd managed to keep their existence secret from the AMT Oversight Committee. "But how is this possible? No one knows about the existence of EMs, not even DEFEND."

Marco tapped her chin. "That's what you think."

"What the hell? Stop with the ambiguity and just spit it out already, Marco."

"First, answer my question about how you know about the EMs. That's only fair."

Cam resisted a growl, but knew he was right. "Fine. My mother told my siblings and me the stories growing up. But apart from my family, I have no idea who else knows."

His grip on her hips loosened and he said, "Which stories did your mother tell you?"

She pushed past the sadness that squeezed her heart at the memories. "She knew hundreds of *Feiru* legends. I think she told them to us to try to make Kiarra feel more accepted, and less like a burden. But whatever the reason, the one that reminded me of you was the story of Konrad Wolf."

Konrad Wolf had been a strong—yet humble—Elemental Water Master from the 16th century. The story that had made him a legend was about how he'd foiled the plans of an army trying to invade his hometown of Vienna, by manipulating the weather.

Marco winked. "Glad to know you see me as a hero." She glared and he laughed. "All right, I'll drop the bullshit. But before I can tell you anything else, I need you to promise me that you won't tell anyone about this—not your team or even your sister. I'm not really supposed to tell anyone, so the fewer who know the better."

The enormity of his confidence hit her. First, he'd listened to her past with the Fed League without judgment, and now he was telling her something that could easily make him a target.

A feeling Cam couldn't described filled her chest. Maybe Marco was interested in her beyond a quick lay.

But then she'd believed the same thing with Richard, and that had ended with her cousin Adella almost dying.

Marco traced a finger down her cheek and she shivered. "Camilla, tell me I didn't just fuck up by telling you this. Tell me you can keep my secret."

The look in his eyes was vulnerable, making him appear younger than usual—and it made her uncomfortable. She knew how to deal with his charm or his temper, but not this. She wanted to make the look go away, but she wasn't about to lie to him. "You didn't fuck up. But if Zalika or Jacek ever ask me about it, I won't lie to them, Marco. They're like family to me."

She waited for him to pull a stunt with his water tricks, to force a promise to keep his secret, but all he did was smile and say, "Well, then, I'll just have to make sure they never see any of my tricks, and they'll never be the wiser."

Chapter Twenty

Marco felt lighter. He'd always known that bearing the secret of being an Elemental Master had weighed him down, but he'd never realized how much. True, he had yet to tell Cam what his fellow EMs did secretly to help the world, but he was starting to believe he would in time. He just had to be careful, and not spook her away.

Cam gave him a puzzled look. "Just like that, you're not going to try to make me promise to keep your secret?"

Marco resisted the urge to brush her cheek again. He'd be doing more than that soon enough. "I'm putting my trust in you, so don't fuck me over, okay? I've seen what goes on inside the AMT compounds, and I have no wish to live there permanently."

She straightened her shoulders. "I'm not sure if I should be insulted by that remark or not, considering the hell my sister went through. You'd really have to piss me off for me to want to send you there."

He smiled. "So I shouldn't get on your bad side?"

Cam extended one of her claws. "Definitely not."

Marco laughed and decided he'd tell her more later. Right now, he wanted to play.

He ran his hands up the sides of her ribcage and Cam's eyes widened. When he rested his hands on the side of her neck and caressed the sides of her jaw, her breathing was fast. "I seem to remember you saying you might let me kiss you if I told you about my powers." He moved one of his thumbs to caress the skin just under her lower lip. "Well, what's the verdict? Has your maybe turned into a yes?"

He could see Cam battling with herself, so he leaned over and kissed where her jaw met her neck. She sighed and he nipped her skin. "I'm not Richard or whoever else fucked you over in the past. I've trusted you, Camilla; won't you at least trust me in this?"

He felt the instant she let go of her tension. When she moved her hands up his chest, he moved to face her again, and saw her vulnerable expression.

He loved that she was revealing a little more of herself to him.

She met his gaze and said, "Don't hurt me, Marco."

His heart tightened. He kissed the scar on her chin and said, "Not if I can help it, Camilla." Then he kissed the one on her forehead. "There's so much more I want to tell you."

He pressed his lips to hers, gently at first, but then Cam leaned forward and delved her tongue into his mouth. His cock grew hard again at her taste, but more than anything, he wanted to feel her skin against his. He'd just worked his hand up under her built-in bra when something in Cam's skirt started to vibrate.

She broke the kiss. Her expression was apologetic as she said, "I'm sorry, but I need to take this." She pulled out a cell phone from her skirt pocket, pressed the screen, and answered. "Zalika? Is that you?"

~~*

The moment Cam had felt her phone start to vibrate in her pocket, she'd wanted to ignore her duties for once even if it were only for a few hours. After distancing herself from most everyone for years, she wanted to enjoy what little time she had with Marco. She knew he'd get fed up with her eventually—most men had trouble with taking orders from her—but even if it lasted for just one night, she wanted to feel normal.

For once, she wanted to feel desired and not have to live as her reputation required.

But her team's safety was one of the few things that took precedence over her yearnings for a normal life, so Cam took out her phone and answered it. "Zalika? Is that you?"

"She's a bit tied up at the moment," said a somewhat familiar male voice she couldn't place.

Cam frowned and said, "Who is this?"

"I think you know, Mel."

Only a handful of people knew she'd ever gone by Mel—the cover name from her years in the Fed League—and Richard Ekstrom had been one of them.

Cam stayed calm. Anger or an outburst would only make the situation worse. She kept her tone steely and said, "Richard, if you harm my team, you know I have the skills to hunt you down."

Marco raised his eyebrows in question, so she leaned over and let him listen in to her conversation.

Richard said, "I have ways around that. You're not as invincible as you think you are, Mel."

"Get to the point, Richard."

"No bullshit—one of the things I loved about you. I have a job for you, and if you do what I ask, then your friends will live. Otherwise, you know I can make their pain last for days before I kill them."

"I'm not going to do anything until I hear from Zalika or Jacek. Actually, I'm a little insulted you think I would just march to your orders without proof of life."

Richard snorted through the line. "I'd heard you'd gone soft and complacent. Good to know the rumor isn't true."

Soft indeed. "Cut the bullshit back and forth. Either prove you have my friends, or fuck off."

Marco patted her hip to cheer her on, and she gave a 'cut it out' motion with her hand.

There was some noise on the other end of the phone line before she heard Richard's voice again. This time it was as if he was holding the phone away from his head. "If I press much deeper, he'll start to bleed out. Let Cam know you're here."

Silence. She knew her friends were loyal, but even when someone held a knife to Jacek, the pair kept silent.

Cam needed to help them.

She said, "Put me on speaker phone, Richard."

"Okay, you're on speaker phone. Now tell them to be good little soldiers and do as I say."

What had happened to him? While there was no love lost between them, the man on the other line barely resembled the Richard she'd dated years ago. "Just tell me you're there so I don't have to waste any more time talking to my asshole ex-boyfriend."

A few beats of silence and then Zalika said, "Sorry, Cam. He sent a team to bring us to this boat, and with my injured ankle—"

Zalika was cut off with some scuffling and the sound of a slap. Jacek yelled in the background before Richard came back on the line. "I've given you something, and now I want something in return."

Since reacting to her friend's pain would be counterproductive, she focused on Zalika's clue of a boat. That limited their range, unless Richard had already taken them out to sea. She'd investigate that later. "What do you want, Richard?"

"Meet me tomorrow at 10 a.m., just inside the entrance to the Lucas de Galvez Market, at the intersection of Calle 56 and Calle 67. Wait for me next to the first general wares vendor you find inside. And come alone. You don't want to know what I have in store for you if you disobey me. All that matters is my end goal, and I'll do whatever it takes to reach it."

Richard sounded like some poorly written villain, and Cam wondered what had triggered the change from the sharp, cunning man she'd once known. He'd been skilled when they'd been together, but never cruel—at least until she'd tried to flee. "I'm guessing this grand scheme requires my help. I want you to promise to come alone as well, because even if you kill my friends, you'll still be without my skills if I don't show."

"Bargaining with your friends' lives, are you, Camilla? You never would've done so in the past."

"Yeah, well, we've both changed."

"More than you know. See you tomorrow at 10 a.m."

The line went dead and Cam powered off her phone.

Goddamn Richard Ekstrom. He'd promised nothing but then again, neither had she. Her best bet was to see if she could convince him to open up to her and find out what had snapped him. While she didn't look forward to it, she might have to play on his memories of them together to get what she wanted.

At least Zalika had given her something to work with.

She looked at Marco. He squeezed her hip and said, "What do you need me to do?"

Cam blinked. Not only had he offered to help, no questions asked, but he hadn't tried to take charge—at least not yet. "Well, Zalika mentioned something about a boat. Can you tap your web of contacts and find out if anyone's seen a tall blond foreigner with accented Spanish boarding a boat in the last ten hours? The boat will probably be as nondescript as possible, ruling out any fancy yachts or expensive sailboats."

"Of course, but what are you planning to do? Are you going to meet with Ekstrom or not?"

She wanted to tell him her plan, but she couldn't risk him getting involved. Cam needed to keep a clear head when she faced Richard, and she wasn't sure she could do that if she had to worry about whether Richard would use Marco against her or not.

Over the last week, Marco had shifted from a playboy nuisance to an intriguing Elemental Water Master. She wasn't quite sure what her feelings were yet, but Marco was at least a friend, and she wouldn't put anyone else in danger because of the follies of her youth.

So, even though she'd longed for a man who wouldn't balk at taking orders from her, she was going to have to turn him down. It was the best chance she had at rescuing Zalika and Jacek.

While she knew in her head what needed to be done, she dreaded what she had to do next.

~~*

When Cam didn't respond right away, Marco took one of her hands and squeezed. "Camilla? What's wrong?"

She pulled her hand away from his and cleared her throat. "I have a plan, but first I need to tell you more about Richard."

He tried to take Cam's hand again, but instead, she slid off his lap and walked toward the fountain.

He knew Cam was upset, but he didn't like her pulling away from him. He only hoped it was temporary, while she focused on rescuing her friends, because if Cam thought he was going to give up after all the progress they'd made, she had another thing coming. It was more than being able to tell her everything, or that he was attracted to her—Cam's complexity both fascinated him and forced him to actually be himself.

When she stopped in front of the fountain, Marco stood up. "So tell me about the asshole ex-boyfriend."

She kept her back to him. "I told you how I used to cover the retreat of other teammates in the Fed League, but what I didn't tell you was that I was usually covering one of Richard's operations." She leaned over and skimmed her fingers across the top of the water. "He's very good at getting into places he shouldn't, and then disappearing without a trace."

So far, so good. Marco could handle that.

Cam straightened and looked over her shoulder. "He's also very good at pinpointing weaknesses, and exploiting them. When I decided that I didn't want to be an assassin, I ran to Richard and asked for his help in leaving the Fed League for good. But instead of helping me, he tried to use Adella again, to try and 'convince' me to stay, saying he couldn't lose me like he'd lost his sister to the AMT. Only because my Uncle Alex had people watching my cousin—people I later learned were connected to DEFEND—did Adella survive."

Richard was a grade-A asshole. No wonder Cam didn't trust people. He was going to have to work hard to fix that.

Marco took a chance, went up behind Cam, and wrapped his arms around her. She tensed, but then leaned back against him. He gave her a gentle squeeze before he said, "Then let's work together to get the bastard." He created a stream of water around them and continued. "No matter how good he may think he is, I'm probably better."

Cam merely leaned against him and watched the water encircling them for a few seconds before she took a deep breath, straightened, and said, "Get rid of the water." When he did, she pushed against his arms and Marco released her before she walked a few feet away and faced him. "Don't underestimate what Richard can do. Something happened to him two years ago that made him snap. My guess is he's more dangerous than before."

"Get to the point, Camilla."

There was a blue streak and then he felt Cam behind him, with her claws on his throat. She whispered, "I'm truly sorry, Marco, but I can't risk him using you as a weakness against me." He felt her claws prick his skin. He was about to draw on his elemental magic to shift the situation to his favor, but then his vision blurred.

He barely managed to say, "What did you do?" before the world went black.

CHAPTER TWENTY-ONE

Millie Ward waited for Larsen to leave again the next morning before she climbed out of the bathroom window and inched her way up to the roof.

Petra asking for her help yesterday had been the last thing Millie had expected. While she and Petra had occasionally been on neutral ground with respect to clients and targets, they'd certainly never trusted each other enough to work together.

Yet a part of Millie hoped Petra held up her end about the call to Jax, because Millie was curious about this "friend" Petra would risk everything to rescue.

She reached the top of the roof and peeked over to see Petra standing on the far end, alone. Millie checked to make sure her heavy can opener was accessible—even an unconventional weapon was still a weapon—and pulled herself up to the roof. "Brandt."

Petra half-turned toward her. "So, Ward, do you have an answer?"

Millie raised an eyebrow. "I won't say anything until I've rung my brother."

Petra took out a mobile phone and offered it. "Just be quick. They're planning to move you tonight, which means we have to leave here as soon as possible."

Petra hadn't slipped the information about moving her from this location on accident—it was a type of down payment of trust. *Good to know.*

She carefully approached Petra and took the phone before dialing the secret number Jaxton had for family emergencies. She heard the, "Your call is being forwarded," before the phone started ringing. One ring, then two. *I know it's early, but pick up, Jax.* Finally, on the fourth ring, Jaxton picked up.

"Hello?"

"Jaxton, it's Millie."

"Millie, where are you? Are you okay?"

Millie heard a sleepy woman in the background. "Is that Kiarra?"

"Yes, she's here, and I'll tell you all about it later. But where are you?"

"Norway, but not for long." Jaxton started to say something, but she cut him off. "I don't have a lot of time, Jax." Petra held up two fingers. *Two minutes.* "I have a job I need to complete before I can go home, but I need you to watch out for a red-haired Norwegian asking about me. He might be sporting a beard, and he carries a pair of Glocks."

"Do I even want to know?"

"Probably not, but I'm kind of escaping him, and he's bound to go looking for me."

Jaxton sighed. "Of course he would. Do you know his name?"

"He goes by Larsen, but I reckon it's not his real name."

A beat of silence and then Jaxton said, "Are you okay, Millie? Did Giovanni hurt you?"

So that was the name of Kiarra's brother. "Giovanni is my concern, Jax. Leave him to me."

Jaxton growled. "What did he do?"

"Nothing." Petra made a motion with her hands to wrap it up. "I need to go. I'll ring you the next chance I have, so make sure you have access to a phone that picks up this number."

"Millie?"

"Yeah, Jax?"

"I'm glad you're okay."

Hearing emotion in Jaxton's voice nearly caused her to choke up. "Thanks. Look after Kiarra. She and I have a lot of conspiring to do against you."

Millie clicked off the phone, removed the battery, and handed it back to Petra. "You've shown your good faith with the phone call, but before I agree to help you, I want to know the name of your brother's new boss, the one whom you don't want to find out about your plan. That way we each have a bit of leverage on the other, and are less likely to double-cross or betray."

Petra raised her brows. "You're a lot craftier than people give you credit for."

She shrugged. "I think that works to my advantage. Now, who is your brother Dominik working for?"

Petra stared at her for a second before she said, "Sean Reilly."

While she only knew about Reilly from word of mouth, the man had a reputation for doing dirty work no one else would take. "Why would Dom want to work with Reilly? Your brother seems clever enough to avoid that disaster waiting to happen."

Petra's face hardened. "That's my affair."

"Fair enough." For now. Millie held out her hand. "I'll help you."

Petra shook and Millie said, "Right. Let's get planning."

FROZEN DESIRES

~~*

Marco opened his eyes and promptly shut them again. Why the fuck was the light so extra bright this morning?

As he tried to roll on his side, he started to remember what had happened—Cam's murmured apology, the prick of her claws, and the world going black.

Judging from the pounding in his head and his sluggish body, he was pretty sure Cam had poisoned him.

He cracked his eyes open again and managed to keep them open this time. The room was a small, bare bedroom with only a large fan and a plain wooden chair opposite the bed. As he slowly sat up, he noticed a note next to his pillow. Marco blinked a few more times until he could focus, and then he read it:

Again, I'm sorry, but R's actions are my fault, and I'll take care of him. I left a message for DEFEND about looking for Z and J, but I need you to tap your web of contacts to try to find out where he's stashed them. I know it's a lot to ask for, after what I just did, but if not for me, then help them because they're your colleagues.

I'll try to contact you as soon as I can.

~C

He fisted the paper. *Shit.* She was going to self-sacrifice herself to protect her friends. If Ekstrom really was as unstable as he'd sounded, then even badass Cam would need some extra help.

He glanced at his watch and saw he still had an hour to reach the marketplace.

She might have a few tricks up her sleeves, but so did he. Marco had conditioned his body to various poisons during his Elemental Master training. Most people would be out cold for

163

another few hours, but thanks to his slight immunity, he could now go and watch Cam's back. He refused to let that stubborn woman get herself killed.

He splashed some water on his face and exited the room. After checking to make sure he still had his wallet, he hailed the first taxi he saw and climbed in.

After negotiating a price to use the driver's cell phone, Marco dialed up one of his DEFEND colleagues in Merida, and explained what he knew about Zalika, Jacek, Ekstrom, and the boat, careful to use as many code words as possible so the driver wouldn't understand his conversation. When his colleague assured him he'd get on it, Marco gave the phone back to the driver and tried to figure out how he was going to play this.

Most people would be angry at Cam's actions and label it as a betrayal, but he was pretty sure he understood the why behind it. After what had happened to her cousin, Adella, and now with Zalika and Jacek, she didn't want Richard to have any more people to use as leverage against her.

Ekstrom probably had people watching Cam's movements, and if they saw him and Cam go into a room together, they would assume Marco was of some value to her, and exploit the weakness.

Hence, the poison. A small part of him hoped Cam's actions last night meant he was starting to mean something to her, while another part warned him to not be fooled by desire.

Whatever the reason, once they'd dealt with Ekstrom, he and Cam were going to have a few words. He'd told her about his powers, and next time, she was going to tell him the finer details of her latent ability, starting with the name of it.

The taxi stopped outside one of the other entrances to the market. Marco took a quick look out of the window to check for threats before he paid the driver and exited the car.

He made his way inside the massive warehouse-like building that held the Lucas De Galvez market. As he walked down the packed aisles toward the entrance where Cam would be waiting, he kept an eye out for anything suspicious. Ekstrom would probably have people watching out for any kind of back up, but Marco was good at blending in.

The crowded marketplace was filled with produce stands, people selling spices, and even clothes and shoe vendors, and he admitted Richard Ekstrom knew what he was doing tactically. With a few rare exceptions for holidays, there were always crowds of people here during the day.

It was hard not to see trouble around every turn, but Marco had been scouting locations for years, and had yet to see anything that set off warning bells. Still, Cam had said Ekstrom was a master of slipping in and out of locations without being seen. There was a small chance Ekstrom would do the same with Cam.

He wished he'd been able to contact Neena, Aislinn, or Jaxton to get more back up, but he'd just have to make do.

He approached the entrance Ekstrom had mentioned, and scoped out his surroundings. His best bet was to loiter near the blended fruit drink stand down one of the aisles. A few people stood with their drinks, watching the soccer game on TV. He went over, ordered a drink, and kept one eye on the TV and the other on the general wares stall Ekstrom had described.

Five minutes later, Cam walked into the building, and started scanning the stalls for one with general wares. Marco leaned closer to the blended juice drink stall and made a murmur of agreement about the ref's call for the game on TV. He waited to see if she'd tell him to get lost, but if she'd spotted him, he couldn't tell.

Marco reached a finger to the west, and waited. Even in this crowded market there were a few things he could do with his elemental water to help Cam without attracting too much human notice.

Just as he took a sip of his drink, a humid breeze brushed against his legs. He tried to step to the side, but something pushed at his feet. Marco tried to resist, but the force was too strong, and he could do nothing but walk away from where Cam was standing or risk falling over, and cause a commotion. A commotion that could end up costing Cam her life if Ekstrom suspected she hadn't come alone.

As he was pushed farther and farther away from Cam, he wondered if Ekstrom had an elemental wind user nearby. He tried to think of what options he had when the invisible force pushed him into a dark corner. He felt a tugging at his ankles before the world went black.

~~*

Cam had made it to the market, but Richard the Asshole was late.

Since she'd run a few errands before arriving, Cam had triple-checked the time at first, but she'd actually been fifteen minutes early. Then she'd realized that not sticking to a meeting time or to a schedule helped disturb the person waiting. It was an old Fed League tactic: If your child or loved one's life was in danger, each second past the deadline would fray a parent's nerves, making a takedown easier and quicker to accomplish.

Precisely because she cared for Zalika and Jacek, Cam wasn't about to fall for that trap. She was not the love-blind woman who, at twenty-two, had expected love to be stronger than ambition and selfishness. Four years later, her eyes were wide open and ready to take on the man who'd nearly destroyed her adopted sister's life.

She'd heard a few rumors over the years about Richard sealing himself off from the world two years ago, but even without knowing the "new" Richard, Cam knew it wouldn't be easy to find a way to save her friends and take him out. Part of her wished Marco was here to help her, since his elemental water tricks would be able to take Richard down quicker. But the last thing she needed was another person to be used by Richard as a pawn, especially as he would exploit Marco's abilities to help with whatever "end goal" he was working toward.

Not only that, if Richard knew of Cam's interactions and intimacies with Marco, he would probably make him suffer just to force her hand.

Even in the Fed League, she'd always put those dearest to her—Richard, her adopted family, and her sister Kiarra—as top priorities. She didn't know what the hell was going on between her and Marco, but given Richard's somewhat disturbed behavior over the phone, she wasn't going to risk Marco's life or sanity.

So she'd used one of her abilities she'd kept secret from Marco, and pumped him full of the venom from her claws. Not enough to kill him, but enough to knock him out long enough for her to meet Richard, and be done with it.

The move had been a tactic, to help her reach her goal. But for some reason, she felt guilty.

Marco had, after all, turned to her for orders and had offered his help. He hadn't tried to take control, and when she'd been trying not to let her past catch up with her, he'd noticed her tension and had wrapped his arms around her, and the contact had relaxed her. She had wanted to stay encircled by his strong arms and watch his water tricks for hours. Then she'd remembered how she'd nearly destroyed Adella's life, and Cam refused to be the reason something similar might ever happen to anyone else.

She only hoped she'd made the right decision. Richard wasn't the man she'd once known, and no matter what had happened in the past, he might kill her. Hopefully, the only old Fed League contact she still trusted, the one she'd contacted before coming to the market, would pull through and help her.

Cam scanned the crowd and counted two male blond heads further down the aisle where she was standing. One was tall enough to be Richard, but as she caught a glimpse of his face, she dismissed him. She was about to check the time again when a familiar voice said behind her, "Follow my lead, and I'll guide you to where we need to go. Don't make a fuss."

Richard Ekstrom had arrived.

CHAPTER TWENTY-TWO

Gio had put off calling his father for as long as possible. He knew if he waited any longer, James Sinclair would get suspicious.

So, even though he hadn't been as successful with questioning Dr. Evans as he'd liked, Gio pressed the call button on his tablet screen in his room and waited for his father to answer.

After three rings, his father's face appeared. "Hello, Giovanni."

Gio nodded. "Father."

"So tell me what you've discovered about the elemental earth user."

"They keep her constantly sedated, so I can't accurately gauge how her abilities have changed. They're working on creating a safe room to test her limits, but it's still weeks from completion."

"Why does she require a safe room?"

"The researchers here think she can manipulate elemental earth without putting her hands to the north, and they're concerned that the usual dampers won't work."

Sinclair leaned back in his chair. "And you mentioned another accidental discovery in your email?"

"Yes. You've been curious about how elemental magic is changing, but I think there's more to it. A man here suddenly gained the ability to heal with a touch."

"What did you find out from him?"

"It took some convincing, but the man with the healing ability—a researcher here named Evans—thinks the ability is related to genetics. Much like how we don't test for certain diseases until the symptoms show up. Evans believes there are others, and they should be found and quarantined."

"But the condition is genetic, which means it shouldn't be contagious."

"Yes, but while the man here has the ability to heal—which isn't something to be overly bothered about—he reckons there are other abilities that could be dangerous."

"Is there a way to test for these anomalies?"

"Evans was less than forthcoming, but I believe so."

"Has the staff there released much information about this man with a healing touch?"

Gio shook his head. "No. The staff are loyal to Evans. I could barely get them to talk to me."

His father paused a second before he said, "If I were to put this project into your charge, what would you do?"

Giovanni sat up a little straighter. He'd given this a lot of thought, in case he was asked this question. "I'd create a section in one of the AMT research facilities specifically for studying and pinpointing the cause of these changes. I've learned firsthand how the various AMT research facilities don't communicate with each other. But if everyone's together, they can easily exchange information."

"Did you have a location in mind?"

"Yes. There's a research facility not far from here, on mainland China. It's not an AMT compound, but it's pretty well isolated, and I'd like to check out the facilities to see if they could accommodate a new project."

"Then do it. If you run into any complications with regard to access, let me know and I'll sort it out." Giovanni nodded and Sinclair continued. "I'm going to send Ramirez to oversee the elemental earth user and the new healer in your absence."

"May I make a suggestion?" Sinclair waved his hand and Giovanni said, "I'd like to take Evans with me. He's started to open up to me, and bringing in a new person like Ramirez would be counterproductive with him."

He knew his father usually didn't like being questioned, but Giovanni was careful to only question him when he had a good reason.

He resisted letting out a breath when his father finally replied. "Explain."

"Evans is a scientist. Ramirez's methods rely on various types of physical persuasion, and I don't think those methods will work with Evans."

Sinclair smiled. "And you've figured out what works, I take it?"

"Yes, Father. I appeal to his need for logic."

"Fine, but I'm having two of my men accompany you."

Gio barely resisted a frown, but he knew his father had spotted it—James Sinclair was very observant. His father continued. "I trust you to scope out the facility, son, but you're new to this. Bodyguards will ensure both your safety and your success."

Since there was nothing else he could do, Giovanni nodded. "Is there anything else?"

"No, just make sure to keep sending me daily reports."

"Yes, Father."

The screen went blank, and Gio stood up. He'd managed to convince his father to let him take charge; but there was still another obstacle that might prevent Gio from visiting the AMT facility on mainland China.

He needed to persuade Dr. William Evans to go with him.

Gio left his room and nodded to one of the guards patrolling the corridor. Since he'd been given a temporary access card, he weaved through the halls and soon arrived at Evans's quarantine room.

Evans was lying on his bed, staring at the ceiling. At least he was no longer tied to a chair. That had to count for something.

Gio tapped on the glass, but Evans didn't acknowledge his presence. Gio moved to the speaker box, pressed the button, and said, "Dr. Evans." Still nothing. "Dr. Evans, since I know you can hear me, at least listen to my proposition.

"I'm going to leave soon for a different facility, one I hope to use for research. I know you were quite dedicated to eradicating elemental magic, but I think your skills could be used better on a different task."

Evans moved a little on the bed, but didn't take his eyes off the ceiling. Gio took the reaction as a good sign. "I want to set up a dedicated team to research these unusual abilities and devise ways to contain them, maybe even eradicate them. Is that something that might interest you?"

Evans still didn't rise from the bed. Gio decided to make it more personal. "If you join me, you can find a way to eradicate your own, Dr. Evans, so you're not constantly reminded of the *Feiru* who killed your fiancée. Unless you enjoy reliving what has to be the most painful memory of your life."

The other man rose from his bed. His voice was quiet when he finally replied. "You know nothing of my life, Sinclair."

Gio raised an eyebrow. "Then go ahead, correct me if I'm wrong."

Gio kept mum, and after about sixty seconds, Evans finally spoke again. "Nothing could ever be worse than Leyna's death."

"Then will you help me?"

"For now."

Chapter Twenty-Three

The world came back into focus just before Marco crashed down onto a cement floor. The combination of the impact, and whatever had just happened, dazed him. Before he could move, his hands were secured behind his back with plastic ties. Rough hands flipped him over, and Marco recognized the man's face. "Who are you and what the hell just happened?"

The Shadow-Shifter he'd chased from the market a few days ago glanced out of the barred window above him, and then back to Marco. His reply was in Spanish. "First tell me if DEFEND is real, or if it's just a rumor."

Marco blinked. "You used some kind of weird shifter magic just so you could ask me that question?"

The Shadow-Shifter drew a long knife out of his boot and held the point between his fingers. "Let's just say the answer is very important to me." The man repositioned his hand and gripped the knife's handle. "Now talk."

Marco instinctively knew his hands weren't pointing to the west. Keeping the man talking would give Marco a better chance of repositioning his hands. If he could just get a finger in the right direction, he could get free.

Even now, Cam could already be in Ekstrom's custody. The timing of Marco's capture was no coincidence—the shifter and Ekstrom had to be working together, and he needed to find out why.

He decided to walk the line of ambiguity and shrugged a shoulder. "I'm sure you've heard the same rumors as me. No one has any proof that DEFEND exists."

The shifter swung his arm with the knife and embedded it into the wall two inches from Marco's face. Thanks to years of training, he didn't flinch.

Marco kept his voice bored. "Don't you know that violence isn't the way to win me over? Try being polite and you might get better results."

The man yanked the knife from the wall and pointed it at him. "Stop with the games and nonchalance bullshit. The longer you play around, the greater the danger you put your lady in. I may have owed Ekstrom, but he's not the same person he once was, and I wouldn't trust him with my car, let alone my girlfriend."

So this man had no loyalty to Ekstrom. Marco could use that. "Let's say, for the sake of argument, that DEFEND exists. Why do you care? Do you need their help? Or do you want to hunt them down? If they exist, no one will help you without knowing your motive. If you've worked with the likes of Ekstrom, then I'm sure you're familiar with that concept."

The shifter said nothing at first, but then he moved close to him and repositioned the knife at his throat. "Do you have a little sister?"

Marco was curious to see where this was going. "Two, in fact."

"Then imagine your teenage sister had been taken, and her kidnapper kept forcing you to use your latent abilities however the kidnapper liked, in order to guarantee your sister's safety." The shifter paused a second, almost as if he was trying to get his anger under control before he continued. "And then imagine

175

you're only one of an ever-growing army of *Feiru* with latent abilities, made to do things against their will, to fulfill one person's greed. I'd think if DEFEND existed, they'd want to stop the bitch in charge of the coerced army sooner rather than later. Especially if the rumors I've heard about the anti-prison activist group are true."

If there were as many *Feiru* with latent abilities as the shifter's words implied, then the Four Talents were closer to awakening than he'd previously thought. Part of Marco's Elemental Master training had focused on the old *Feiru* legends. According to those legends, by the time all of the Talents awoke, nearly one out of every eleven or twelve *Feiru* would have a latent ability of some sort.

They'd been able to hide those abilities in the past. But this was the first time since the advent of TV and the internet that anything like this had happened. The *Feiru* High Council had been strict before, and it was only going to get stricter in the future if they wanted to keep humans in ignorance.

Did Neena and Aislinn already know about the surge in latent abilities? If not, this would start a shitstorm flurry of activity—DEFEND against this unknown party, fighting for control, all while trying to keep out of the High Council's notice.

As if all of that wasn't enough to take in, Marco also now realized the Shadow-Shifter hadn't been after their information about the Talents, that first day back in the market. "You're here for Cam, to take her back to this person gathering *Feiru* with latent abilities."

The shifter pressed the knife hard enough against his throat to prick his skin. "If you don't answer my question about DEFEND, you'll never find out the answer."

Marco took that as a yes. "Killing me won't accomplish anything. If I'm not working with DEFEND, then you've murdered an innocent. And if I am working with DEFEND, well, they'll never help someone who murdered one of their own." Marco raised his eyebrows. "So how about you lower your knife, and stop with the threats. I'd much rather have a conversation."

The shifter stared at Marco, but eventually he lowered his knife. "You have no fucking idea what that woman—she calls herself the Collector—is planning to do. Any *Feiru* with a latent ability is in danger."

"See, talking like that may get you somewhere." Marco motioned with his head. "So, how about you tell me what you want."

"Are you going to actually listen, or are you plotting how to move your hands to the west, so you can take me out."

The corner of Marco's mouth rose. "Not a stupid one, eh?"

"I wouldn't have been sent after Camilla Melini if I were."

He sobered at Cam's name. "As long as you give me actual information, I won't try to reach to the west." The shifter stared, and Marco resisted a sigh. Did everyone have to be so suspicious? "I'd cross my heart and hope to die, but I'm a little tied up at the moment."

The shifter shook his head. "Your reputation is true, then, about not taking things seriously."

"So it seems. Now that we've gotten the displays of manliness out of the way, tell me what you want. My ass is getting cold here on the floor."

The shifter took a step back and leaned against the wall. "I want my sister free of the Collector's prison, and stashed away some place where the bitch can't find her."

"And what about yourself?"

"While I'd like to live, that probably won't happen once my sister is free. I'm not the only Shadow-Shifter the Collector has in her camp. I'm disposable."

At the mention of other Shadow-Shifters, Marco remembered the one back in Washington State. "By any chance, did this Collector have a Shadow-Shifter working for her named Vanessa?"

The shifter kept his face expressionless. "You need to tell me what you can do to help my sister before I tell you anything else. I'm not about to give away all of my information for free."

Marco needed something more concrete before he risked exposing DEFEND's existence. "Answer this last question, and I'll see what I can do." The shifter started to shake his head, so Marco said, "All you've told me so far are vague statements about a woman collecting *Feiru* with latent abilities. I need something specific to work with, something that isn't easily investigated."

The shifter stared at him a moment. When he finally spoke, his voice was quiet. "Just tell me if rescuing my sister is even possible."

The look of desperation in the shifter's eyes was genuine. "I believe so, yes."

His answer must've convinced the shifter, because he continued. "What I'm about to tell you can't be shared with anyone you don't trust. The Collector is a powerful woman, and she'll hunt you down if she sees you as a threat." Marco nodded, and the shifter continued. "Vanessa was the previous shifter assigned to Cam's capture, but once V disappeared, the assignment fell to me."

Everyone—including Marco—had assumed Vanessa had been after Kiarra. But if Vanessa had known Kiarra was Cam's sister, then capturing her to use as leverage made sense. How

Vanessa had found out about Kiarra's escape from the AMT so quickly was proof she either she had powerful connections, or this Collector woman did.

He now not only needed to see what he could do about this shifter's sister, he needed to find a way to get in touch with Darius. His friend was currently working with Vanessa, and no doubt he could corroborate the story, if it were true. "Do you have a cell phone?"

"Why?"

"In order to see what I can do for your sister, I need to make a call."

~~*

Cam walked beside Richard in silence, taking note of the surrounding landmarks and street names. She didn't expect a rescue and escape attempt to be easy, but she'd use every little thing she could.

Her hatred of what Richard had done to her cousin Adella outstripped any lingering fear from yesterday. Her adopted sister had gone through hell twice. The first as leverage to make Cam accept her assassination assignment, but the second time because Cam had run to Richard for help after refusing to kill her child targets in Merida four years ago.

Her adopted sister had spent days curled into a ball after the second attempt, refusing to eat or speak, no matter how much her family coaxed her. It'd taken months before she'd even talked with her family, let alone functioned normally again.

Even now, years later, Adella still had trouble going to new places by herself.

In truth, part of the reason Cam had joined DEFEND was to avoid seeing her cousin. Even though Adella had long forgiven her for what had happened, each time she'd seen her, it had brought back painful memories for them both.

Cam had never been able to let her fuck-up go.

She'd long accepted Adella's pain had been her fault—all because she'd trusted the man now walking beside her. Somehow, some way, she wanted to make sure that Richard couldn't hurt anyone else ever again. But until Zalika and Jacek were safe, she'd have to be patient.

Richard stopped in front of an old yellow VW Beetle, unlocked the passenger door, and motioned with his hand. "Ladies first."

She decided to test some boundaries. "So, I'm a lady now?"

"You may hide it well, but I know firsthand that you are." He motioned again. "Now, get in the car."

The thought of being in an enclosed space with Richard wasn't a pleasant one, but since he hadn't frisked her, she still had her weapons strapped to her thighs. She only hoped she didn't need them until she knew that Jacek and Zalika were okay.

Cam peeked into the car, but while it smelled faintly of cigarettes, it was empty. Taking one last glance at her surroundings, she slid inside.

But as she settled her weight on the seat, something pricked her through the thin fabric of her skirt, and she jumped back out. On closer inspection, she saw the silver tip of a needle poking out of the crease between the top and bottom halves of the seat.

She half expected to fall unconscious, but nothing happened.

She looked to Richard, but he was smiling. "Obviously your trick didn't work, so why are you so happy?"

Richard's smile turned devious. "It did what it was supposed to do, now get in the car."

Cam glared, and careful not to sit on the needle, she slid into the Beetle and shut the door.

She wondered what had been inside the pressure-triggered syringe. Richard obviously wanted her conscious, so the only possible answer she could come up with was that she'd been pumped with rowanberry juice—an illegal truth serum of sorts for the *Feiru*.

She needed to test that theory, because while she'd had training to resist answering questions while under the influence of rowanberry juice, she could put DEFEND and its people in danger if she didn't prepare her mind properly.

Richard started the car. "Take out your cell phone, remove the battery, and toss it out the window."

She waited to see if she felt compelled to follow his order—one of the side effects of rowanberry juice—but nothing.

Shit. Now she really was worried about what he'd injected into her body.

Of her own free will, Cam took the phone out and did what he asked. "So now that you know I'm not being tracked, care to tell me where we're going? Or are you going to be vague as hell, and continue acting like some caricature of a bad guy?"

"Just shut up and sit there. We'll be there soon enough."

Chapter Twenty-Four

Marco waited to see what the Shadow-Shifter would do. Time was ticking, and the longer he was here, the longer Cam was on her own.

The shifter finally said, "If I let you make a call, you're going to do it on speaker phone, just to make sure you're not trying to play me."

Relief washed over Marco, but he didn't let it show. He shrugged a shoulder. "Fair enough. Put in this number." He rattled off the number, and the phone rang.

After three rings, Aislinn—one of the DEFEND co-leaders—picked up. "Hello?"

Marco switched to English. "Hey, I have a situation. What do you know about a woman called the Collector?"

Aislinn paused, and then said, "Why am I on speaker phone?"

He glanced at the shifter. "Caught that did you?"

"Answer the question."

"Well, there's a guy here who claims that he works for this Collector woman, and he wants to strike a deal to rescue his younger sister."

"Humph. Mysterious stranger, are you there?"

Aislinn could sound like a drill sergeant when she wanted, so Marco moved his head in encouragement, and the shifter said, "Yes, ma'am, that would be me."

"Tell me in three sentences or less why I should help you."

Marco tried not to laugh at the shifter's face. Aislinn's orders brooked no argument—you followed them or you knew something bad would happen.

The shifter cleared his throat. "I have inside information about how the Collector works, and I also know the number of *Feiru* with latent abilities that she has under her control."

"That was one sentence, bravo. Care to use the other two?"

"I know how the Collector plans to capture Camilla Melini. We need to work fast, because once the Collector obtains Melini, she'll be forced to kill to protect someone she loves."

Marco couldn't resist asking, "Who?"

The shifter shook his head. "I won't say anything else until I get a sign of goodwill that you'll see to my sister's safety."

He was tempted to move so that he could use his elemental magic, but he knew that breaking his promise to the shifter could end up hurting Cam in the long run. Instead, he said to Aislinn, "What do you think, boss?"

There was some typing on the other end of the line. "Give me five minutes, and I'll call you back."

"But what about Cam? The longer we wait, the more time we give the Collector to capture her."

"The longer you argue with me, the longer it's going to take me to verify and put things in place. I'll call you back."

The line went dead.

Marco pulled against his ties, but they held firm. Cam had barely escaped killing someone against her will once. He hated to think she might have to go through with it again. Especially since he knew that if the targets she had to take out were innocent, she'd never forgive herself.

There was little he could do to help Cam right now, but in order to be prepared for when Aislinn called back, he needed to negotiate his release. He looked at the shifter. "I need to be ready for when my friend calls back, so either I can get rid of my bonds myself, or you can cut me free."

The shifter stared at him a second, and then said, "I think you care for Melini."

Marco decided to play dumb at the random change of topic. "Of course I care about my friends. Now, are you going to free me?"

The shifter backed away, to the other side of the room, and he took out his gun. "Go ahead and free yourself. But if you try anything funny, I shoot first and ask questions later."

Marco shifted his body until he could point his finger to the west. He drew the elemental particles to the bonds around his wrist, and froze them. A quick tug and the plastic snapped.

Waiting for Aislinn to call was torture, and as the seconds ticked by, all he could think about was helping Cam. He knew she was a DEFEND soldier with skill, but skill mattered little when dealing with a person that might be mentally unstable—like Ekstrom—or with a potential sociopath, like the Collector.

He had more than a few words to say to Cam when this was done. Even if she didn't trust him enough to ask for his help, which irritated him, she surely could've asked Aislinn or Neena for some kind of back up.

What the fuck had she been thinking, going into this alone? Her former life in the Fed League must have scarred her deeper than Marco had thought. It would explain her irrational and illogical behavior.

Sitting around, doing nothing wasn't his style. He decided to spend the remaining time he had until Aislinn called back by questioning the Shadow-Shifter. "Since we have a few minutes to kill, how about you tell me why you wouldn't trust Ekstrom with anything."

"First, you tell me why I should. Who is Melini to you?"

"Cam is my co-worker."

"Bullshit."

"You know, if things were different, you and I might've gotten along."

He rolled his eyes. "Best buds, I'm sure." The shifter peered at him. "If you want information about Ekstrom, just tell me the damn truth."

Marco raised an eyebrow. "You're awfully demanding for a man who needs my help."

"After what I've seen during my time with the Collector, I've learned that beating around the bush or hesitating is a waste of time."

Wow, this guy is confident. But, in truth, he had a point. Marco had spent a good chunk of his life pretending to be someone else, never taking the plunge to trust someone. At least, until Cam had come along.

And now he might lose her.

For once in his adult life, Marco wasn't going to try to hide his true self with a stranger.

He eyed the shifter. "Truthfully?" Marco shook his head. "I'm still trying to figure that out."

"See, now was that so hard?"

He resisted rolling his eyes. "Tell me about Ekstrom."

The shifter's ease disappeared, replaced by anger. "We used to be friends, years ago. But ever since his sister died inside the AMT, he's changed. He doesn't care about anyone anymore. He just wants vengeance for his sister's torture."

And yet again, the fucking AMT was complicating his life. "While I'm sorry for what happened to his sister, it doesn't allow for kidnapping and threatening people."

"That's not the worst of it by half. Ekstrom plans to pick off the AMT head wardens one by one."

Marco leaned forward. While he wanted to bring the AMT system down, violence was sure to ignite greater hatred toward the first-borns. "When is Ekstrom planning to do that?"

The shifter shook his head. "Not until I know my sister will be taken care of."

Marco growled. He was about ready to try a little intimidation, but Aislinn chose that moment to call back. The shifter answered the call and put it on speakerphone. "Yes?"

Aislinn answered. "Marco, your newfound friend there is indeed working for the Collector. Am I right, Jorge Salazar?"

The shifter—apparently named Jorge Salazar—blinked. "How do you—"

"No time for that," Aislinn said. "Now, here's what you're going to do, Jorge, if you want us to help your sister, Alejandra."

~~*

Between the Fed League and DEFEND, Cam had nearly a decade of experience when it came to reading people. A nervous twitch or erratic tapping could tell someone a lot about that person's mental state. Most people had a way of showing their agitation or unease, but unfortunately, she couldn't get a read on Richard. That was the problem when a person had training similar to yours—they became unpredictable.

The longer she sat in the passenger's seat of the Beetle, the more logic and reason returned to her brain. Sure, she wanted to stop Richard, but without the most powerful tool in a soldier's arsenal—knowledge—she'd never be able to make that happen. She had no choice but to tolerate Richard, which meant acting in a somewhat civilized manner toward him.

Several of her past missions had made her play the part of spy, so she had some experience with pretending to be someone she wasn't. However, her emotions were going to make it trickier with Richard.

Maybe once all of this was over, she should ask Marco for some tips. That man had fooled everyone, including her.

Determined not to feel guilty again about what she'd done to Marco, Cam focused on Richard. Whether she liked it or not, they shared a past, and she could use that. Her best bet was to pretend Kiarra was still trapped inside the AMT, and act as if she'd be willing to do anything to get her free. The Richard Ekstrom of her past would've offered to help her, so it was time to find out if that part of him had stayed the same.

She selected the best method to get Richard talking and cleared her throat. "So, this thing you want me to do, will it help to free your sister?"

Richard voice was flat. "Daniela's dead."

Cam's surprise was genuine. "What?"

"Two years ago, the AMT researchers finally tortured her to death."

Oh, shit. She needed to tread carefully. Daniela had been Richard's only living family, and after Cam had left, his only lifeline to sanity.

His change in behavior now made sense.

"Then if she's dead, what are you planning?"

"Didn't I tell you to sit there and shut up?"

She did a quick study and decided that since Richard needed her alive, he probably wouldn't hurt her if she pushed.

The old Cam-the-girlfriend wouldn't have been afraid of the threat, so she decided to go with that. "Listen, asshole, my sister is still being tortured by those AMT bastards. So, if you're planning on blowing up an AMT, or some such bullshit, then I need to know, because I'll kill myself before I'll kill thousands of innocent first-born prisoners."

Richard finally glanced her way. "So leaving the Fed League to work for the squeaky clean DEFEND organization didn't help you to free your sister?"

She needed to be careful not to reveal too much. Cam shrugged a shoulder. "The Fed League had failed me, so I tried something different. But I'm seriously considering a new path."

"How do I know that you're not just bullshitting me?"

"Would I ever do something to put my sister in danger?"

She waited one second, then another. She was almost afraid she had made a mistake, but then Richard gave her a sinister smile. "Well, we'll see if you're telling the truth or not tomorrow, when you'll have the chance to try something new."

"And do what?"

"You'll just have to wait and see."

CHAPTER TWENTY-FIVE

When Aislinn finally hung up, Marco went over to the window. He checked outside and said, "We need to get to Campeche. I'm assuming you have a car?"

"Yes, but it's parked across town."

"Perfect. "Then get it and meet me across from the second-class bus station. Oh, and leave me your phone."

"Look, just because I said I'd help you doesn't give you the right to order me around."

He moved his gaze to Jorge. "Maybe so, but there are other reasons you should listen to me."

Jorge put a hand out. "Such as what? Are you going to try and charm me to death?"

He resisted tossing the shifter across the room with his powers. "Let's just say that if Camilla Melini ends up dead—or even damaged—I'm going to take it out on you."

"But I'm—What're you going to do with that?"

Marco had made a sliver-like dagger of ice in his hands, one that just about any elemental water first-born could construct. "If you cooperate and give me your phone, then nothing." He took a step closer. "You may be helping us in order to get your sister free, but until I have Camilla back, I'm holding you just as much responsible for her safety as Ekstrom."

Jorge's confidence flickered for a second, but as he took out his phone and offered it, his lapse faded. "Here, take it. But don't take too long. I'll be across the bus station in about thirty minutes. Look for a ten-year-old silver sedan."

Marco took the phone. "Fine. I'll meet you in half an hour."

Jorge shook his head and left. It was a good thing the Shadow-Shifter could only shift once every twenty-four hours, or Marco might have had to deal with more than flippancy. He'd have to remember to be careful when the twenty-four hour mark came around tomorrow morning.

He dialed Darius's number and hoped like hell his friend would pick up. Marco had no idea where in the world Darius was, and therefore, had no idea what time zone he was in, or if he even had a phone.

The call forwarded and started to ring. On the second ring, Darius picked up. "Yes?"

Thank goodness. "Hey, D, it's me. I have a situation, and I think you can help me. Can you talk right now?"

A pause, then Darius said, "Okay, now I can. Make it quick."

Did Darius sound a little annoyed? Marco put aside that concern. "Did Vanessa work for someone called the Collector?"

"Yes, but how did you find that out?"

"The Collector is after Cam, and I sort of coerced one of Vanessa's former colleagues—a Shadow-Shifter named Jorge—to help me rescue Cam. Can Vanessa tell me anything about Jorge, or about the Collector for that matter, that might help?"

Darius's voice was distant, as if he'd lowered the phone from his head, and said, "Nessa, what can you tell Marco about Jorge the Shadow-Shifter?"

There was some mumbling, and then a female voice came on the line. "Watch your back. The Collector has no conscience whatsoever, and has a habit of using someone and then discarding them. Jorge is as good as a dead man."

"What about weaknesses? Or holes in her security?"

"Believe it or not, she never confided all of her evil plans in detail."

Marco resisted a sigh. "Tell me specifics, Vanessa. I know you were after Camilla back in the States, and I need information to help free her."

"Oh, *her*. She's been marked for retrieval for a while. The Collector really wants Melini for some reason, so I wouldn't get your hopes up."

"Yeah, well she hasn't had to deal with me."

Vanessa laughed. "Yeah, I'm sure a pretty boy like you can take down a woman with an *army* at her disposal."

Marco took a deep breath to rein in his temper, or he might say something he regretted. Whether he liked it or not, Vanessa had information he might need again in the future. "Can you at least tell me if it's true that this Collector uses hostages to force members of her army to act?"

There was a beat of silence, and then she answered, "Yes."

For a second, Marco believed she sounded sad. But he brushed it off. He didn't have a lot of time. "Put Darius back on the phone."

Her usual attitude returned. "Fine with me."

There was some mumbling again before Darius said, "I think she likes you."

"Yeah, whatever. Listen, if Jorge is telling the truth, then Richard Ekstrom is taking Cam to a marina in Campeche. Can you reach out to our contacts there, and have them put together a retrieval kit? I want to pick it up at the usual location in about three hours."

"Sure. But do you really think you can take him on alone?"

"You know what I can do, Darius."

While it wasn't obvious, he and Darius had more in common than most people realized.

"Yeah, I know, but I wanted to check and make sure. Just because we're on different missions doesn't mean I don't consider us on the same team anymore."

Marco had yearned for years for missions of his own, but he was starting to realize how much he'd enjoyed working as part of a team. "Okay, I need to go. I'll call you if I need you."

"FYI, don't call within the next few hours, because I won't be able to pick up."

He wondered what his friend was up to, but if Darius wasn't telling him details, there was a reason.

Besides, he had more than enough to worry about. "Okay." And he clicked off the phone.

~~*

Cam stood on a dock in front of a medium-sized boat and decided that yes, her day could get worse.

Richard pushed her toward the boat. "Get on."

She crouched down and slowly slid onto the boat. She managed to get herself upright, but then the boat rocked, and it took everything she had not to vomit the contents of her stomach. Hopefully, their stay on the boat would be brief, because without her seasickness bands, she was useless on the water.

No doubt, Richard had remembered that.

He jumped down beside her—which rocked the boat again—and he guided her toward the cabin.

They reached the door and he pushed her into a small, dark room. "I know how much you love the water, so I've put a bucket on the floor for you. The window is big enough that you can empty it out when needed, but small enough that you can't escape. Since I need you alive, I'll have some bottled water and sports drinks brought down."

Despite the queasiness in her stomach, Cam could be sarcastic like the best of them. "How nice of you."

Richard shook his head. "Just don't die on me, or I might have to hunt down your adopted sister. What was her name again? Adella?"

"You couldn't get to her if you tried, Richard."

He shrugged. "Zalika and Jacek, then. I was just trying to spread the pain around a little."

The boat pitched to one side, and she nearly lost the battle with her stomach. She wanted nothing more than to curl into a ball on the bed and will her stomach into submission, but instead, she forced herself to stand up straight again. "As fun as all this threatening back and forth is, don't you have other things to do? I know how you like to triple-check everything before making a move, and there's not much time until morning."

"You may know a few things about me, Cam, but the same goes for me, but about you. Remember that." He turned and exited the door. One lock clicked, followed closely by another, and she collapsed onto the bed.

Now alone in the darkness, she took a few deep breaths to calm her stomach and look around the mostly dark room. She tried to make out the vague shapes on the far side of the room, but they remained nothing but shadows. Strange. Thanks to her latent abilities, she could usually see just as well in darkness as in daylight.

Then it hit her—maybe her latent abilities had been affected by whatever Richard had had inside that syringe in his car. She decided to find out.

She tried to extend her claws, but nothing happened. Next, she picked up the blanket at the end of the small bunk she sat on, and tried to rip off a piece, but no matter how hard she tugged, it stayed whole.

Fuck. Her strength, her claws, and her keen vision were gone, no doubt because of whatever Richard had put into that needle back in the car.

Not only was she going to be seasick for who knew how long, but without her super-speed, strength, and reflexes, Cam might be in more trouble than she'd counted on.

She started to wish that she hadn't poisoned Marco.

She should've heeded his warnings about watching out for herself. Yet despite Marco's lessons to humble her, such as using his powers to restrain her on the jungle floor, she'd never really taken his warning to heart. She was good, but she'd somehow forgotten that she wasn't invincible.

When it came to operations like the ones she did for DEFEND, she should always have back up, because Cam never knew when she'd end up on a boat, barely able to function. Or, against the odds, someone found a way to suppress her latent abilities.

Working with others didn't signify weakness, and it'd taken a powerful, yet easygoing young man to finally drill that into her thick skull. If she got out of this alive, she was going to break down and thank him for that. The walls she constructed to keep others from getting close had finally succeeded a little too well, and she was now paying the price.

The boat rocked harder, and she grabbed the bucket. While waiting to see what Richard planned to do with her, she would search her room and see what she could use as a weapon.

CHAPTER TWENTY-SIX

Marco looked through the binoculars he'd borrowed from Jorge and scanned the marina, looking for the right boat. "You said it was the tenth one down?"

"Yes. Ekstrom called a mutual acquaintance of ours, and he was very clear about needing a boat."

"I'm starting to think that you need new friends." Marco found the tenth boat down, and saw that it was completely dark. Of course, that didn't mean anything. Ekstrom's crew probably had orders to keep a low profile.

He lowered the binoculars and unlocked his door. "I'm going to check it out." But before he could open it, Jorge put a hand on his arm. "Aislinn said she needed until morning to get my sister free, and I won't let you endanger her life."

Marco needed to wait until he knew Zalika and Jacek were safe anyway before he could try to outsmart Ekstrom. Not that he trusted Jorge enough to tell him that.

He shook off Jorge's hand. "I have no plans to endanger your sister. But I need to plant a tracking device."

"And how do you expect to do that? It's not like we have scuba gear for you to sneak under the hull, or some other type of sneaky spy trick."

"Leave that to me." Jorge remained skeptical. Marco added, "We're in front of an ocean, and I'm an elemental water first-born. You do the math."

"I could say that we're in front of a marina, and I can sail a boat, but that doesn't mean I'm about to sail away to freedom."

Marco slid out of the car and squatted down so that his head wouldn't show. "Your pessimistic attitude explains a lot, but I have experience with this, so let me handle it. I know what I'm doing."

He didn't wait for Jorge's snarky reply, but shut the door as quietly as he could and inched to the rear of the car.

Planting a tracking device wasn't his main aim. Rather, he wanted to let Camilla know that she wasn't alone, and that he was going to help her if she needed it.

Ekstrom had left about thirty minutes ago to run a few last minute errands. Jorge knew the guard on duty, and after a quick call and some blackmailing, the guard had agreed to not investigate any noises coming from the water for thirty minutes. Marco wasn't about to let the man see his face, but he had other ways of contacting Cam without boarding the boat.

Using the shadows to his advantage, he made his way to the marina. Confident the coast was clear, he walked to the water's edge and dove into the sea.

The ocean was chilly, but the night air was warm. Having grown up near the Colombian coast, Marco had no trouble making his way to the first boat on the same dock as his target. He stopped and listened for noises while he checked for any signs of life before moving to the next boat. He continued stopping behind each one until he reached the tenth boat, which was the one that should have Cam on board.

He took out the small waterproofed tracking chip he'd picked up from his contact on his the way to Campeche, and affixed it to the underside of the window. No sooner was the chip in place than the window opened, and someone tossed something into the water; the smell told him it was vomit.

He was about to move his position when he heard, "Fucking hell."

He froze—that was Cam's voice.

The window stayed opened, but Marco waited to see if she was alone. But apart from the sounds of dry heaving, he heard nothing. He'd been careful to make sure no one on deck was facing this side of the boat before swimming up. He was tempted to talk to her, but considering Jorge had negotiated with blackmail, he wasn't going to risk it.

Instead, he created an ice flower on the windowsill—the same carnation as he'd made back in the park—and waited for Cam to return to the window. Except with each minute that ticked by, Marco knew he was putting himself in greater danger of discovery.

Hoping that he was right about her being alone, he sent a stream of water into the room, and then back out to land into the ocean. A few seconds later, he saw her fingers tracing the petals of his flower. Knowing she'd seen his message, he melted the flower and started swimming back to shore.

~~*

After nearly six hours of driving through the mountain roads of Sichuan province in mainland China, Gio nearly bolted out of the car when their driver finally stopped in front of the AMT research facility entrance.

He might finally find some answers here.

He'd managed to sleep on the plane ride to Chengdu—the nearest airport to this place—but as he glanced at Dr. William

Evans, he reckoned that the researcher hadn't slept in days. If he didn't do something about that soon, Evans wouldn't be able to help him in the future.

The driver unlocked the doors and he motioned for Evans to exit the car. The pair of them headed toward the heavily guarded entrance, where a man stepped forward and gave a slight bow of his head in greeting. "Welcome, Mr. Sinclair. My name is Liang, and I manage this facility." He motioned toward the door. "Come, I'll show you to your rooms."

Gio nodded and followed. Liang was middle-aged, and shorter than even Dr. Chan back in Hong Kong. While his outward demeanor was calm, Gio wasn't about to dismiss the man—his father probably had Liang watching him. He needed to be careful about what he said or did. He didn't want to be reassigned before he found out the truth.

He still had no idea what he'd do if he found out they were mistreating the *Feiru* children he suspected they kept here, especially if Gio discovered that his father already knew about it. James Sinclair's support and influence were powerful things, and it wouldn't be easy to work around them.

Don't think about that yet. There was still a chance that his father was ignorant of the pediatrics facilities, where they hid all of the children born inside the AMT compounds. Many of the children were the results of experiments conducted clinically with the first-borns, but Gio had a feeling at least some of the children were the result of rape.

He still believed in the good intentions of the AMT—to keep first-borns from harming themselves or others—but somewhere along the line, corruption had taken hold.

He didn't think dismantling the AMT system was the answer, but there had to be a better way of doing things. He hoped he could come up with an alternative solution while he was here.

As they walked down the long steel corridor, there were no outward signs of this being anything other than a research facility. If he wanted to find out information, he needed to start asking questions. "Is this the empty wing I was told about back in Hong Kong?"

Liang nodded. "When there used to be activity here, visiting researchers and inspectors had needed a place to stay. I've assigned you to the biggest spare rooms. Since any employee that stays full-time at this facility stays in one of the other wings, you'll have this section to yourself."

If the rumors were true, he doubted that any inspectors had ever come to this place. But he kept his mouth shut.

As they continued to walk down the long hallway, Gio noticed the numbers above the doors. Unlike the AMT compound he'd seen back in Scotland, the numbers here weren't sequential, and jumped around in no discernible pattern. He knew Liang wouldn't tell him the meaning of the numbers, but he could aim for more general questions. "When was the last time you used this wing?"

Liang glanced at him. "A few years ago, at least. The number of mentally disabled first-borns holds steady, and the other potential inmates—first-borns with mutated abilities—have been pretty much nonexistent for the last few decades. But if what I've heard about the emergence of strange abilities is true, then I look forward to filling this wing again."

There was an undertone of glee to Liang's words, and Gio started to get a bad feeling about the research facility manager. Could he enjoy mistreating the prisoners here? He added that to his ever-growing list of questions.

Liang turned a corner and stopped in front of an unmarked door. He slid the access card through the slot on the side, a light blinked green, and the door opened. "As requested, this is a shared room. Your two other associates will be in the room directly across the hall. Someone will come along after you've had a chance to rest, and bring you to my office. We can discuss the details of your proposed project then."

Gio nodded, and Liang disappeared. Once the door shut behind him and Evans, he motioned toward one of the beds. "I need you to try and take a nap, Dr. Evans, before we meet with Liang."

The man didn't reply. He looked to be trapped in his own thoughts, much as he'd been the whole ride here. He needed to snap Evans out of it, and soon, or he could lose him as an asset.

He hadn't punched someone since he was a teenager in sixth form, but Gio walked over to Evans, pulled back his arm, and punched the man in the jaw.

Pain radiated up his arm as Evans regained his balance and put a hand to his face. "Why the hell did you do that?"

"I'll do it again if you fall into another bout of self-pity." He hoped not, as his hand bloody hurt. "I understand your dislike of your new ability, but you need to get past that if we're to be successful here."

For the first time since he'd met Evans, the man looked genuinely interested. "What is so important to you here? The mentally disabled are under tight security, with no chance of escape, and looking at a few empty rooms isn't exactly groundbreaking."

Gio wanted to share his hypothesis with Evans, but he didn't trust the man. Not yet. Besides, he had no idea if Liang had the rooms bugged or not. "Get some sleep, clean yourself up, and maybe I'll tell you."

He waited, and finally Evans moved toward the en suite toilet. He stopped at the doorway and said, "I'm only doing this so I can help find a way to get rid of my ability and the other unusual ones. I don't care about you or your plans, just so we're clear."

Evans would change his mind, but for now, Gio said, "Fine by me."

Evans nodded and shut the toilet door.

He waited a few minutes until he heard the shower turn on, and then he moved to the in-room console and tapped the surface. A password screen appeared. He typed in the password he'd been given in Hong Kong, and instantly had access to the local files. Aware that someone could be tracking his searches, he flicked through the basic information about this facility. Maybe he could narrow down where they were keeping the children.

Chapter Twenty-Seven

It was a little after 6 a.m.. Aislinn was on the phone, and Marco was not happy. "What do you mean Jorge will take over the investigation into the arson fires? I'm this close to getting the bastard in charge of it."

Aislinn said, "Are we really going to do this? You know I'll win, especially since Neena's on my side."

If there was one rule inside of DEFEND, it was never to cross Neena Chatterjee unless you had a good reason. Marco himself had learned that lesson the hard way.

Jorge spoke up. "There's no love lost between me and Harry Watkins. He's in charge of these fires, and I have no problem bringing him in."

Marco raised an eyebrow. "How do you know about Watkins?"

Jorge shrugged. "I've heard things. Working with Ekstrom has put me back in touch with some of our mutual former co-workers."

Aislinn added, "And that's why Jorge is going. With Jorge's sister Alejandra in custody, and a few other things in the works, Neena's confident he'll pull through. Besides, you need to focus on Cam and her mission."

Aislinn had yet to mention Cam and her team looking for Talents in front of Jorge, so Marco decided to keep it vague. "Speaking of Cam, what about the boat I asked for?"

There was some typing on the other side of the phone line. "Jorge, give Marco the phone and step outside for a few minutes."

Jorge handed over the phone and went outside. Ever since Aislinn had sent a short video of his sister, showing her safe and sound, the Shadow-Shifter had been a hell of a lot more cooperative.

Even so, Marco was glad that it was still a few hours before the man could shift again.

He tapped off the speakerphone function and put the phone to his ear. "Well? I can't do anything without a boat. At least, nothing in broad daylight."

"It's going to take another hour."

"An hour? Cam was seasick last night, and the longer we wait, the weaker she'll be."

"I'm aware of the situation, Marco. Can you listen for a few minutes without getting emotional?"

"I'm not—"

"Yes, you are. But don't worry, Cam's tough. She can last a little while longer."

He knew that, but the thought of her suffering longer than necessary didn't sit well with him. Still, Marco forced himself to become the DEFEND soldier he knew he could be and said, "Okay, so what do you need to tell me?"

"Ekstrom is going to use Cam to trade favors, and I need you to let her be taken."

~~*

Cam hugged the pillow to her chest, thankfully, too exhausted to even dry heave. Unable to sleep last night, she'd spent most of her time thinking about the ice flower in her window.

Marco had found her.

She'd been a fool to take charge and make decisions, not even bothering to confer with him to see if he had any ideas she could use. The man was a fucking Elemental Master, and yet that hadn't been good enough for her.

Cam was a cocky idiot.

The next time something happened, she would talk with Marco and work out a plan.

The next time? Yes, she wanted there to be a next time. Marco was smart, strong, and full of tricks. He could be fierce one moment, and able to lighten the mood in the next. Around Marco, she could almost be…playful. Not even when things had been good between her and Richard had Cam acted that way.

And considering her latent abilities were still absent, and her team members were still missing, she might need a sense of humor to face her future.

Don't think about that. Worrying about "what if" was a waste of time. She refused to believe Zalika and Jacek were dead, and her abilities would either come back or they wouldn't. She'd been a good soldier before they appeared. Cam had no doubt she could learn to be creative without them.

Maybe she'd even discuss working together with Marco, and lead a team. With Zalika and Jacek to help them, of course.

She was still floored by the trust he'd shown, by telling her about the Elemental Master academies. She had a feeling there was more to it, as she'd heard nothing about his family. For all she knew, his past could be as screwed up as hers.

As interesting as Marco was as a person, she was also attracted to him more than she'd ever been to another man. She

205

decided that if she survived this, she was going to reward him with more than a kiss. After the preview of what had happened back in the park, she was curious to see what he'd do with her when she was naked.

She stopped herself from having another fantasy of Marco naked over her—she'd relived that fantasy far too often over the last few hours. It was amazing what being dehydrated and off-kilter would do to your brain.

The boat went over a rough patch of water. Cam clutched the pillow tight to her chest, breathing in and out until the water calmed.

At this rate, she'd never have the chance to help her friends, let alone see Marco again. Another few days on the water without something to help with her seasickness, and she might die of dehydration.

The locks clicked on her door, and Cam gripped the heavy-duty flashlight that she'd found inside one of the cubbyholes in her room. Her energy levels might be low, but she wasn't about to let someone kill her without a fight.

The door opened, and Richard stood in the doorway. "Time to come out on deck."

Before she could reply, he walked over to her bunk, pulled her up by her arm, and started dragging her.

"Can you slow down? I've been puking my guts out for the last however many hours I've been on this damn ship."

Richard yanked harder. "We have an appointment and can't be late."

Asshole. But struggling would use up energy, and she couldn't afford to spare any in case she needed it for this "appointment."

Somehow, between Richard's grip and her strength reserves, Cam managed to walk onto the deck without stumbling. The sudden brightness of the sun hurt her eyes, but after blinking a few times, she noticed that not only were they in the middle of the ocean, but there was a ship anchored not that far away.

She had a bad feeling about this.

Richard released her arm. "You said that you wanted to try something new since DEFEND hadn't been able to free your sister." He gestured toward the ship in the distance. "If you were telling the truth, then the people on that ship are your new chance."

When she'd made the bluff, Cam hadn't foreseen her current circumstances—mainly the lack of her latent ability and her seasickness. Her best bet was to keep bluffing and find out what she could. "How do you know that they won't just kill both of us, and take your boat?"

"Oh, I know they won't kill me."

That was comforting. "Is that why you brought me on this damn boat, to make me weak so they could kill me?"

"You'll just have to wait and find out."

Okay, that was it. She wasn't going to try to pretend to be anything but herself.

"Richard." She waited until he looked at her. "Look, I'm sorry that your sister is dead, but all of this vague bullshit needs to stop. Just tell me what you're trying to do, and maybe I can help."

Richard shook his head. "No, you abandoned me when I needed you, and I won't risk it again."

She had a feeling Richard was a lost cause, but she couldn't leave it there. "You were the one who let me down, Richard. I went to you for help, and what did you do? You tried to force me to stay by going after Adella. If you can't see how wrong that was, especially after what happened after my skills placement, then I feel sorry for you."

Richard raised an eyebrow. "Sorry for me? You're the one I feel sorry for."

Before she could reply, he picked her up and tossed her overboard.

Her first thought was that she was going to die without ever seeing her sister, Marco, or her team ever again. But as the shock of hitting the water faded, Cam started swimming upwards and made it to the surface.

She used the last of her strength to reach the side of the small, inflatable boat sitting next to Richard's boat, and she crawled in. As she lay panting on the floor of the boat, Richard descended from the foot of the stairs and sat in front of the motor.

She glared at him. "Thanks for trying to kill me, asshole."

"I knew you'd make it. Now, shut up. Your mouth will likely piss off the people on that boat, you really don't want to do that. The Collector's people make the Fed League recruits look like spoiled children."

She wondered who this "Collector" was, but considering a good third of the Fed League recruits from back in the day had been a little crazy, Richard's words worried her a little.

Richard started the motor and headed for the large boat in the distance.

~~*

Gio sat with Evans in a well-organized office, waiting for Liang to show up for their meeting.

FROZEN DESIRES

There was nothing in the room that revealed anything about Liang or what he did here—just a few art pictures on the walls, office supplies on a mostly bare desk, and a locked filing cabinet. Liang was either extremely careful, or extremely tidy.

Evans started drumming his fingers on the arm of his chair, and Gio took a good look at the researcher. After several hours of sleep, he looked a little less like a corpse and was functioning somewhat normally again. He'd even trimmed his close-cut beard and put on a set of fresh clothes. At least for now, his self-pity act seemed to have disappeared.

The door opened and Liang walked inside. "Evening, gentlemen. Did you find your room to your liking?"

Gio didn't want to waste time on small talk, but it was necessary, as he'd learned from watching his father over the years. He forced down his impatience and said, "Yes, everything was fine. The facility is quite modern."

Liang nodded. "Some overseers resist change, but technology has its uses." He sat down in the chair behind the desk. "The people in Hong Kong rarely tell us anything that doesn't deal with the mentally disabled. So, tell me more about these *Feiru* with strange abilities, and why you chose this facility as a possible site for these special cases."

They'd decided earlier that Evans would be better at explaining this—albeit with a few exclusions—so Gio nodded for the scientist to go ahead.

Evans said, "While all first-born children of *Feiru* mothers gain their abilities through chemicals absorbed while in their mothers' wombs—chemicals all *Feiru* females are born with, but don't regenerate after the first pregnancy—it is my belief that other abilities exist among the *Feiru* as a result of genetics and a different type of chemical change."

"Such as?"

"Well, all I have at the moment is a hypothesis, but my hypothesis is that latent abilities appear in groups, often around the same time. An hour ago, I was able to confirm three other cases, which all manifested in the last few weeks."

Liang folded his hands over his slightly round stomach. "Were all of these people working in other AMT facilities?"

Evans shook his head. "So far, only one AMT employee has shown signs of a latent ability."

"Okay, so if the AMT or exposure to first-borns doesn't trigger a change, then what does?"

"I still need to conduct a series of tests to prove it, but I think the change is triggered by something invisible, possibly a chemical reaction in the air."

Gio had first heard this hypothesis about thirty minutes ago. And while it made sense to him—after all, first-borns controlled elemental energy particles in the air to do their "magic"—it would take a little bit of faith to accept such a radical idea.

Liang looked at Evans, then to Gio, and back again. "So you would gather these *Feiru* with strange abilities, place them in my empty wing, and conduct tests on the sources of their power?" Gio and Evans both nodded. "That's all fine and well, but how will you contain these abilities? I have no idea what these 'latent abilities' entail, and I'm not about to have my compound explode or whatever else they can do to destroy it."

Gio spoke up. "Before bringing them in large numbers, I'd like to have one or two with milder abilities brought here and tested by Dr. Evans. That way he can find a way to contain their abilities, much like how the elemental dampers stop elemental magic." Gio paused, but since Liang looked unconvinced, he added, "Of course, you would approve or deny any new entrants into your compound before they would be brought here."

He waited. If Liang said no, they'd have to leave tomorrow. If he said yes, Gio could finally ask for a tour of the facilities and do a little snooping around.

Liang unfolded his hands and leaned forward on his desk. "I want to know, in detail, about what types of abilities have appeared and their dangers. Once I see the list, I can determine if any of them are safe enough to allow here for a trial run."

At least that wasn't an outright no. Gio nodded. "We'll do that today. But in order to better pitch possible dangers and risks, is it possible to have a tour of the whole facility, not just the empty wing?"

"While you were given clearance, Mr. Sinclair, Dr. Evans was not. If you wish to have a tour, you'll have to do it alone."

Gio looked to Evans, and Evans said, "I have work to do. Just show me to a lab with computers, a secure phone line, and database access. I'll start compiling the list for you straight away."

"Done." Liang pressed a button on his desk and stood up.

The door opened to show a short woman, and she said, "Yes, sir?"

"Set up a lab for Dr. Evans in the empty wing, and give him what he asks for." The woman nodded, and Liang looked back to Gio. "I'll have someone come round to your room later and give you a tour. Will that work?"

"Yes. Thank you, Mr. Liang."

"I'm looking forward to maybe working together. The sooner I get the list, the sooner I can give you a more definitive answer."

Evans nodded. "I should have a full report ready for you in a few days."

"All right, gentlemen, if there is anything else you need, just ask Mrs. Wu. She can schedule a meeting once you're ready."

The woman named Mrs. Wu motioned for them to follow her, and they started walking.

So far, so good. Things were going according to plan.

CHAPTER TWENTY-EIGHT

Richard stopped the little inflatable motor boat next to the large yacht, and someone threw down a rope ladder.

He nudged her to get up, but Cam couldn't manage it. She felt like she'd just woken up from a severe bout of food poisoning, and even lying down, she felt woozy. "I can't do it, Richard, I just can't."

He frowned down at her, and for a second she thought he might care if she lived or died, but then a hard expression returned to his face. "I think you have gone soft with age." He shouted to the people above for something to haul her up.

She was too exhausted to reply. A stretcher board secured on all four sides with rope came into view. Richard picked her up, placed her on the board, and strapped her in.

As they hauled her up, she wondered what the hell had happened to Marco. It'd been hours since she'd seen the ice flower in her window. And no doubt he'd done more than just put a flower. If she'd been in his place, she would've planted a tracking device, too.

Yet as far as she could see, there weren't any other boats on the water. He had to know her current location, so where was he?

When she was nearly to the railing on the ship, Cam tried one last time to extend her claws, but nothing happened. She truly was going into this as an underdog.

A man finally came into view—lean with a long torso and broad shoulders—and he hauled her up and over the railing. There was no way to tell if he was human or *Feiru*, but since Richard had said these people would give her a new way to get her sister out of the AMT, she reckoned the man was *Feiru*. And with her luck, he was either a first-born or someone with a latent ability.

The man undid the last strap, stood, and frowned down at her. "So this is the great Camilla Melini, eh? I had expected more."

These people knew of her, so no sense trying to play the part of a weakling. Besides, in her experience, showing attitude earned respect with mercenary-types. "Fuck you."

The man chuckled and looked to a woman with short blond hair standing behind him. "Her spirit is the first thing that's got to go."

Over her dead body.

A third person came into view, and the pair addressed the middle-aged Hispanic man as "captain." He merely stood five feet away from her and stared.

They all kept silent until Richard jumped over the rail and said, "I brought her to you, just as you asked."

The man who'd hauled her up replied, "First we're going to test her. If she passes, then we'll discuss terms."

Richard took a step forward. "If you couldn't tell, she's seasick. Besides, the formula won't wear off for another few hours, and I don't plan on waiting around."

The blonde woman who'd been silently watching from the shadows finally spoke up. "Leave her test to me."

Cam didn't like the sound of that. Using her peripheral vision, she tried to spot something she could use to get away—a life jacket, a life ring, or even an automatic inflatable boat would do. But the closest life boat, where she could find some of those supplies, was twenty feet down the deck.

The blonde woman was now standing over her, and she looked to be about twenty years old, reminding Cam of her own fuck-ups in her early adulthood. She wondered if this woman had been coerced into helping, or if she had joined of her own free will.

The woman opened her mouth, and her blue eyes started to glow as she sang:

"*Sister of my race, heed my call. Let your claws grow as nature intended.*"

At first, nothing happened, but the woman kept singing the same two sentences over and over again. Her eyes grew brighter with each pass, and Cam tried to remember the stories from her childhood, desperate to place what kind of latent power this might be so that she could exploit its weakness.

But on the eighth time around of the woman singing those words, Cam felt the area just below her fingernails start to tingle. Usually, she would feel nothing more than a light stretch when her claws extended, but as they began to grow ever so slowly, it felt as if someone were tearing her fingernails off with a pair of pliers.

Cam gritted her teeth. She'd experienced worse, and she wasn't about to give these people any sort of sick satisfaction.

The blonde woman stopped singing. Cam looked down and saw that her claws were fully extended.

The tall man leaned down, grabbed her hand, took out a mini-metal flashlight from one of his pockets, and used one of her claws to slice through it.

215

As he dropped her hand and stepped away, the woman said, "Only Blue Demons have claws strong enough to slice through titanium." She looked to Richard. "You did as you said you would. The Collector's handler will be in touch."

Cam tried not to blink. How in the hell did they know about Blue Demons? More than ever, she wished she'd heard of this Collector person before.

Richard replied, "And when is that supposed to be? I don't want to leave until I have some sort of proof that the Collector will follow through."

The woman opened her mouth again, but the middle-aged captain spoke up. "You've delivered the cargo, and it's time for you to get off my ship."

Richard opened his mouth to argue, but the captain whistled, and ten crew members appeared with guns in their hands.

Great. She had been hoping that since they were doing an illegal exchange that the ship would have minimal staff. Apparently, she'd been wrong.

She watched Richard stand his ground. Maybe he'd be cocky, and she could see what these people could do.

Richard eyed the crew. "I want to hear from the Collector's handler by tomorrow."

The captain said, "You're a bit of a fool. But the Collector wishes to use you again, so I will pass on your words. That will have to be good enough."

"Fine." Richard headed for the ladder on the rail, but stopped, turned around and looked at her. "Don't worry, Cam, they want you alive. I wouldn't have traded you otherwise."

As if that was comforting. But before she could reply, Richard was gone.

216

Unsure of how long she could get such a good look at everyone, Cam memorized as many faces as possible before the tall, lean man unstrapped her from the board, picked her up, and carried her inside to one of the cabins. As they passed the captain, she swore that the man's face flickered, but she brushed it aside—she'd never met anyone who could change their appearance before. And if such a person existed, Neena would've let them know about it.

~~*

Marco sat in a small boat that he'd surrounded with a low wall of water to hide them from the prying eyes of the other boats.

As soon as Aislinn had told him that his boat was ready, he'd gathered the two local DEFEND soldiers who'd agreed to help him and headed toward the location of his tracking device. They'd arrived before Ekstrom had traded Cam, so he'd had to sit and merely watch as the bastard had tossed her over the side of the ship. Luckily for Ekstrom, Cam had surfaced, otherwise Marco might've had to disobey Aislinn and teach the other man a lesson.

But Cam was still alive, at least for now.

He moved the water to create a small hole in the protective wall. He then used his high-powered binoculars to check and see if Richard Ekstrom was still on the other vessel or not. Because of Aislinn's order, he couldn't do anything for Cam until Ekstrom was safely away.

He spotted Ekstrom back in his own little inflatable boat. The man started the motor, glanced over his shoulder, and drove away.

Marco gripped the binoculars tight as he pulled back and filled the hole with water. Just like that, Ekstrom had left Cam behind. If he hadn't already promised Aislinn that he'd let Ekstrom get away, he'd be tempted to use his elemental water magic to capsize the man's boat.

Just a little longer. She's alive, you saw her not five minutes ago. The sight of her being tied to a stretcher and hauled up to the deck wasn't something he was going to forget any time soon.

He turned toward the two DEFEND soldiers he'd borrowed for this rescue operation and nodded his head. "Let the other two boats know that Ekstrom is on his way, and that I'm going to attack soon. Double-check that they're in the safe zone I designated. I'm not taking any chances."

The woman named Santos nodded, and took out her satellite phone. While she focused on sending the message, Marco turned toward the other person, a man named Jimenez. "Give me two of the inflatable life preservers, and then put on your own."

Jimenez opened the back seat and handed him two of the instant inflatable preservers. "Are you sure Santos and I need one? We grew up along the sea, and have been swimming since we could walk."

"This boat isn't meant to survive a major storm, and I'm not about to put your lives in danger." Marco motioned to the low wall of water that surrounded them. "This is child's play compared to what's coming next."

Jimenez looked skeptical. But Marco had worked with Santos a few times before, and, thankfully, she spoke up. "Usually Marco is more charming with his explanations. Just do what he says, because the sooner we get his lady friend back, the sooner he'll stop growling at us."

He resisted a growl. "Are you done notifying the others yet?"

Santos took her free hand, made an exaggerated show of raising her hand, pressed a button on the phone, and said, "Done."

Marco sighed. He was starting to understand why his old boss Jaxton had sighed and rolled his eyes so often—Santos was irritating him on purpose, much like he had done with Jax. "Take a jacket, stow the phone and the guns in the waterproof, inflatable bag, and wait for the signal."

Once both Jimenez and Santos nodded, he put both of his hands to the west and concentrated on the elemental energy in the air. He was going to need massive amounts of it to pull this off, and he'd only used this much elemental magic once, during his training years ago.

While there was always a possibility he'd burn out, Cam's life was at stake, and he'd do anything to save her.

CHAPTER TWENTY-NINE

Petra handed Millie her fake UK ID card. She glanced down at it, and frowned. "Do I really look like a Donna?"

"Does it matter? Now, hurry up or we'll miss the check-in for the ferry."

Millie tucked the card into the pocket of her jeans. Once they'd gotten off Lofoten Island, Petra had surprised her with a full suitcase of clothes, toiletries, and now an ID card. Good thing, because they were taking the overnight ferry from Norway to Denmark.

They made the rest of the way to the check-in station in silence.

She hoped that once they were inside their private cabin, Petra would start talking. While she was grateful to be free, there had to be loads that Petra wasn't telling her, and that made her uncomfortable.

Ten minutes before the check-in station closed, she handed over her fake ID card and waited. She knew that having one made in less than a day would cost a small fortune, which told her that this person they were going to help meant a great deal to Petra.

After clearing the check-in process, they found their cabin. It was small, with two sets of bunks attached to the wall and a small toilet en suite off to the side. There was barely enough room for her to lay down on the floor, but at least it was an inside cabin and they didn't have to worry about someone peeking into a window. While she was pretty sure they were in the clear, there was always a risk that Larsen or someone he knew could've followed them.

Tossing her stuff on the bottom right bunk, Millie crossed her arms over her chest and leaned against the top bunk. "Right. We made it, so now it's time to talk."

Petra tossed her stuff on the top left bunk and laid down on the bottom one. "There are limits to what I'll tell you, but go ahead, ask me some questions."

"First, where is this research facility we're supposed to break into?"

"Hong Kong."

Millie kept her face expressionless despite her curiosity. She knew the locations of most of the AMT compounds, but she knew very little about the special standalone research facilities. "Do I need to ask specific, in detail questions? Or can you just tell me the general gist of this place, its purpose, and anything else I might find relevant."

Petra looked up at her. "And here I thought you knew everything."

"Just tell me already, Brandt. We have seventeen hours on this bloody ferry, and I, for one, would like to get some sleep before our little adventure."

Petra stared up at the bunk above her. "My friend has spent the last year working in a high-rise research facility run by the AMT Oversight Committee. He's been trying to find a way to eradicate elemental magic."

Millie's eldest brother, Garrett, had spent the last five years imprisoned inside the AMT. Her other brother, Jaxton, had only rescued him recently, alongside Kiarra Melini. Garrett and Kiarra still bore the scars of the torture and experimentation the AMT researchers had conducted on them. She had yet to see her oldest brother, but according to Jax, Garrett couldn't stand to be touched or he'd start thrashing to the point of hurting himself and others. Pain squeezed her heart at thinking of how Garrett, the brother that had always coaxed away her tears as a child, might not ever recover.

She clenched a fist and narrowed her eyes. Since Petra probably didn't know about her brother's escape, she focused on Kiarra's mental and physical scars. "So you want me to help the bastards that treated my friend as a guinea pig?"

"You promised to help me, remember."

She clenched her jaw and took a few deep breaths. If she couldn't get free, she couldn't help Garrett, plain and simple. Until she came up with another escape plan, she needed to work with Petra and not tear her to shreds.

When she had her temper under control again, she said, "So why does this person need you to swoop in and save his arse? He chose to work with those people, and should've known the risks of working there ahead of time."

"He did know the risks, but there was no way he could've foreseen what happened to him."

Curiosity started to overpower her anger. "And what, pray tell, happened to him?"

Petra continued to stare above her, and Millie wished she could see her eyes. "One day, his own latent ability emerged."

"Let me get this straight. The man who had been working to eradicate elemental magic developed his own type of magic, and now he's being given a dose of his own medicine?" Millie shook her head. "If I believed in karma, I'd say she was a bitch."

Petra rolled off the bed and stood opposite her. "Listen, you agreed to help me. I didn't ask for your opinions or commentary. You're here to do your job, and that's all."

"I can say whatever I bloody well please. This person may be your friend, but if you don't want him to know that you're alive, then you need me. So deal with it, or find somebody else."

Petra took a step closer, her eyes flashing. "Without me, you'd still be a prisoner. And I can easily call up Larsen and tell him where you are, and then ditch you. Once Larsen has you, I won't have to worry about you telling my brother or his boss anything because Giovanni Sinclair wants to keep you hidden from the world."

"What? Why?"

Petra shook her head. "No, I'm not telling you anything until this assignment is complete. Once this rescue mission is a success, I'll tell you some details, but not before."

Petra had the upper hand, at least for the moment. Millie might not have much of a choice in the matter, but she wasn't going to just blindly agree to do anything. "Fine. But listen closely, because if I find out that this friend of yours did anything—*anything*—to hurt innocent first-borns, I don't care who he is or what past you two had together, I will find a way to make him atone for his wrongs."

"Will may be many things, but he always tries to make the best decisions he can with the information that's provided to him."

Okay, that sounded like this Will had been misled over the years.

Petra had turned away from her, and was now rummaging through her pack, probably to find the concealed gun Millie knew she had in her luggage. "So that signals the end of our

223

conversation? What about logistics? Or tactics? I'm not about to go into this blind, Petra Brandt."

Petra turned with a file in her hand and held it out. "Here. Review this."

She took it. There had to be at least a hundred pages in the file. "This is going to take a bit to go through."

"Consider it a 'welcome to the job' present. You can go through it while I take a nap."

She watched as Petra curled up on the bottom bunk, slid her gun under the pillow, and closed her eyes. Petra mumbled, "And don't try anything. I'm a light sleeper, much like you are."

"I won't try anything as long as you don't."

"Sounds good to me." Then Petra snuggled into the blanket and went still.

Right, time to get to work.

Millie searched through the files until she found the profile pages about the man they were going to help. Apparently, the bloke who'd recently discovered his latent ability was named Dr. William Evans.

Millie continued to read, curious to find out how this man was connected to Petra.

Chapter Thirty

The man carrying Cam shifted her weight so he could open the door to a small, windowless room. Once he laid her on the bed against the wall, he said, "I'll bring you some drinks to help you rehydrate. The last thing I need is for you to die."

"What are you going to do with me?"

"I can't tell you. But take a bit of advice—just do what they ask, and your life will be a hell of a lot easier."

"I'm guessing you aren't here by choice either."

The man remained silent, which told her all she needed to know. Cam decided that this man hadn't completely crossed over to the dark side. Maybe, just maybe, she could get him to recognize it. "There are ways out of this, you know."

The man snorted. "Sure, tell yourself that. You have no idea what you're talking about. Forget everything you thought you knew about our world because the Collector doesn't follow any laws—human or *Feiru*. She makes her own, and given her army, no one is about to mess with that."

Cam knew she didn't have much more time. This man seemed to think the Collector was invincible, but she clearly hadn't heard of Neena Chatterjee.

The best she could do was plant a seed of doubt. "This Collector might be powerful, but I bet I know someone who is more so."

The man shook his head. "Do you think you're the first person to try to bluff your way free?" He turned toward the door. "Enjoy your optimism, because I assure you it won't last."

He exited the room without another word, and locked the door behind him.

While she hoped that she'd stoked the man's curiosity, she'd also had time to memorize his features—dark hair, tan skin, an intricate tattoo on his neck. All of those things might help, if she could ever fall asleep deep enough to dream and contact Neena. If there was anyone who could stand up to the Collector and her army, it was Neena Chatterjee.

After all, the DEFEND co-leader had her own army at her command.

Cam had also succeeded in distracting the man who'd carried her, and he hadn't noticed that her claws were still extended. It hurt like hell to have them out for so long, but she instinctively knew that if she retracted them, she wouldn't be able to extend them again of her own free will until the formula suppressing her abilities wore off.

The sound of rain started to beat against the hull, followed by the boat pitching up and then back down. She willed her stomach to behave—it was easier to do on an empty stomach—and wished she had a window in her room so she could see outside. When she'd been out on deck not five minutes ago, the sky had been bright blue and cloud-free.

Wait a minute. She didn't want to get her hopes up, but maybe Marco hadn't abandoned her after all. The only way to ascertain if he'd come or not was to get to a window or balcony, and see if the storm was only something an elemental first-born could create.

Cam closed her eyes a second to gather her last vestiges of strength. If she met someone while trying to get to a window or balcony, she was fucked, plain and simple. But anything was better than her lying here helpless and wondering "what if."

She opened her eyes and slid off the bed. She crept to the door and listened, but all she heard, apart from the rain, was the slow creaking of the boat rising and falling with the water.

Good enough. She couldn't be a hundred percent sure there was no one in the hall, but she'd take her chances.

She focused on her next obstacle—the locked door. It had a sideways-extended handle and an insert for a physical key. She put one of her claws into the small space between the door and the door frame, held her breath to make sure there wasn't anyone walking down the hall, and then cut through the lock bar with a small clicking sound.

She counted to ten, and then gently eased the door open. The hall was empty.

Leaning heavily against the wall, Cam scanned for the nearest life ring and emergency kit, and saw one at the far end of the corridor.

Using the wall to remain upright, she slowly made her way toward the emergency kit station. All of the other doors she passed were closed, but she'd deal with breaking into one after she had something to keep her afloat.

While the ship was a little less steady than when she'd arrived, thankfully, it hadn't jolted again since she'd left her room. She reached the kit station and carefully unhooked the life ring and grabbed the small emergency kit. She had no idea what was inside the bag, but there was bound to be something she could use.

Now, all she needed to do was to find a balcony or a window.

All of the sudden, the floor jolted under her feet, and she fell to her knees.

Her insides were a mess, and the exaggerated rocking was not helping matters. But she was nothing if not determined.

Cam laid on her stomach and started to crawl along the floor. There were noises and shouting coming from up above.

The boat rocked hard to the left, and she crashed against the wall. No doubt the crew would be coming downstairs any minute. She needed to find somewhere to hide.

She eyed the closest room and doubled her efforts, using her claws to help pull herself along the floor. As the boat continued to pitch, Cam was grateful that there was nothing left in her stomach.

She finally made it to a door, reached up, and turned the handle.

The door swung open on the next pitch, and she tumbled into the room.

After crashing into the bunk at the far end, small pinpricks of light dotted her vision. She shook her head and blinked until she could focus. While the room was dim, there was light coming from a sliding glass door next to the bed. If she could just make it to the door, she could try to escape.

Dragging herself across the floor, Cam reached the door just at the boat rolled dangerously to one side. This time she slammed into the glass door, hitting her left elbow against the glass. She sucked in a breath at the pain, but it would pass. She could move all of her limbs, so nothing was broken. A better assessment would just have to wait.

As the boat slowly righted, she moved her hand up to the latch and flicked the lock on the glass door. She gave a tug, and nearly whooped when it opened.

Now that the door was open, she could see why the room had been so dim—not only was rain coming down in sheets, there was also snow, hail, and crashing waves. But the odd thing was that it looked clear and calm a few miles away.

She heard a voice and glanced over her shoulder to see the man who'd carried her earlier standing in the doorway, gesturing with his hands to come inside. *No way in hell.* The odd weather, combined with the calm waters in the distance, all pointed to one thing—Marco was using his Elemental Master skills.

She could be wrong, but as the ship rocked far enough that she could jump from the balcony and possibly hit the sea, she made the split-second decision to slide the life ring down around her middle, wrap the strap of the emergency kit around her wrist, and with one last deep breath, jumped over the railing.

~~*

Marco watched as the small cruise ship continued to rock and pitch. He was careful to keep the boat from tipping over, but the more extreme he made the situation, the more the crew on board the other ship would start to panic. And he was counting on their panic for his rescue mission to work.

Santos stood next to him, peering through the high-powered binoculars. He heard her whistle, so he asked, "What is it?"

"Your lady friend just jumped off one of the mid-level balconies."

It took everything he had not to drop his hands and grab the binoculars. "Did she hit the deck or the sea?"

"She jumped when you had the boat tilted."

"And?"

"She hit the sea."

A sense of relief washed over him, although, Cam wasn't safe yet. "Did you see her surface?"

"These binoculars are good, but not that good. You're going to have to ease back on your magic, Alvarez, or you might kill her."

Damn it, Santos was right. But the trick was how to confuse and contain the threat on board the Collector's ship long enough to find Cam.

The trick he'd shown her back in the park gave him an idea. He never would've attempted it if he'd been in plain view of humans. But he had a feeling that even if there were humans on board the Collector's ship, no doubt she'd take care of them rather than expose the *Feiru* world.

Marco stopped the rain and snow falling from the sky at the same time he stopped moving the water around the boat. He now had enough concentration to start moving elemental water particles around the top section of the boat.

As he started to create a shield, he willed the water to freeze. There was a slight delay, but within a few seconds, the water turned solid and an ice dome started to take shape. Even if the crew were brave enough to jump ship, it was now too late. No one, save a Talent or another Elemental Master, would be able to break through his ice barrier.

Keeping the ice in place was much easier than creating it, so once the ice finally met at the top of the oval shaped-dome, he turned his head toward Santos. "That should keep them occupied. Tell Jimenez to start searching the water for Cam."

Santos looked to the small cruise ship, now covered by a two hundred foot high ice containment dome, and then to Marco. "Where the hell did you learn to do that?"

He'd deal with the repercussions of showing his Elemental Master training later. "Contact Jimenez. Now."

His steely tone worked, and Santos picked up her long-range walkie-talkie and said, "Cam's in the water. She jumped off one of the balconies on the east side. Find her and bring her in."

"Roger."

Now, all Marco could do was wait.

After what seemed like an eternity, he finally saw Jimenez's small boat heading toward them. It took everything he had not to lower his hands, dive into the water, and swim over to find out what had happened to Cam. Apart from Jimenez, he couldn't see anyone standing or sitting upright.

That worried him.

No, he wouldn't think like that. Instead, he checked the ship in the distance. But his dome was still in place. It was going to be tricky to remove the dome and cover their getaway, but he would do whatever it took to get Cam to safety.

Jimenez finally pulled alongside their boat and cut the motor. Santos rushed to the side and said, "Fuck, is she okay?"

Marco's heart clenched. "What's wrong with her?"

Jimenez answered. "She's cold to the touch and unconscious, but her heartbeat is strong. If we can just warm her up, she should be fine."

He clenched the hand at his side. "Jimenez, get her on the boat and wrap her in the emergency blanket. Santos, once they're aboard, start our getaway. When we're in the safety zone, I'll finish warming up Camilla."

Santos went to the driver's seat and turned on the engine as Jimenez hefted up Cam and climbed into the boat.

Santos turned them around and started heading back to the coast, but Marco turned to keep his hand to the west or his ice dome would collapse too early. When the cruise ship was a dot in the distance, he decided they were far enough away. He stopped controlling the elemental water particles and let them go free. A sense of exhaustion slammed into him. But he pushed it aside and raced to Cam's still form in the back of the boat.

He motioned for Jimenez to keep watch from the front of the boat before he looked down at Cam.

Her face was pale with dark circles under her eyes. He cupped her cheek, and was grateful that it was only slightly chilled.

Deeming the air warm enough—they were in the Gulf of Mexico after all—he removed the blanket and slowly lifted Cam up against his chest, not caring if he'd get wet in the process. When he finally had her cradled against him, he leaned down and kissed her forehead, letting his lips linger on her skin.

He closed his eyes and breathed in her scent. With Cam unconscious, it was almost easier to admit how scared he'd been when Santos had told him about Cam jumping into the churning ocean. He knew she was a capable soldier or she never would've been able to escape. But he was fast discovering his protective and possessive streak when it came to the woman in his arms.

Cam stirred and nestled into his chest, and he smiled. He'd never really had someone to care about before, and he sure as hell wasn't about to give her up. No doubt she'd make a big fuss when she woke up—either because of poisoning him or some other excuse—but he was ready to fight for her.

CHAPTER THIRTY-ONE

Gio was back in his assigned room, pacing. Evans had left straight away to hide in his new lab. Not that he minded since the lab would hopefully keep Evans focused and prevent him from lapsing back into a depression of self-pity. Gio wanted to know more about these latent abilities, and only a focused Evans could give him that information.

Earlier, Evans had told him about the two other cases he'd discovered. One of them—about a woman using her singing voice to command others—had triggered the long-lost memory that had been nibbling at the back of his mind, a memory of his mother telling him and his two sisters one of her grand bedtime stories:

Gio leaned against his sister Kiarra, and pinched himself to stay awake. He was so sleepy, but tonight his mama would finally tell them the story he'd waited so long to hear—the story about Loreley the Siren.

His mother tucked a blanket around him and his two sisters before she sat down at the foot of the bed. "Gio is looking a little tired. Maybe I should put off this story until tomorrow."

Gio shot up. "No! Please, mama, I want to hear it."

His mother smiled and patted his leg. "If you think you can stay awake…"

"I can, mama, I can!"

His sister Cam poked him in the ribs and he yelped. She snickered. "I'll make sure he stays awake."

FROZEN DESIRES

"Mama, make her stop. Her poking hurts."

Their mother simply gave them a "look" and the three of them settled into place. When they were calm and waiting patiently, she nodded. "I think we're ready. Let's begin.

"Many years ago, a young woman named Loreley lived in Western Germany with her father and two older brothers. Even though she was the youngest child, Loreley had always secretly longed for elemental fire, like her eldest brother. And one day, just after her twenty-first birthday, her wish almost came true."

Kiarra interrupted their mother's story. "Are we going to hear about her brother using elemental fire?"

"No, Kiarra, not today. Now shush, so I can tell the story."

Kiarra didn't look happy, but she nodded and their mother continued. "Loreley was sitting in her favorite place, on one of the ledges of a huge rock face that sat on the river not far from her house, when she noticed a huge wooden ship coming around the bend. Since she came to sit on the ledge at least a few times a week, she knew all of the usual ships that came down the river. But this one had a strange flag on it, one that she'd never seen before. Recently, she'd heard tales of raids in other parts of Germany, and afraid for her family, she murmured to the ship, 'Go away.'

"Of course, the ship kept coming toward her. She repeated the words, but for some reason, she felt the urge to sing them. Over and over, she sang them; wondering why she felt this need. As the ship drew closer, she noticed that it started to change course—it was now heading straight for the huge rock outcropping she was sitting on.

"Not wanting to find out if the ship crashed or not, Loreley climbed down as fast as she could to reach the ground. Once she made it, she ran all the way home and straight into her papa's study. She'd always been close to her papa, so when he asked her what was wrong, Loreley explained everything—including her urge to sing and how the ship had changed course."

Gio's mother paused, as she always did at important points in the story, and asked, "What do you think happened next?"

He always hated this part. He didn't want to guess, he wanted to know. But his sister Cam always took a guess. This time Cam said, "She has a special power. Maybe she'll lead an army."

Cam always wanted the women to lead armies, and if he didn't say something, Cam would keep on guessing, so Gio said, "Tell us what happened, mama."

His mother smiled. "Camilla is correct; Loreley did have a special power. She was a Siren, which meant that she had the ability to command people with her voice. But you'll never guess what her father did next."

Kiarra leaned forward and asked, "What did he do, Mom?"

"You'll have to wait until tomorrow night. It's bedtime."

All three of them groaned and begged her to continue, but like always, she never gave in. She put her arms out for Gio, and he jumped into them. After kissing his sisters goodnight, she carried him to his room, tucked him into bed, and said, "Sweet dreams, Giovanni."

"Goodnight, Mama."

Gio had tried for so long to block out the memories of his childhood. After his parents had died and he'd been separated from his sisters, all he'd ever wanted was for his adopted father, James Sinclair, to accept him. Even as young as he'd been, Gio had known that he couldn't be happy with his new father if he kept trying to remember his real parents.

For more than ten years, he'd succeeded in severing ties, and putting aside any tender feelings for his past life. But hearing about a real-life Siren from Evans earlier, had been too much. In some ways, he was grateful for the memory because now he remembered another important fact from the second half of Loreley's story.

FROZEN DESIRES

Centuries earlier, Loreley had only been one of thousands of *Feiru* with latent abilities that had gone on to protect the legendary Four Talents.

If the new abilities were as widespread as he was beginning to believe, it meant that the story of the Four Talents and their periodical reappearances might be true, too.

There was a knock at his door, and Gio decided he'd have to mention the possible connection between the Talents and the emerging latent abilities to Evans later.

For now, he needed to focus on his upcoming tour of the facilities. Maybe he'd finally see how all of the children who had been born inside the AMT compounds were treated.

Chapter Thirty-Two

Cam snuggled into the soft, warm bed and groaned. The last thing she remembered was being cold—freezing—and wet, yet now she was warm and toasty. But as she rubbed her head against a soft pillow, it all came back to her—the ship, the man reaching out for her, and jumping into the sea.

She tried to sit up, but the action was met with a combination of resistance and a small pinch in her right arm. She remembered crashing into the glass door, but after moving her left arm again, slowly this time, it barely hurt, and she knew it wasn't broken.

Still, she didn't know where she was. She wondered if that man with the tattoo on his neck had retrieved her and taken her somewhere. There was only one way to find out, so Cam opened her eyes. But the room was full of overly bright light, so she promptly shut them. The brightness was like daggers stabbing into her eyes.

"Camilla Melini, open your eyes right now or I'll force them open."

Wait a second. "Zalika, is that you?" Cam blinked her eyes until she adjusted to the brightness. Sure enough, her friend was sitting next to her, smiling. "You're alive."

"Of course I am. A team of DEFEND members rescued Jacek and me."

"Is Jacek all right?"

Zalika rolled her eyes. "He's fine. Although, you'd guess from the way he goes around, showing everyone the tiny scab on his neck, that he'd barely escaped with his life."

Because Zalika had always been good at hiding her true feelings—a thing Cam had in common with her—she pushed. "Tell me the truth—are you okay? Did Richard do anything to you?"

"I'm fine, I swear. There was a hairy moment when I thought your asshole ex might actually slit Jacek's throat, but things turned out all right in the end. Richard Ekstrom is now in the custody of the *Feiru* Enforcement. Your hottie new boyfriend, Marco, set up his capture, so make sure to thank him."

She was too exhausted to correct her—Marco wasn't her hottie boyfriend. At least, not yet. "Where's Marco?"

Her friend merely stared at her, assessing something. She didn't think Marco would've abandoned her, and she refused to think of the alternative. "Well, where is he?"

Zalika raised an eyebrow. "Impatient to see him, are you?"

Cam growled, noticed the IV in her arm, plucked it out, and sat up. "You don't want to fuck with me right now, Zalika. Tell me where he is."

Her friend put her hands up in defense. "Geez Louise, calm down. He's alive. It's Wednesday evening—you were knocked out for nearly a day—and he had to go and retrieve the clue from that Rosa Elena person at the *Novia del Mar* statue."

A sense of relief washed over her, but she was careful not to let it show on her face. Now that she knew he was still alive, she focused on the other shitload of problems that needed to be handled. "What about the Collector's crew? Did DEFEND or Enforcement capture them?"

"No, somehow they managed to escape. Probably by jumping out of one of the windows lower down. Marco had only created an ice dome on the top part of the ship, to serve as a distraction to rescue you, rather than contain the whole thing."

Cam stopped breathing. "Marco created another ice dome, in front of everyone?"

Zalika gave her a look. "What do you mean by 'another' ice dome? Did you know he could do that?"

She gave a noncommittal shrug. It wasn't her secret to share. "You'll have to ask him."

Zalika leaned close. "What is going on between the two of you, Cam? And don't you dare say nothing."

"I'm still trying to figure that out, so don't push me."

They stared at one another until Zalika let out a sigh. "Fine, I'll accept that—for now. I'm more concerned about your recovery. You need to eat something and get some more sleep. You're no longer dehydrated, but food will give you strength."

Speaking of strength, she wondered about her latent abilities. Were they back? She was about to try, then hesitated. Despite her earlier convincing and acceptance, she was nervous. If her abilities were gone for good, she might be pulled from her mission to continue looking for any of the Talents. Marco might be sent to complete it on his own, and she might not see him for a long time. The thought made her sadder than if her latent ability was gone for good.

What's wrong with me? She'd made out with the man once. Okay, almost twice. And despite sharing his secrets, despite his willingness to accept her, despite her attraction to him, in reality, she had no claim. Besides, considering she'd poisoned him between then and now, he might have decided that she wasn't worth it.

Stop it. She wasn't that girl who worried about men and feelings. She was Camilla Melini, soldier and DEFEND commander.

It was time to start acting like it again.

She lifted her hand and tried to extend a claw. When she felt the slight stretching, and saw her claw come out, she let out a sigh of relief. Her abilities were intact. Things could go back to normal.

But the question was—did she want them to?

She felt Zalika's gaze on her, but she refused to look her in the eye, afraid of what her friend might see. Instead, Cam tossed the blanket aside and scooted to the edge. "Food sounds good, but I'm going to take a shower first."

Her friend was quiet, probably trying to figure out what was wrong. Zalika was one of the few people who knew that when Cam didn't look at you straight away, it was because she was hiding something.

Much to her relief, she heard Zalika walk across the floor before she said, "I'll be back within the hour. There are a few protein bars in the duffel bag if you get hungry and a satellite phone next to your bed if you need either me or Jacek."

She glanced at her friend, but her face was unreadable. "Sounds great."

Zalika nodded and was gone. Cam grabbed one of the protein bars and forced herself to eat. She also started humming to herself, hoping that music could help distract her like it had done so many times in her past, and she could avoid thinking about Marco Alvarez.

~~*

Marco approached the large statue of a woman sitting with her knees up to her chest, gazing out at the ocean. The *Novia del Mar* was situated along the Campeche seaside walkway, which was currently filled with walkers, joggers, and bike riders. It was nearly 7 p.m., the weather had finally started to cool down, and he could see about twenty people with their yoga mats rolled out around the statue, waiting for the instructor to begin.

While he knew it was important for him to be here, he wished he were back at the safe house, watching over Cam. The memory of her cold, still body from yesterday still haunted him.

Cam had yet to wake up. The doctor in the area used by DEFEND had suggested keeping her unconscious until she was hydrated again. The doctor had experience with stubborn DEFEND soldiers and hadn't trusted Cam to stay still long enough to recover on her own.

Marco had stayed as long as he'd been able, but he knew the importance of this mission to both Cam and DEFEND. The coin collector in Merida had probably shared his details, including what he looked like, with whoever was waiting for him here. He couldn't risk someone else coming and not getting the information.

Cam would want to see her mission through to the end, and he'd make sure it happened.

Right before coming here, he'd had a call from one of Aislinn's second-in-commands. Apparently, Cam's sister Kiarra was the Fire Talent, meaning that if he and Cam succeeded in finding another Talent, that would give DEFEND two out of the four.

According to the legends, when all four of the Talents were assembled they would have to stop some kind of catastrophe.

Marco hadn't heard of anything brewing yet, and that scared him a little.

But he would worry about that later. For now, finding even one more Talent took priority.

He arrived at the statue, and did a general sweep of the area. The space was wide-open with the ocean on one side, and the walkway and wide-lane street on the other. Satisfied at his safety for now, he pretended to read the sandwich sign on the ground advertising the weekly outside yoga classes. A minute later, a woman came up next to him and said in Spanish, "You look like you're from out of town. Can I help you?"

Time to tread carefully. This woman could be the Rosa Elena he was looking for. "Yes, I'm on vacation with my girlfriend. We're trying to decide if we should stay in Campeche for another week, or if there is somewhere else we should go."

"Have you already been to Chichen Itza?"

"Yes."

"And how about the beautiful city of Merida?"

He nodded. "We especially loved the Sunday Market."

"Hmm, in that case, I have a well-kept local treasure you might want to visit if you're interested in going somewhere without a lot of tourists."

"That sounds lovely. The crowds in some of these places have really started to get to my girlfriend."

"Give me a second, and I'll write it down for you." The woman took out a piece of paper and a pen from her purse, wrote something down, and handed it to Marco. He glanced down and saw the message was written in the old language: *If you need a guide to see the San Rafael Waterfall, go to D&D Tours in Quito, and ask for Diego to take you via the scenic route.*

When he looked up, the woman was gone.

He read it one more time to memorize it, and then tore the paper into little pieces and put it into the pocket of his jeans. He'd burn it the first chance he got.

He'd heard of the San Rafael Waterfall somewhere before, but he couldn't quite place it. All he knew was that it wasn't in Mexico.

Cam would need a day or two more to recover before they left anyway, which suited him fine because they had much to discuss. It was going to take a combination of charm and stubbornness to prevent Camilla from shutting him out again. It'd taken him days of being constantly around her, and a lot of arguing, before she'd started to trust him. He just hoped that his delay to rescue her hadn't broken what fragile trust still existed between them.

Marco picked up his pace, anxious to find out.

CHAPTER THIRTY-THREE

Cam finished drying her hair with a towel and tossed the long nightshirt she'd found inside the duffel bag over her head. Normally, she'd arm herself with something before heading out of the bathroom, but Richard had taken the gun and knife she'd loved. Her latent abilities would do until she acquired some new weapons. Hopefully, that would be soon, because she was anxious to not only get out of Mexico, but also to continue her mission.

Had Marco found the clue they needed? Judging by the dark sky she saw through the small window in the bathroom, enough time had passed that he might have come back.

She put her hand on the doorknob, and her heart started to pound. What if he was on the other side of the door? The last thing she wanted to do was open the door and see hatred in his eyes.

Cam straightened her shoulders. Standing here, wondering this or that was ridiculous. If Marco were on the other side of the door, she'd buck up and talk to him. She might have poisoned him, but they were still both fighting on the same side.

She twisted the knob and opened the door, but the sight of the empty room filled her with disappointment. She'd never voice it aloud, but after being alone and locked up for nearly two days, she'd missed the company of Marco and her team.

While she had no way to contact him, she could at least find out about Zalika. She moved over to her bed and picked up the phone, but before she could dial, a key turned in the lock of her door. Her soldier instincts kicked in.

Cam moved silently to the left side of the door and extended her claws.

The handle turned, and the door opened inch by inch until she could see a crouching Marco on the ground. She sighed. "Couldn't you have knocked?"

As she sheathed her claws, his eyes met hers and he smiled. "Trying to poison me again, Camilla?"

At his teasing tone, all of her apprehension seemed to disappear. She couldn't resist extending a claw at him. "If I were, you'd already be unconscious."

He snorted. "So does that mean I can come in?" He raised a bag. "I brought dinner."

She lowered her claw. "I thought Zalika was getting dinner."

Marco stood and shrugged a shoulder. "I knew a great place, and it wasn't that hard to convince her to let me get you dinner and take over the next shift."

She straightened her shoulders. "I don't need anyone to watch over me. Now that I'm on dry land, I'm strong as ever."

He raised an eyebrow. "You might not be puking your guts out, but you're weak. If I need to restrain you and force feed you, I'll do it."

So this was what it felt like to have someone want to take care of you.

Cam wasn't good at mushy feelings, so instead, she fell back on challenging him. "I'd like to see you try."

His gazed raked over her and back up to her face. "Are you sure about that, beauty?"

Her cheeks heated, and she cleared her throat. If she wasn't careful, she might end up naked before she'd learned about the latest clue. "Maybe later. Right now, I want to know if you met Rosa Elena or not."

Marco walked past her, and she closed and locked the door. Since there wasn't a table, he sat down on the bed and patted the space beside him. "I'm not going to tell you anything until you eat something."

A week ago, she would've barked some reply and dismissed him. Now, after everything he'd done to help rescue her, she decided that she would stop fighting his common sense suggestions.

She moved to the bed and sat down. Marco handed her a container, and he shook his head. She took a plastic fork and asked, "What?"

"I'm not sure if I should be scared that you didn't fight me on this or not." He placed a hand on the bed and leaned in close. "Did something happen to you on that boat that I need to know about?"

His face was only about six inches away, and it took everything she had not to stare at his lips. "While being seasick is annoying, I'll live."

He raised a hand and tucked her still damp hair behind her ear. "That's not what I'm asking. Did Richard or any of the Collector's henchmen hurt you?"

"Why do you care? Considering I poisoned you, I expected a lot more anger. Or yelling."

He lowered the hand from her ear, and placed it near her hip. His arm might be a few inches away, but she was keenly aware of Marco's heat and scent surrounding her.

His gaze turned hot, with his eyes half-lidded, and her heart started to pound in her chest. Since he was good at playing the charmer, she'd wondered about his true feelings. But as he moved even closer, Cam started to believe that he didn't hate her for poisoning him.

She cleared her throat. "Well? Why are you being so nice to me? It's a little weird."

"I'm not being nice. It's taking everything I have not to toss you back on this bed and kiss you. Knowing you were on that boat, and they could be doing who the hell knows what to you, scared the living shit out of me."

She stopped breathing. "Oh."

The corner of his mouth rose. "I was expecting a little more than 'oh,' Camilla." He moved his hand to her hip and she nearly jumped at his touch. "Maybe something along the lines of, 'I knew you'd come for me. You're so strong, and brave, and smart, there's nothing you couldn't do.'"

His high-pitched mocking tone broke the spell of his touch, and Cam snorted. "You must be thinking of some other Camilla, because never in a thousand years would I say something like that."

He leaned in, his voice husky as he said, "There is only one Camilla in the world that I want next to me, and she's right here."

She swallowed at the possessive look in his eyes. All the years of name-calling and put-downs chipped at her heart, and she had a hard time believing him. "You could have anyone. Why me?"

"Because, woman, you're mine."

Her heart skipped a few beats at his tone. She couldn't look away from his gaze as he took the dinner from her hands, and placed it on the table next to them. When he placed a hand on either side of her hips, caging her, the heat of his breath tickled her cheek, and she grew wet.

Since she wasn't wearing any underwear, she clenched her thighs together. Marco noticed. He nuzzled her cheek and whispered, "Are you well enough for me to fuck you right now?"

Her belly tightened. She was done dodging their attraction. She'd had a lot of time to think about Marco naked while she'd been on board that damn boat, and she wanted him. Now. "Yes."

"Good answer."

He took her mouth in a possessive kiss, thrusting his tongue into her mouth as he threaded his fingers through her hair. She ran her fingers up his back, dug in with her claws, and pulled him closer. When her breasts brushed his chest, he growled and used his weight to force her back and pin her to the bed.

She parted her thighs, loving the feel of a hard, muscled man pressing against her. She tried to loop a leg around his waist to bring him even closer, but Marco broke their kiss to look into her eyes and caress her cheek.

She growled. Cam didn't want gentle right now. "Why did you stop? I want you inside of me. Now."

"In time." She was about to protest some more when he took her wrists and moved them over her head. "If you move your arms before I say so, I'll stop. Follow my orders, and I'll reward you. Disobey them, and I'll pull away. How much pleasure I give is entirely up to you."

Her first reaction was to break his hold. But much like how she'd been intrigued by the show of exhibitionism back in *La Noche*, she started to wonder what it would be like to allow Marco to call the shots.

Since she was eighteen, Cam had been in control of nearly every aspect of her life. For once, the idea of letting someone else take charge—in the bedroom and nowhere else—excited her.

She nearly started at that thought. Where had it come from?

However, as Marco stroked the soft skin of her wrist, Cam nearly squirmed at the idea of ceding control and allowing Marco to dictate her actions.

She tried not to think of how much she'd grown to trust the man currently pinning her to the bed. But considering he'd created a fucking snow storm in the middle of an ocean to rescue her—risking it all by using his abilities—she wasn't afraid of handing over her trust.

She decided to give him a try. If things got out of hand, she could always take him out. She nodded. "Okay."

Marco gave a wicked smile. He rose from her body and moved to the side. "I want to see how ready you are for me, Camilla. Spread your legs."

~~*

Marco palmed his cock through his jeans as Cam moved her legs. While all he wanted to do was pound her senseless, he was going to have a little fun with her first. He wanted to make sure she understood how precious she was to him, and how much he desired her.

Her legs were apart, but her fucking nightshirt was in the way. He needed to fix that. "Bend your knees and spread them further."

She flushed, but she obeyed. As her knees inched wider, her glistening, pink folds came into view, and his mouth went dry.

Even from a few feet away, he could see how wet she was for him.

Time to reward her.

He pulled his t-shirt off and tossed it aside. He extended his arm and brushed the back of his fingers against her inner thigh. When he removed his hand, Cam started to squirm, but she caught herself and clutched the pillow under her head.

She stared down at him with smoldering brown eyes. He brushed the inside of her other thigh and said, "You look nice and wet, Camilla. Shall I taste you?"

Her voice was husky. "Yes."

He traced the outer lips of her core. "Yes, who?"

"Yes, Marco."

She moved her legs even further apart in invitation, and his restraint snapped.

He moved between her legs and spread her open. He looked up into her eyes before he gave a slow lick up her core, but stopped just short of her clit. Cam moved her hips toward him, and Marco pulled away. He deliberately licked his lips before he said, "Patience. Keep still until I tell you to move."

He could see she struggled to obey, but eventually she nodded.

He kissed the inside of one thigh, and then the other, before he tasted her again. With her scent invading his nose and her juices on his tongue, his cock hardened to the point of pain. To share his frustration, he nipped her clit gently between his teeth. Cam moaned and arched her back, drawing attention to the pointy buds of her nipples poking through her nightshirt. Suddenly, all he could think about was sucking them deeply.

He gave one last flourish of his tongue. Then he put his hands just under the hem of her bunched nightshirt and slowly lifted it, caressing her skin in the process. When he reached her breasts, he deliberately used the material to rub across her nipples.

Cam moaned. He smiled, because he was just getting started.

"Release your grip on the pillow and lift your head and neck."

She obeyed, and he tossed the nightshirt aside. She put her arms back over her head and gripped her elbows. The fact she did so without a fight showed just how much she was starting to trust him.

He maintained eye contact as he pinched her hard, little nipples. "While I've told you how I admire your intelligence, I'm going to make sure you understand how beautiful you are to me." She blushed and looked away. He pinched her nipples again. "Look in my eyes and see I'm telling the truth."

She slowly turned her head and met his gaze. He leaned down and took her lips in a brief, rough kiss. "I don't like it when your confidence falters. You're beautiful to me. Learn to accept that."

~~*

Cam had never thought of herself as beautiful, but as Marco said the words with desire burning in his eyes, she started to believe him.

Her core was already throbbing from the attentions of his tongue. Part of her wanted him to just fuck her already, but she was starting to like not knowing what he would do next. She couldn't remember being this wet in her life.

252

Not sure how to respond to his statement, she merely nodded. But when he moved away from her and stood up, she nearly whimpered. Had she done the wrong thing?

Marco leaned over her and traced her jaw. "Don't worry, beauty, I'm far from finished."

Relief washed over her, and Cam tried not to think about the power he had over her.

He unbuttoned his jeans before slowly unzipping them. Each inch revealed not underwear, but dark hair and his hard cock. When it finally sprung free and reached toward his belly, she licked her lips, wanting to taste the salty masculine essence that was Marco Alvarez.

He took something out of his pocket and kicked off his jeans. He moved back to the bed, and kneeled between her legs. He placed an unused condom next to her head and said, "For later. For now, I want to cover my cock with your juices and feel how wet you are for me."

Holy hell, his dirty talk just made her hotter.

He took his cock in hand and held it an inch from her core. She watched and waited, her clit starting to throb in anticipation. She wanted to shout for him to get on with it, but she didn't want to risk him stopping.

Finally, he said, "Close your eyes."

Cam always liked to know what was going on, but deep down, she knew she had nothing to fear from this man. She closed her eyes and was rewarded with a brush of ice across her nipples.

Then it was back to nothing. She was just about to squirm when Marco's hot mouth took her nipple into his mouth and sucked. The heat of his mouth after the chilliness of the ice sent a jolt through her body.

When he bit her a little roughly, she clutched the pillow tighter to avoid threading her fingers into his hair. He released the first nipple to take the other, and at the same time, she felt his cock start to rub against her. Not being able to see Marco's actions made her body more aware of them, and as his cock circled her clit—never touching it—the pleasure/pain started to overwhelm her.

Then he released her nipple and took away his cock. She couldn't help but cry out, "Why?"

She heard a chuckle, and it took everything she had to keep her eyes closed. She didn't want to risk him stopping now.

A rustle near her head and then a tearing sound gave her an idea. When Marco spoke, his accent was thick. "Because I want to do this."

He thrust into her and Cam cried out. But he didn't move. Instead, he flicked one nipple, and then the other. She was about to tell him to get on with it when he put his hands under her ass, lifted her, and started pounding in and out so hard she moved up the bed.

The combination of his rough thrusts and hearing the slap of flesh on flesh without being able to see it was the most erotic thing in her life. She arched to help with the angle, and Marco moved one of his hands on her ass away, only to come back hard, leaving a little sting.

"Let me be in charge just a little longer, Camilla. I'll hand it back after you come."

"Then make me come, Marco. Please."

He growled and thrust harder before she felt a pressure on her clit. He started to move his finger back and forth. Lights started to dance across her closed eyelids. When she felt something cold pinch her nipples, she let go.

254

As she started to spasm, Marco redoubled his efforts. His movements prolonged her orgasm into some kind of blissful state she'd never experience before.

Soon he stilled before his weight settled on top of her. She felt his breath on her cheek. He kissed her gently and said, "Open your eyes."

She did, only to see his dark eyes staring at her with a mixture of lust and tenderness. He brushed her cheek. "Relax, Camilla. You did well, and as promised, I'm giving you back control."

She lowered her arms and burrowed her head into his neck. He put his arms around her and moved so that she lay on his chest. She listened to his heartbeat, not quite ready to look him in the eye again.

It scared her how much she'd enjoyed what they'd done. The only question was if Marco was really going to be able to leave his control in the bedroom. If he couldn't treat her as an equal in the field, and let her be herself, it would break her heart.

CHAPTER THIRTY-FOUR

Marco laid his head against the top of Cam's and played with the long strands of her soft, black hair. Half of him was content to lay like this all night. The other half wanted to take her again, this time with her on her hands and knees in front of him. Maybe she'd even wear a blindfold.

His cock stirred to life, and he realized just how far they'd come.

When he'd first met Cam two weeks ago, he never in a million years would've imagined he'd be lying with her naked right now. Just thinking of her calling him a "horny sidekick" made him chuckle.

Cam brushed her hand against his chest, and asked, "What's so funny?"

Good, she was finally ready to talk to him again. She'd been silent ever since they'd finished, and he had started to worry that he'd pushed her too far.

Hopefully, his memory would help lighten the mood. "I was just thinking about how you'd dismissed me as a horny sidekick."

She raised her head to look at him, the fire back in her eyes. "Well, what was I supposed to think? You acted as if you were the world's greatest gift to womankind. How was I supposed to know it was all an act?" She poked his rib. "I'm curious, what did you think of me at first?"

He smiled. "You were so indifferent to my charm, I wasn't sure if you preferred women, or a man to boss around and do your will."

She rolled her eyes. "Yes, because the only reason a woman wouldn't want you is because she is a lesbian."

He slapped her ass. "Scamp."

She grinned, and the sight sent blood straight to his cock. She opened her mouth to say something, but Marco rolled them over and trapped her beneath his body. "Maybe I need to prove to you why you're the luckiest woman in the world right now."

He lowered his head to kiss her, but Cam put her hand over his mouth and said, "Believe me, I want you." She reached down, gripped his cock and squeezed, making his cock go from semi-hard to rock hard in a matter of seconds. "But neither one of us can spare a night of hot, sweaty sex until our missions are done. You need to tell me about what you found at the *Novia del Mar.*"

He groaned. Leave it to Cam to stay focused, even when they were both naked and horny.

But he knew her well enough to know that she wouldn't be deterred until she had the information she needed. Still, he couldn't resist moving her hand away and giving her a quick, rough kiss. "Just to remind you of what you're turning down."

She brushed his lips with her fingers. "The sooner you start talking, the sooner we can get going. I'm sure we'll have some travel time to kill along the way, and there's a high chance I'll be naked for some of it."

He nipped her fingers. "If it means I can be inside you again sooner, then fine." Needing to put a little distance between them to help him focus, Marco rolled off her, propped onto his side, and said, "At the *Novia del Mar* statue, a woman came up to me. After some chitchat that I'm pretty sure was a test, she wrote out a vague message written in the old language. At first I wasn't sure what it meant, but while waiting for your dinner—" He looked at the untouched container of food on the nightstand next to the bed. "Camilla, you must be starving. Go ahead and eat while I debrief you."

~~*

Touched by Marco's thoughtfulness, Cam laid a hand on his chest. The lingering dampness and hard muscles under her fingers reminded her of earlier, and it took everything she had to focus and not reach out for his still-hard cock. In all honesty, she wanted nothing more than for him to fuck her again.

But she had duties, as did he. She was grateful that he was still helping her but no doubt he wanted to focus on his mission too.

Since Marco was male—a plainly aroused male—it was going to be up to her to keep them focused while they were naked. Although with all of his smooth, tan skin in front of her, even she was having trouble when it came to caring about their missions.

However, sex wouldn't help them find a Talent.

She focused. What had Marco been talking about? Oh, right, eating dinner. "I ate a protein bar earlier. Just tell me what you discovered so I can finish my mission and help with yours, if you still want my help."

He reached out and tucked her hair behind her ear. She was starting to love when he did that. "I'll always want your help, but right now, the only mission I have is yours. Aislinn gave the arson fire investigation to someone else."

She sat up. "But why would she do that? You're the one who found the witnesses that led us to Harry Watkins. Moreover, I'm the one with the contact to help us catch up with him. My contact is a little paranoid and isn't going to work with just anyone."

"I don't know who your contact is, but I met someone else who can lead DEFEND to Harry Watkins." He explained about the Shadow-Shifter named Jorge Salazar, and his connection with the Fed League.

Cam frowned. "I've never heard of a Jorge Salazar. He must've joined after I left. Are you positive that Aislinn and Neena vouched for him? Using his sister as blackmail—even if it's to save her—doesn't exactly inspire loyalty."

He raised an eyebrow. "You can try asking that to either one of them, but that would mean questioning them, and I don't think you have the proof to do that."

Since Neena could see visions of the future, a person only questioned her when they were positive of something, and Cam had nothing to make Neena change her mind. "I know, but it just seems unfair that they'd take this from you, especially when you've done such a good job with it."

He laid his hand on her hip and squeezed. "Thank you."

"For what?"

"For being on my side."

She refused to dwell on why she'd done it, and decided that since she didn't handle gratitude well, it was best to brush aside his thanks and push on. "What about your family? Will you still be allowed to help them?"

Marco ran his hand down from her hip to rest on her thigh, and it took everything she had to concentrate on his response.

"Yes, and you can help me with that after we get to the bottom of the clue I got this evening."

Just knowing that he wanted her to help with his family warmed her heart. Maybe this thing between them would work after all. "Okay, so tell me about the clue."

He recounted his meeting with the woman and the message, then he said, "At first, I wasn't quite sure what or where San Rafael was, but while waiting for your dinner, I looked it up. We need to head down to Quito, Ecuador to ask for this Diego person to take us on a special tour to the San Rafael Waterfall."

Cam tried to remember what she knew of the area down there. "Aren't parts of Ecuador crawling with drug traffickers, guerrilla groups, and all sorts of gangs?"

"Most of that is near the border with Colombia. Quito does have some crime, but we're experienced enough that we should be safe."

She definitely needed to get some weapons before they went looking for this Diego person. "What about contacts? Do you have any down there? If not, I got a few from the vendor back in Merida that we could use."

"Colombia is my home turf, so I have plenty of contacts, but I'll use whatever you've got too. Will you share them with me later?"

There he went, asking her for something and including her in his plans again. Maybe he really was different, and he'd become the first man she'd met who could keep his control and desire to dominate for when they were naked.

She started to think of what he might do to her if she gave him more rein in bed. He'd restrained her with ice in the jungle; maybe he could do it in bed too.

FROZEN DESIRES

The image of cool ice around her wrists and ankles, restraining her while Marco licked between her thighs made Cam wet.

Marco waved his hand in front of her face. "Cam? Are you with me?"

Her cheeks flushed, but she did her damnedest to act nonchalant. "Yes, of course I'll share the contacts with you later."

He brushed the side of her breast. "Are you sure we can't spare fifteen minutes? You're as distracted as I am right now." He ran a finger over her nipple. "What was on your mind, Camilla, that made you blush?"

Her nipples tightened, betraying her. But she knew if she didn't set this boundary now—that finishing missions was more important than anything else—she'd be fighting an uphill battle for the rest of their time together.

She batted his hand away. "We can have hot, kinky sex later. Right now, every minute we waste is a minute someone else could discover this Talent we're hunting. And we can't allow the pro-AMT side, or even worse, a human, to have a chance of finding the first one."

Marco's look sobered. "Haven't you heard, Camilla? DEFEND already has the first Talent. Your sister Kiarra is the Fire Talent."

She blinked. "What? Since when?"

"Since a few days ago. Aislinn told me while you were with Ekstrom. I was going to tell you, but it sort of slipped my mind."

Kiarra was a Talent?

The brief few hours Cam had seen her sister back in the States, Kiarra had barely been able to hold a conversation. Now she was one of the four most powerful *Feiru* on the planet. "How is she handling it? Is there a protection strategy in place? And who would be in charge of that?"

"Jaxton. He and your sister are a thing now." Marco smiled. "I pity the person who tries to harm the woman Jax loves."

She twisted her hair to one side and then tossed it back over her shoulder. She'd noticed how protective Jaxton had been around her sister, but she never thought he'd fall for one of his trainees. "Love? Bossy and straight-talking Jaxton Ward?" Cam blinked again. "Well, shit. He'd better not hurt her, or I'll have to cut off his balls."

Marco snorted. "From what I've heard, she can take care of herself. But she's only the first, and you're right, we need to focus on the others. I'll call one of my buddies to make travel arrangements." He leaned forward and placed a gentle kiss on her lips. "If you want to take another shower, now is the time to do it. No doubt we'll have to leave tonight."

The first chance she had, she would call Kiarra and find out how her sister was doing—no excuses this time.

Cam remembered about her team. "What about Zalika and Jacek? I want them to come with us."

"I can call them, if you want."

"Since when do you have their phone numbers?"

He grinned. "I can be quite persuasive."

She slapped his arm. "I don't want to know. Make your calls, and if you're quick enough, maybe you can join me in the shower before we have to meet up with my teammates." She stood up, and walked across the room. Marco whistled, and she gave him a look before deliberately bending over to pick up the duffel bag.

"Woman, you're killing me here."

Cam smiled. "Well then hurry up, and maybe you'll get lucky in the shower."

Marco whipped out his phone and started dialing. "I'm going to hold you to that."

She laughed and made her way to the bathroom. Provided there was a Talent at the end of all this clue chasing, things were looking up for her.

She was a skeptic at heart, but Marco was starting to worm his way inside, making her a little more optimistic. A week ago, being influenced by a man would've scared her, but now, she was actually content. Maybe even happy.

Hopefully, her track record of things going to hell whenever she finally felt content with her life was finally broken.

CHAPTER THIRTY-FIVE

Gio and his guide—a security officer named Xu—approached yet another locked door. They'd been walking for nearly thirty minutes, and he had yet to see much of anything apart from hallway upon hallway of doors with random serial numbers.

The facility must wind through more of the nearby mountains than he'd originally calculated.

He noticed that the sign above the door here had more Chinese characters than any of the others they'd gone through before. Maybe this one would finally lead to the section of the facility he was anxious to see.

Xu slid his keycard through the slot and entered a password. Just like with the other doors, Gio heard a click before it slid open, except this time, instead of another empty hallway, a man and a woman stood in the space in front of them.

Xu—like most *Feiru*—spoke some English, and said, "Yang and Wallace will take you from here."

The female nodded at Xu, and the security officer left. Once alone, the man at her side reached out a hand to shake. "I'm Gregory Wallace." He motioned to the woman at his side. "And this is Crystal Yang."

The man's Scots accent reminded him of home. "Giovanni Sinclair." He shook and released Wallace's hand. "Are you two going to give me a proper tour? Xu was less than forthcoming."

Wallace handed him a clipboard. "First, while you've been given top level clearance, I need you to read this nondisclosure agreement and sign it. Once you do that, we'll answer any questions that you might have."

He took the clipboard and read the one page document. He'd seen similar agreements before, although this one was stricter. Gio was prohibited from sharing the information he learned inside the facility for life. If he violated the agreement at any time in the future, his case would be decided by the *Feiru* High Council. Penalties included up to a death sentence.

If this was the kind of protocol that had been used with all of the AMT researchers then no wonder the general *Feiru* population didn't know anything.

Careful to keep his face expressionless, he skimmed the important details one more time and committed them to memory in case he needed to figure a way out of it later. Satisfied, he signed his name at the bottom.

Wallace took the clipboard and nodded. "As you might've guessed from the form you just signed, this section of the AMT system is top secret."

It would be best to play ignorant. "What kind of research do you do here?"

The woman motioned for them to start walking. "Given your clearance, I'm guessing you know about the experiments being conducted on the first-borns?"

"I've only recently acquired my clearance. I know there are three types, but could you give me a quick overview?"

Wallace took over. "Each first-born is assigned to one of three types of experiments during their first year inside the AMT, and continue undergoing treatment for life. The three experiment tracks are: psychological, gene therapy, and breeding."

Luckily, Gio already knew about the breeding experiments, so he could keep his expression bland. "Is that what you do here?"

Yang shook her head. "No, we do something much more important. We raise the children born inside the AMT compounds, and monitor them for genetic shifts. Our ultimate goal is to use them to eradicate elemental magic."

The pair must not yet know about the other abilities emerging, and he wasn't about to share it with them. "What happens to the non-first-born children born inside the AMT compounds?"

Wallace motioned for them to turn a corner. "The records aren't always kept up to date with which first-born is bred with who, and each of the three experiment tracks have their own set of secrets, so it was decided to just transport them here, for everyone's safety."

"Have any of the children shown dangerous side effects that could endanger others?"

"Not yet," Yang answered. "But would you want to risk everything the AMT Oversight Committee has worked so hard to protect? Here we can monitor them closely, in case something goes wrong."

So the children were guilty until proven innocent.

To mollify Yang, he said, "I'm just trying to understand what goes on here."

They reached another door that required both Yang and Wallace to put their thumbs to a scanner to unlock it. Once the door opened, Wallace motioned both Yang and Gio ahead of him.

They walked a few more feet before Yang opened yet another door—he had to commend them on their security protocols—and Gio followed. Inside the small room were computers, chairs, and monitors. Yang did something on a keypad, and a screen lifted from the inside to show a dormitory-style room with six sets of bunk beds. The beds were empty, but as he scanned the room through the glass, he noticed twelve children sitting around a table, drawing pictures. They all looked to be between the ages of five and ten. "Are those some of the children?"

"Yes. This is group 5A."

He wondered if the children were raised with serial numbers from birth, but now wasn't the time to ask that question. "How do you raise the children? Are they brought here as infants?"

Yang replied, "They're moved to this facility at eight weeks of age. We have a special wing for the infants, but once they're two years old, they're transferred into a room with other children. The interaction with others their age helps keep them preoccupied. They're also allowed to play, draw, sing, or any other number of harmless hobbies."

"But what about social interaction with adults? Or an education?"

Wallace gave him a strange look. "An education is the last thing we want to give them, or they'd start asking questions. We treat them well, but we do what we think is best for them."

It took everything he had to keep from reacting to Wallace's words. "Who decides their activities or their upbringing?"

Yang answered, "The AMT Oversight Committee."

Gio had never given much thought to the Oversight Committee, but after the number of times they'd been mentioned today, he was going to have to look into it.

Yang closed the window screen and motioned toward the door. "Most of this wing is a collection of rooms like the one you just saw. We'll visit one of the research rooms, and then Xu will return to take you back to your quarters."

As Gio followed the two researchers down the hall, he braced himself for what he might see. The researchers had been less than ethical with the adults, and he truly hoped they did better with the children.

Yang and Wallace opened another room by pressing their thumbs onto a scanner. Gio took a deep breath and walked inside.

The two-way mirror didn't have a screen this time. It looked into a sterile exam room, similar to the one back in Scotland he'd used to interrogate Millie Ward. Instead of an adult, however, there was an unconscious child strapped to a metal table in the center of the room.

One scientist was standing next to the table, injecting a syringe into a young boy who looked to be about twelve years old. Even if he was a first-born—which didn't seem to matter in this facility—there were some things that shouldn't be done.

Experimenting on children was one of them.

While he wanted to charge in and release the child, the action would accomplish nothing. He needed information if he was ever to have a chance of freeing the children. Gio kept his voice calm and asked, "What experiment are they running here?"

"The boy is a first-born on the cusp of magical maturity. We're trying an antibody serum, developed from the chemical lining of a young woman's uterus. Our hope is to prevent him from feeling elemental particles in the air, and thus nullifying his abilities."

He surprised even himself when his voice came out devoid of emotion. "Was there anything special about the young woman they used to make the serum?"

Wallace shook his head. "Other than the fact she was sterilized to preserve the chemicals in her uterus, no, there was nothing special with the young woman."

They were sterilizing children now? Gio couldn't believe how these two talked about living, breathing *Feiru* as if they were nothing more than lab mice.

Now, a much bigger goal was forming in the back of his mind, and he forced down his anger. "Dr. Yang, Dr. Wallace, thank you for showing me around. But I need to be heading back so that I can confer with my colleague."

"Of course," Yang said. "We'll take you back to the entrance of this wing, and Xu can show you back to your room. If you have any more questions, just call one of us and ask."

"Thank you."

As they led him back down the hallway, Gio hoped that Evans had put together a docile enough list of latent abilities to appease Liang. While Gio had seen a few abuses today already, he wanted to dig deeper.

He needed to gather evidence if he ever wanted the chance to change the things he'd seen today. He also needed to see how much his father knew about this because if James Sinclair supported the actions they were conducting on the children here, Gio was going to have to reevaluate his goals and figure out how to deal with his father.

CHAPTER THIRTY-SIX

After a number of buses and several plane transfers, Marco was finally on the last plane that would take him, Cam, and her team to Quito International Airport in Ecuador. As their plane left Panama City behind—the place of their final layover—Marco took a good look at Cam and tried not to frown.

She did better on planes and buses than on boats, but he could tell all of this flying was getting to her. She looked pale and had refused to eat much of anything over the last twelve hours.

Cam and Marco had spent most of their time separated from Zalika and Jacek, in case one group needed to back up the other. He'd managed to ask Zalika about how Cam usually traveled. She'd told him that if Cam had someone she trusted to look over her, she'd take a sleeping pill and wake up refreshed and ready to go once they reached their destination.

She'd yet to take any kind of sleeping aid, which made Marco wonder if she didn't want to appear weak in front of him again, or if she just didn't trust him outside of the bedroom.

The thought of it being the latter grated at him.

They hit some turbulence, and Cam clenched her jaw. He decided she was being ridiculous. He leaned toward her and growled. "Take your damn sleeping pill. You'll be no use to anyone if you keep being stubborn."

She gave him a startled look. "How do you know I have sleeping pills?"

"I was tired of seeing you suffer for no reason, so I asked your friends for some help."

She shook her head. "Anything could happen, and if I'm unconscious, that would be a huge liability. I'll survive this. I've done it before, you know."

He kept his tone low. "What the hell are you trying to prove? I know you could sit through this and suffer in silence. But, woman, seeing you do it for no reason upsets me. Take the fucking pill, and I'll watch over you. Unless you don't trust me to keep you safe."

Cam hesitated, and it was like a stab into his heart. He whispered, "You don't trust me."

She placed a hand on his arm. "No, it's not a matter of trust."

"Then what is it, Camilla? Because I don't see any other explanation." She bit her lip, and some of Marco's tension eased—Cam never bit her lip. He took her hand and said, "What is it? You can tell me."

She looked away. "The last thing I want is for you to think I'm one of those clingy, needy women."

He smiled. "Somehow, Camilla, I doubt that is possible."

At his amused tone, she shot him a look. Good, her fire was back.

"Maybe I should become one, just to piss you off then."

He squeezed her hand. "You're deflecting. Tell me what's wrong, because I'm not going to let you off the hook, even if it takes me the entire plane ride to wheedle it out of you."

She sighed. "And you would, too. Fine. Ever since I've woken up from the whole jumping-into-the-ocean thing, whenever I try to close my eyes, I feel as if I'm back on that boat, helpless and weak. Unless…"

He brushed her cheek. "Unless what?" She mumbled something he couldn't hear, so he said, "Louder, Camilla."

She blurted out, "Unless I can feel you next to me. For reasons I can't explain, your scent seems to calm me."

Marco blinked. He'd worried about her trusting him, and here she was, telling him he was the only thing that helped chase away her nightmares.

He knew how hard that admission was for her, so for once he wasn't going to tease her. Instead, he raised the armrest between them. "Then come here and lean against me."

She hesitated, and he had a feeling he knew why. "Denying a weakness is far more dangerous than admitting one. If sleeping against me will help you get the strength you need for our upcoming visit, then do it. Seeing as I haven't showered in nearly a day, there's plenty of eau de Marco to chase away even your worst nightmares."

Cam smiled, and he knew he had her. She eased against him and he pulled her close with his arm before laying his head on top of hers. "Do you think you can sleep now, even without a sleeping pill?"

She nuzzled against his chest. "Yes, I think there's enough eau de Marco to lull me to sleep."

He chuckled. "Good girl. Now sleep, I'll wake you when we're about thirty minutes from landing."

"Marco?"

"Yes, Camilla?"

Her voice was sleepy when she answered. "Thank you."

He sat up and leaned his head against the seat. "Hush and go to sleep."

She stilled and soon her breathing started to even out, telling him she was asleep.

He brushed her hair back with his free hand and studied her face as he thought about what she'd admitted to him. Even though they'd only known each other a short time, she'd given him her trust both in and out of the bedroom.

And considering all of the shit she'd gone through with her ex, he wasn't about to take it for granted.

Cam mumbled something in her sleep and snuggled closer against him, if that were possible, and her actions shifted something inside of him. It'd been a long time since he'd had a woman to look after. Too long, in fact.

She'd given him something, so Marco decided he'd give her something in return. Once they landed and were some place secure, he was going to tell her about the other Elemental Masters.

~~*

Cam suddenly appeared in the middle of an empty water park. Looking down, she noted the skimpy bikini, and was grateful that no one was around to see it.

But while she could see the sun in the sky, she didn't feel any warmth. Determined to find out why she was half-naked at an empty water park, she started walking. When she passed a large jungle gym-like structure standing in the middle of a shallow wading pool, she heard a unique whistle.

She looked over and noticed a woman in a bright pink bathing suit, her curly hair plastered against her head as a large tub of water poured over her. Once the water stopped flowing, the woman climbed down the structure and headed over to Cam.

When the woman was close enough, Cam said, "Neena, care to tell me why you decided to bring me to a water park?"

Neena grinned. "Well, I needed to dream-speak with you, and I didn't know how long you were going to take to get here. So I decided to find a place to play and relax while I waited."

Dream-speaking with Neena was old hat by now, so Cam knew to just push on and avoid distracting her. "Just tell me what you need."

Neena rung out her long hair. "For once a, 'How are you Neena?' or 'I love the location you choose, Neena' would be fantastic. But I guess that's asking too much."

Cam shrugged. Arguing would only distract her.

"Fine," Neena said. "What I need from you are images of the people you saw aboard the ship, the one with the Collector's people."

She wondered how much Neena knew about the Collector. "Am I allowed to ask why? Or, maybe even, what you know about her?"

"Well, the Collector is a recent thorn in my side, mostly because I can't see her face in my visions. I'm hoping I can use one of her people to lead me to her, hence, why I need the faces of the people you saw on that ship."

While Marco and her team had told Cam a little about the Shadow-Shifter and the Collector, she wanted to know more. She chanced a question. "Why does DEFEND need to track down this Collector woman?"

Neena gave her an impatient look. "Because she's a pain in my arse, and I need to take care of it. Why else?"

That didn't tell her anything. Getting an answer out of Neena was close to impossible, but Cam was going to try one more time. "But how is she a pain in your ass? Is she poaching future recruits or something?"

Neena waved her hand in dismissal. "Enough chit-chat, I need you to concentrate and show me all of the people you saw aboard that ship, and what happened."

Great. When Neena said 'no,' then getting anything out of her was akin to banging your head against the wall. It was best to give her what she wanted, and get the hell away as quickly as possible before she asked for some kind of strange favor.

Cam had shared images with Neena before and knew the drill. She closed her eyes and recalled the details of the man, woman, and ship captain. Once she had as many details as she could remember, she let the events play out in her head. When Cam reached the part about jumping into the ocean, she opened her eyes to see the last of her memories fade away. She didn't know how Neena did it, but she could make the memories recalled during one of her dream talks play on a free-floating movie screen in front of her.

Cam waited, and finally Neena said, "How positive are you that you saw the ship captain's face flicker for a moment, revealing a glimpse of pale skin?"

"I remember the flickering, but I just assumed it was related to my weakened state. You think it could mean something else?"

"Possibly. But don't worry yourself about it. I want you to focus on finding that Talent."

"Speaking of which, I was wondering—" Cam started moving, as if someone were shaking her shoulder. "Damn it, already?"

Neena winked. "Your lover boy awaits."

Before Cam could reply, the world blanked out.

Cam heard Marco's voice say, "Camilla, we're nearly there. Wake up."

She snuggled into his chest, not wanting to wake up. Then his fingers flitted over her sides. She started to squirm and opened her eyes to see Marco grinning. Because she wasn't the cheeriest person when she first woke up she pinched him and said, "You interrupted my dream. I'd found the golden temple, and was in the process of taking the treasure."

His grin faded. Dreaming about "the golden temple" was the code for dream-speaking with Neena, and "taking the treasure" meant getting information.

Marco asked, "Do you want to tell me about your dream?"

Cam sat up and stretched her arms over her head. "Maybe later, once I've had some coffee and we're in a more secure location."

The loudspeaker came on, informing them in English and Spanish that they were approaching Quito International Airport. Cam put her seat in the upright position and tried to remember the ship captain's flickering face. Thanks to her mother, Cam knew a lot of the old stories about the *Feiru*, but she'd never heard of anyone being able to wear a false face.

Chapter Thirty-Seven

Marco sat next to Cam inside a taxi and resisted pulling her up against his side. They'd arrived late last night in Quito, and barely had time to reach out to their contacts and put together their plan before going to sleep. Sex, once again, had been put on the back burner. But, at least, Cam had let him hold her through the night as they slept.

He hadn't had a chance to tell her about the other Elemental Masters yet, but that was something else that would just have to wait. Their mission took priority. For now.

Since it was Friday, and he'd learned from one of his contacts that not all tour company offices were open on the weekend in Quito, they'd woken up early and were now heading to meet this mysterious Diego. Cam and Marco were to play friends, not lovers, to avoid showing a possible weakness to Diego or anyone he worked with.

However, not being able to touch Cam was proving to be harder than he'd thought. He'd barely gotten a taste of her, and he was hungry for more.

The taxi stopped in front of a door on the corner of a building, and he focused. The dilapidated sign above the door said, "*Agencia de Viajes, D&D Tours.*" The same company the note had mentioned. Cam gave him a look, and he nodded.

He paid the taxi driver, and exited the car. Once the car drove away, he looked at Cam and said, "Ready?"

Cam, decked out in an oversized t-shirt and cargo Capri pants, nodded and tugged at her t-shirt. "Yes."

Since he'd watched her load up this morning, he knew every weapon she had tucked under her shirt or inside the pockets of her Capri pants. If Diego were human, and things turned bad, they wouldn't be able to use either of their powers. Even so, Cam would only use her weapons as a last resort.

He opened the door of the travel agency and entered the small shop first, to check out the interior. Since nothing jumped out or attacked him, he motioned Cam to follow him.

Inside, he saw faded tourism posters on the walls in a mixture of English and Spanish. There was also a single desk in the corner, with two chairs in front of it and a man sitting behind it. The man spoke to Marco in Spanish. "Can I help you?"

"Yes, a friend recommended this place as the go-to place for tours of the local area. My friend and I just wanted to see what you had, and go from there."

The man behind the desk stood up. "You're in the right place, my friend. My name is Diego." He moved to a display of pamphlets. "What did your friend recommend? A tour of the historical Old Town? A visit to the Maquipucuna Cloud Rainforest Reserve? Or maybe my custom tour of the famous churches and buildings in Quito?"

Marco had to admit that Diego was enthusiastic about his job. He shook his head. "No, she mentioned a private tour to San Rafael, via the scenic route. Is that something you still do?"

Diego put his hands in his pockets and studied him. "Maybe. Where was this friend from? And who was it? I only ask because I give certain friends of mine bigger discounts than others."

"Rosa Elena, back in Campeche, Mexico."

The man darted his eyes to Cam and then back to him. "I see." He walked to the front door and flipped the sign from "open" to "closed."

He motioned toward the chairs and went to sit back behind his desk. "Tell me how you found Rosa Elena, and I'll tell you if I still do that special private tour."

He and Cam sat down, and he noted the slight irritation in her manner. Diego wouldn't pick up on it, but Marco was fast becoming attuned to everything about the woman next to him.

He had an idea of why she was irritated, so he asked Diego, "Since you cater to foreign tourists, I'm assuming you speak English. So can we finish this meeting in English?"

Diego switched. "Okay, so tell me how you met this Rosa Elena."

Cam looked at him and he nodded for her to take over. She turned back toward Diego and said, "Does the Great-Tailed Grackle mean anything to you?"

"Perhaps."

"And what if I also mentioned the observatory?"

Diego glanced at the two of them, and then nodded. "So you found the message. But before I say anything else, I need to know why you went looking for it in the first place." Cam leaned forward. "You haven't earned the right to that information."

Diego raised an eyebrow. "I don't need to earn anything. You're the one who needs my help, so give me an answer or you can leave."

Cam opened her mouth, but Marco put up a hand to silence her. This man seemed a little overprotective for a mere messenger, but then he put it together. "You're acting this way because you're close to the person who left that message. Am I right?"

Diego's eyes widened a fraction before his face returned to a neutral expression. "Then you understand my caution."

Cam touched Marco's knee to silence him, and she said, "Yes, if the wrong person got to this person you're protecting, then things could get bad. But we're trying to help. You have no reason to trust us, but the Four Talents are meant to be protected."

The man leaned back in his chair. "And how do I know that you're not just putting on an act? Just because you mention the Four Talents proves nothing. For all I know, you're one of those people who want to use their powers for your own personal gain."

Cam extended a claw. "Because I've got my own 'special skills' and I'm part of the damn army that's going to help protect them."

The man stared at Cam's claw and Marco waited to see how he'd react. Mentioning the Four Talents was their last card to play before they resorted to force, and personally, he wanted to avoid that.

The man studied them for a few more seconds before he smiled and started whispering something Marco couldn't hear. The man started to blur before his eyes, and Marco felt the urge to look away.

Before he could react, the whispering stopped and the man came into focus again, except this time he was smiling. "Then we have a lot in common, because so am I."

Marco had no idea what kind of ability he'd just seen, but it put him on his guard. Latent abilities now made him think of the Collector, and while they'd been careful to cover their tracks—the giant DEFEND network of contacts was on alert for anything suspicious—he couldn't let down his guard. Especially since thanks to Cam, he now knew that even Neena was on the hunt for this Collector woman. And any person who gave Neena trouble was dangerous.

Still, trying to charm the man in front of him would be useless. Maybe a more direct method would work, so Marco asked, "Okay, so where does that leave us now? Are we going to sit here and dodge questions, trying to outsmart the other into revealing information, or can we discuss how to help this person you're protecting?"

"I was never a fan of beating around the bush. I think it's time to take a little trip and meet Eduardo."

CHAPTER THIRTY-EIGHT

Cam sat next to Marco in the back seat of an old jeep, their wrists cuffed together with some kind of special handcuffs. She didn't know how it worked, but they prevented her from using her abilities. She reckoned that the same went for Marco, but with his elemental magic.

Diego had offered them a now-or-never ride, and since they'd predicted this might happen, they'd taken it.

The prep work she and Marco had put into place last night and this morning should pay off, and help them survive no matter what happened to them. While Diego had confiscated her weapons earlier, he hadn't found the tracker hidden inside one of Marco's buttons. Unless Diego had a signal jammer in the jeep, Zalika and Jacek should be tracking their location.

The jeep went over another rough spot and she resisted leaning against Marco to help keep her balance. They were still playing the role of friends, and they needed to keep it that way to avoid becoming weaknesses to one another. The thought of Marco being tortured in front of her to gain her cooperation made her sick to the stomach.

She tried not to think about how quickly he'd come to mean something to her.

Assuming Cam was merely battling carsickness, Marco tapped her foot in sympathy, and she resisted a sigh. She usually had no problem riding in cars, but they were on something she'd call more a path than a road, and the ride wasn't pleasant.

They'd been at it for hours, traveling through the mountains. She'd had little else to do than to watch the scenery and keep track of how far the sun had sunk in the sky. Even the foliage was different now, which told her they had traveled to a different elevation.

Diego finally turned onto a slightly smoother road, sparsely lined with small shack-like houses. He stopped at one that was at least a mile from all of the others, and said, "We'll rest here and eat. Then we'll continue on."

Because Diego had appreciated Marco's straightforward manner earlier, Cam decided to try that tactic again. "If we have to go back onto that road again, I'd suggest getting me some motion sickness medicine, or I might throw up in your car."

Diego turned around in his seat and asked Marco something in Spanish. When Marco replied in the same language, she decided then and there that she was tired of not being able to understand what was going on. As soon as they were free again, she would ask Marco to start teaching her Spanish. She'd need it if she were to make any sort of good impression on his family.

She resisted a frown. That was the last thing she should be worried about right now.

Diego switched back to English. "The rest of our journey is on foot." He exited the car and opened her door. "Now, come on."

She gave Marco a quick glance, and he gave two slow blinks, telling her that he was ready to attack if she gave the right signal. She blinked in return to confirm the same, and climbed out of the jeep with Marco right behind her.

Diego shut their door just as some frantic Spanish starting blaring from the in-car radio. He reached in and said something. Judging from his facial expression, the radio reply wasn't good news.

~~*

Marco listened as the man on the other side of Diego's radio detailed a recent ambush by one of the drug cartels in the area. Apparently, some trucks filled with gun-happy lackeys had spotted them, and were nearly at their location.

When Diego started to reply, Marco took advantage of the distraction to lean over and whisper in Cam's ear. "Some angry drug cartel guys are heading in this direction. Blink twice if you're ready to fight."

He leaned back and saw Cam blink twice right before Diego signed off on the radio and turned toward them. "Promise me that you won't run, and I'll release you. One of the local cartels is heading this way, and I need your help in case we're ambushed."

Marco wasn't about to agree to something without question. "How do we know that you won't use us as bargaining chips to secure your own safety?"

"You don't. But unless I remove those special cuffs, you'll be facing the cartel guys at a serious disadvantage."

He was right, of course. However, as long as he removed the cuffs, Marco would agree to anything. "Fine. But if you turn on us, don't expect me to go easy on you."

Diego shrugged. "I'd like to see you try." He unlocked their handcuffs, and then headed toward the small shack. "Come on. We need to grab some supplies and get out of here ASAP."

As soon as Diego turned around, Marco touched Cam on her lower back and said, "If you're captured alone, play up your American-ness. That way you have a chance of being held for ransom, giving you time to contact Neena via dream-speaking."

Cam touched his arm and whispered, "But what about you?"

He grimaced. "I'll have to find a way to use my elemental magic without them noticing. Of course, I hope it doesn't come to that."

Diego opened the door of the shack and Marco reluctantly moved away from Cam. He wanted to kiss her and tell her, well, something. "Good luck" was inadequate. So was "be careful."

In reality, he wanted to tell her to protect her ass so he could kiss the living shit out of her later. But that would reveal his doubts about surviving capture.

Even for an Elemental Master, drug cartels were definitely on the 'don't fuck with' list of enemies.

They entered the shack. Inside there were three backpacks sitting on a table, with a few cupboards off to one side. Diego pulled his head out of one of the cupboards and produced two handguns. He motioned toward them. "Take these, and I'll get you some extra bullets."

Marco took one, handed it to Cam, and then took the other. He decided that since Diego needed their help, he was going to ask him for details. "Did you do something to anger these people? Or do we just have the bad luck of being in the wrong place at the wrong time."

Diego strapped on his own pair of guns and said, "Some of our people tried to run the drug traffickers further north, away from some nearby villages. My guess is that's why they're here."

Cam frowned. "But I thought most of the drug activity was further north, near the border with Colombia?"

Diego moved toward the packs on the table. "They've started coming a little more south to avoid the authorities and rival cartels. We'd hoped their presence was temporary, but apparently they're back."

Marco strapped on his own pack. "So where are we heading now?"

"We're going to meet up with Eduardo. He lives hidden in the jungle—both for safety and because of his preference—but we're just going to have to hustle. Once we reach his place, we'll be safe."

No doubt because this Eduardo was indeed a Talent, and he had abilities that would make even Marco's abilities look like child's play. Or at least so went the stories.

Cam clicked the strap around her waist and looked back to Diego. "To have our best chance of surviving, from here on out, you tell us everything."

Diego nodded. "But if you betray me or try to back stab me, my colleagues will deal with you."

Cam nodded. "Fine. Now that we've finished with the threats, let's go."

She went to the door and looked out to make sure the coast was clear.

He fought a smile. Even with only half-knowing the situation, Cam had jumped in to take charge. He looked over at Diego, and Marco could tell the man was less than amused, so he slapped him on the arm. "Forget whatever preconceptions you have about female soldiers. Cam would probably kick your ass in any type of drill or challenge. Believe me when I say that you want her on your side."

Cam motioned for them to head out, and he heard Diego mumble a less than enthusiastic response before they followed her.

~~*

Gio was inside his quarters with Evans when the screen beeped with an incoming call. He reached over and touched the screen. Liang's face appeared. "Hello, Mr. Sinclair, Dr. Evans. I've evaluated your report."

Gio forced himself to act nonchalant. "Ah, I was wondering if you'd made a decision."

Liang nodded. "Well, Dr. Evans was quite thorough, and while I appreciate the details, it took some time to wade through."

Evans moved so that he'd be visible to Liang. "And did you have any questions, Mr. Liang?"

"No. You set out all of the possible scenarios, and provided sound solutions. I think bringing the two latent abilities you mentioned into this facility won't cause any extra danger to my staff or the inmates here."

Gio jumped in before Evans could say anything. "So when can we arrange to bring in the new inmates?"

"Well, security measures need to be installed, and we'll have to do some new training; provided you and Dr. Evans help with that, I'd say a week, maybe two."

Gio nodded. "We'll help in any way we can. My father will be glad to hear of your decision."

Liang replied, "Yes, I've already talked with your father. He mentioned for you to call him to help arrange the details. Once he gets the all clear from the AMT Oversight Committee, he'll let me know. That will be the last major hurdle to admitting the new type of inmates."

Gio didn't like that Liang had talked to his father behind his back, but there was nothing he could do about it. He'd just have to play the part, and see if he could fool James Sinclair into thinking Gio was sincere. Since he'd only be communicating with his father via phone and teleconference, it might just be possible.

Liang started speaking again. "In the meantime, I want Dr. Evans to assist some of the other scientists here to see if any of them would be able to help him with the tests he laid out in his report."

Evans glanced at Gio, and then to Liang. "If you could have someone make a list of those who might suit, I'll start making the rounds."

"Good, good." Liang said. "Mr. Sinclair can fill you in on what they do here, as your clearance has been boosted, Dr. Evans. I'll have one of the lead researchers meet with you tomorrow."

Evans nodded. "Yes, sir."

The screen went blank and Gio turned to face Evans. They'd checked for bugs earlier and knew the room was clean, so Gio spoke frankly. "As dedicated as you are to eradicating elemental magic, I'm not sure you're going to like what they're doing here, Evans."

Evans raised an eyebrow. "Tell me anyway, because I'd rather be prepared."

Gio took a deep breath. "You know the experiments they've been conducting inside the other AMT facilities?"

"Yes."

"Well, they're doing the same thing here, except to children."

Evans blinked. "What?"

He hadn't planned on telling Evans his plans so soon, but with him meeting with the researchers tomorrow, the sooner Gio got Evans on his side, the better. That way Evans could go into this with his eyes wide open—and get Gio the information he needed.

He turned fully toward the other man and explained about how the children born inside the AMT prisons were shipped to this facility at eight weeks of age. Evans stayed silent a moment before he replied. "I'm going to put aside for a minute how wrong that is and simply ask why this matters to you?"

"I believe in the law. Imprisoning first-born *Feiru* at the age of magical maturity is fine because a law was created to help protect them and others from the dangers of their elemental magic. But to experiment on the first-borns, and not protect them as the law states, is wrong." In a rare show of emotion, Gio clenched a fist. "Not only that, non-first-born children—even if they are born inside an AMT—should be adopted out to parents who want a child. But since I suspect the AMT Oversight Committee doesn't want anyone to find out how they're breeding first-borns inside their compounds, they will continue to keep the children locked away for life."

Evans put his hand out. "So you're planning to find a way to let the children free and stop the experiments?" Evans shook his head. "That will never happen. Even if I wanted to stop what was happening to the children, I still believe finding a way to eradicate elemental magic is the only way the *Feiru* can survive in the future. If the AMT system was dismantled and elemental magic exposed, humans would either use the first-borns for their wars, or find a way to make us second-class citizens."

"I don't want to dismantle the AMT system. I just want to make it function as it was intended—to help protect the first-borns from harm."

He could see Evans was teetering, so Gio decided to make the final push. "Dr. Evans, I believe we can find a way to continue conducting experiments in a humane manner, with volunteers. Shouldn't we give first-borns the choice of living secluded away for life with their peers on one hand, or the option to rid them of their elemental abilities on the other?" He leaned forward. "Just think, if the rogue first-born who'd killed your fiancée had had a choice, she might still be alive."

Evans went still. After a few minutes he replied, his voice low and even. "If you want my help, you'll never bring Leyna up ever again, is that understood?"

He believed Evans would act on that threat, too. While Evans wasn't a warrior, neither was Gio. That didn't mean they couldn't be powerful in their own right.

He nodded. "But just remember, if you tell anyone about my plans, I will share your little secret. You are unique, Dr. Evans, and many a person would value your healing abilities."

As soon as he'd said the words, Gio realized how much he was starting to sound like his adopted father, James Sinclair. But he pushed that thought aside. He wasn't fighting for his own gain; he was fighting for law and order.

Evans said, "I don't think hanging that threat over my head is going to work, Sinclair. I'm sure daddy dearest would love to hear what you're planning behind his back."

"I had expected as much from someone as intelligent as you're reputed to be." Gio leaned back in his chair and crossed a leg over his knee. "Threats and blackmail aside, I need an answer now, Evans. Are you with me or do I need to find someone else to help me?"

Evans crossed his arms over his chest. "So, what did you have in mind, Giovanni Sinclair? How are two people supposed to fix a corrupted system as large as the AMT?"

"I'm still working on that bit. For now, your goal is to make sure we can stay at this facility for as long as possible while I look for a way to force the AMT Oversight Committee's hand."

"And how do you plan to do that?"

"I need to find a way to blackmail them."

CHAPTER THIRTY-NINE

Once they were out of the cabin, Cam let Diego take the lead. She had no idea where they were going, but she had wanted to make a point. Despite the act she'd put on inside the jeep, she could handle herself.

She'd overheard Marco's compliments—in English, luckily—and was still glowing on the inside. Unlike other people, his words had been genuine, not laced with judgmental bullshit. If they ever got alone again, she was going to reward him with her mouth.

A noise to the left snapped her back to their surroundings. Diego made a halt sign with his hand, and motioned for Cam and Marco to take the left side while he'd take the right.

This close to the equator, the foliage was thick on the ground. While no doubt someone could track them if they tried, she and Marco moved with as little sound as possible. They needed the element of surprise.

Soon they reached the edge of a pool of water, about fifteen feet across. It didn't look that deep, and as she scanned the surface, she didn't see any telltale signs that someone was hiding under the water.

Diego peeked his head out from the tree cover and motioned for them to continue along the edge. She and Marco retreated a few feet from the shore to use the coverage of the trees and started moving again.

They were nearly to the top of the pool when rain started to fall. She tapped Marco's arm and pointed up toward the sky, but he shook his head. He wasn't responsible for it.

Well, at least the rain would help hide the sounds of their approach.

Another few feet, and Cam started to get the feeling that someone was watching them. But since the tops of the trees were so thick, they'd never be able to spot someone hiding up there. All they could do was remain alert.

She pointed to the west, signaling Marco to stand at the ready. He gave a slight nod, and they pressed on. They finally reached the far edge of the pool, but she didn't see any sign of Diego.

Maybe he'd abandoned them, or maybe he'd been captured. Either way, they needed to hide.

Just as she gave the signal to retreat into the trees, the water in the pool started to move. A foot-wide column rose from the surface and barreled toward them.

Before Cam could even suggest it, Marco created an ice shield just in time to stop the water from crushing them.

The water started pounding on the shield as if a person were knocking. Trusting Marco to protect them, she scanned the surroundings for any sign of the elemental water user. However, because the light was fading fast, she could only make out the trees and the pool of water.

When the water started banging harder against Marco's ice shield, she noticed Diego making a beeline straight for them. Unsure if he'd drawn them into a trap, Cam extended the claws on one hand and cocked the gun in the other.

Marco must've noticed Diego running because the ice shield extended all the way toward the ground. In an effort to make it under before the ice touched the ground, Diego dove and rolled toward them.

But Marco was fast, and Diego didn't make it in time.

Diego started knocking on the ice shield and said, "You need to get down and find some cover."

Cam never broke eye contact with Diego. "Why?"

"We're trying to save your asses. The cartel is coming."

"Then why leave us without a word?"

"Because I didn't have a choice."

Cam kept her sights trained on Diego, but directed her question to Marco. "What do you think?"

As his answer, Marco melted the ice toward the bottom. Once Diego jumped up off the ground, the water stopped pounding the top of the shield and quietly retreated.

Diego motioned for them to move, and Marco melted the last of his shield before he said to Diego, "You go in front to prove its safe."

"Fine."

After about ten feet, Diego laid down on the ground inside some bushes, on his stomach, and Marco and Cam followed suit.

As the minutes ticked by, she started to wonder if this was a trap. Even when she heard voices, she didn't know whether it was the cartel lackeys or Diego's people. She kept her claws out, ready to use her super-speed if needed.

A high-powered light shone through the trees, moving around the area where they'd been standing minutes before. There was some more shouting before two men walked into the light and studied the ground.

The rain was coming down harder now, and with any luck, they wouldn't see their tracks.

Frozen Desires

~~*

Marco waited beside Cam and Diego. No doubt they were holding their breaths just like him.

The light swooped from one side and back again before going out. The two men retreated into the cover of the trees, but that didn't mean they were alone. Their retreat could merely be the set-up for a trap.

Marco might've grown up in Colombia, but Cartagena was far from most of the cartel and guerrilla skirmishes, and he didn't know any of their plays or tactics. He might not know what Diego's motives were, but he was their best bet for information.

Diego was on his left side, so Marco leaned over and whispered into his ear. "What should we do now?"

"Let me use my latent ability to scout the surroundings."

Marco remembered Diego blurring back in the travel agency. "Blurring is nice, but it won't make you invisible."

"I'm a Concealer. Do you know what that means?"

The name sparked a memory from his training during his teen years. A Concealer could blend in with the surroundings, and if the person was powerful enough, could even blur the surroundings enough to make a person go in circles and lose their way.

Marco nodded his head. "Concealers can be useful, but how do we know that you won't just flee and leave us here?"

"You don't, but I'm curious enough about your little ice dome trick to not leave you behind."

At least the man was honest. "All right, go. If you're not back in half an hour, we'll make our own way."

Diego nodded, then scooted a few feet away before he started to blur. Within seconds, Marco felt compelled to look away.

Cam touched his arm and leaned in to whisper, "Do you think he'll be back?"

He'd forgotten about her supersensitive hearing. Undoubtedly, she'd heard every word. "For the sake of our mission, I hope so."

As they waited, Marco made sure that he had one finger pointing to the west, and because there was no one else around, he sidled closer to Cam until they were touching.

She glanced at him, pressed closer to his side, and then looked back in the direction that Diego had gone.

He loved how she didn't hesitate with him anymore, and actually sought out his touch. If she'd have him, Marco wanted to continue working with her. Combining his elemental powers with her considerable strength and brain, they could become a phenomenal team.

He couldn't wait for this mission to be over so he could show her around his hometown. He'd never wanted to do that before, but he wanted Cam to know everything about him. Cartagena would be the perfect place to explain about the other Elemental Masters.

A rustle came from the east, and Marco looked over, but didn't see anything. He nudged Cam, and she whispered, "Every time I try to focus, I can't see anything. It's almost as if I'm forced to look away."

Marco whispered, "Diego."

~~*

As soon as Marco said, "Diego," Cam forced herself to look over to where she'd heard the sound. Something kept trying to force her to look away, but her keen vision did more than see in the dark. Apparently, she could also pick out the blurry form of Diego the Concealer.

She didn't have to keep fighting to focus on his location because a few seconds later, Diego appeared plainly in front of them and said, "They left a few minutes ago. One of their cars broke down, but otherwise, I didn't see any sort of trap or signs of hidden lackeys."

Cam stood up. "Did you check the vehicle for suspicious activity?"

Diego frowned. "No. By the time I got to the car, the men were just leaving. I thought it more important to follow them and make sure they'd gone."

She touched Marco on the arm. "Unless you've had some sort of bomb squad training I'm unaware of, I'll take a look and make sure the vehicle isn't a threat. I had some training in my old life."

The last thing she needed was for Diego to learn about her past.

Marco touched her cheek. "No, I don't know anything but generalizations when it comes to bombs or trip wires. But I can stay close, in case I need to try and protect you if things go wrong."

Not caring if Diego saw, she kissed Marco and said, "Thanks for having my back."

Marco grinned at her. "Anytime."

Diego cleared his throat. "Wouldn't it be better to just leave the car in the jungle? The lackeys might've left, but they'll probably be back. We shouldn't linger longer than necessary."

Cam shook her head. "Just in case it's armed, I can't leave it for an innocent bystander to find. Now, take me to it."

Diego shrugged, and started walking. She followed, with Marco right behind her. She kept an ear out for the cartel lackeys. Even if Diego had been telling the truth—that they'd gone—she wasn't about to let her guard down. In the middle of an operation, that was the easiest way to get yourself killed.

After walking for five minutes, they came to a bare patch of the jungle where an old jeep-like vehicle sat with its doors open. Cam motioned to Marco. "Stay back here, and duck behind the trees if things go wrong."

Marco nodded and she approached the car. She looked inside, then under it, and finally under the hood. The car was clean.

She let out a sigh and turned around. "There's nothing there, so let's get out of here."

Diego came forward to stand next to her. "We need to hurry. Follow me."

He circled to the back of the car and headed toward a faintly worn path. Just as he was about to enter the trees, Cam saw it—a clear fishing line-type trip wire.

She dashed toward him. "Diego, stop!"

But as he turned, his leg pushed against the wire and something exploded behind her.

CHAPTER FORTY

Marco took the split second between Cam yelling and the blast to try to construct a protective ice wall at Cam's back. But he only managed to make it a few inches before something near the car exploded.

He was thrown back and hit a tree.

It took him a second to jump to his feet, and then he raced toward the smoldering remnants of the car.

He was relieved to see that his wall was still standing—elemental ice was stronger than real ice—but his relief faded when he saw Cam on the ground.

No.

As he raced to her side, he melted his ice wall and put out the car fire. Marco knelt down next to Cam, who was unconscious, and checked her pulse. But while erratic, it was strong.

He checked her over, but when he got to her midsection, he found out why she was on the ground. A four-inch piece of shrapnel had blasted through his ice wall and into Cam's side.

Diego raced out of the trees he'd taken cover inside, and stopped next to him and Cam. Only because Cam was hurt and needed help did he restrain himself from punching the man in the face.

Still, Marco couldn't resist asking, "Why the fuck didn't you pay more attention to your surroundings? You claim to be part of a Talent's army, but if you're the best this Talent has, then he or she isn't going to last long."

Diego wasn't fazed by his anger. "Are you going to insult me some more, or would you like me to go get some help?"

Marco took a deep breath. *Think of Cam.* "Is there a hospital nearby?"

Diego shook his head. "No, but if we get her to Eduardo, he should be able to save her."

Diego's words only confirmed his suspicions about Eduardo being a Talent. But now was not the time to get the guy to admit it. "How far away is he?"

"Maybe ten minutes, if we hurry." Diego gestured toward Cam. "Do you think you can carry her?"

Marco looked back down at Cam. It took all of his training and experience as a soldier to keep from panicking at the amount of blood on her shirt. "Yes, give me a second."

He went around to her good side, placed his arms under her shoulders and her knees, and lifted her. He leaned her weight against his chest, careful not to jar her more than necessary. He looked back up to Diego. "Take me to Eduardo."

Diego nodded and started walking.

As they moved through the jungle, Cam kept making small grunts of pain. The part of Marco that had come to care for her wanted nothing more than to lay her down and whisper sweet nothings. But, the solider part of his brain understood that such an action would probably kill her.

Don't you dare fucking die on me, woman. He tightened his grip and pushed on.

In another five minutes, Diego suddenly stopped and put up a hand. Marco was still angry with the man who'd put Cam in this position, but he knew Diego was his best chance of getting her medical attention. If Eduardo was a Talent, and the legends were true, then the man should have extraordinary healing powers.

Marco waited to see what Diego would do.

Diego blurred in front of his eyes until Marco was forced to look away. When he looked back, Diego was gone. "Fuck." The bastard had ditched him.

He was alone, the woman he cared for possibly dying in his arms. He well knew that emotions could kill in an extreme situation, such as this one, but it took him a little longer than usual to focus on what he could do rather than what he couldn't.

All he could do was try to patch Cam up.

He kissed Cam's forehead and said, "Hang on, beauty. I need you to hang on. I'm going to try and stop the bleeding."

Marco knew some basic field medicine, but not enough. All he could do was remove the metal and create some kind of makeshift bandage.

Reluctantly, he laid Cam on the ground. He checked her pulse, and while it was weaker than before, it wasn't yet in the danger zone.

Okay then. He brushed her cheek and leaned down to take a better look at her injury. He ripped her shirt away and sucked in a breath. While the metal wasn't embedded that deep, there was a real chance it'd hit one of her kidneys.

If he'd thought waiting for Richard Ekstrom to trade Cam back on the ocean had been bad, this was a hundred times worse. Because if Cam died it could very well be Marco's fault.

He took a deep breath, pushed aside his emotions, and focused on the wound. He had no way of knowing if the metal embedded in Cam's side was straight or jagged. Since pulling out a jagged piece of shrapnel could make things exponentially worse, he hoped for the former.

Of course, he was damned either way. If he left the shrapnel in, it could kill her. Or if he pulled it out, it could also kill her.

Because he had a trick from his teenage training years that might help, he decided to take his chances with removing the shrapnel. He shucked his shirt to use as a compress, and took a grip on the metal. "Don't you fucking die on me, Camilla, do you hear?"

Of course, she didn't respond, but Marco only hoped her subconscious heard him. It was important that she knew he was fighting for her.

He exhaled, and on his next inhale, he started to pull out the shrapnel. Cam made a faint noise, and he paused. "I'm sorry, Camilla." Marco pulled a little more, sweat trailing down his back as the metal came out centimeter by centimeter.

At least Cam hadn't started to hemorrhage.

Judging by the marks toward the bottom of the shrapnel, the next pull would take it out completely.

He checked her pulse. Her heart rate had dropped slightly, but he hoped not enough to cause her to crash. He needed to finish this. Now.

Marco readied his shirt and pulled the metal free. Blood started to flow out of her wound—at least it wasn't gushing—and he applied his shirt compress. It was time to try his trick.

He moved one of his fingers to the west and moved some elemental water particles to just under the compress. With everything in place, he removed the compress, pressed the two sides of her skin together, and used his elemental water to create ice staples to hold her skin in place. He knitted one through her skin, and then another, until he had enough to stitch the wound closed.

This wasn't a long term solution, but it was the best he could do.

Marco checked her pulse again, but there wasn't any change. He was going to take that as a good sign.

He brushed back the stray hairs that had escaped Cam's braid before cupping her cheek. She was pale and motionless, which was a huge contrast to her stubborn, argumentative self.

The sight squeezed his heart.

He had to do something, anything, to prevent fear from taking hold. So, he took a firm tone and said, "I can insult your effectiveness as a soldier, if that will rile you into waking up." He brushed her cheek with his thumb. "Or I can tell you that a woman's place is in the kitchen, cooking for her man. Anything you like, Camilla, as long as you'll open your eyes."

But, of course, nothing happened.

Marco hated this. He was used to always having an out, or at least a strategy to try. Unfortunately, in this case, nothing he could do would help. Either Cam would last long enough to heal, or she'd die.

"Right, Alvarez. Time to stop moaning, as Jax would say, and focus on what you can do." And right now, the only thing he could do was try to find a village or someone to take him to a village where he could get Cam help. Even if there wasn't a major hospital nearby, this area was on the edge of the Amazon rainforest, and there were all kinds of unique medicines here that could help with infection.

He maneuvered himself to pick Cam up again when he heard a noise. Marco looked up. As he scanned the area, someone said, "Don't attack. This is Diego, and I've brought Eduardo with me."

Marco felt a sense of relief. Diego hadn't abandoned them after all. "If you're here to help, you'd better hurry up."

Diego came into view, followed by a lean young man around Marco's age.

The man he assumed was Eduardo rushed to Cam's side, and knelt down next to her. He moved to touch her, but Marco grabbed the other man's wrist. "I don't know anything about you, so tell me what you plan on doing to her before I let you touch her."

The man put up his hands. "I only want to heal her. Will you let me do it?"

"She needs more than a superficial healing. She might've been injured internally. Can you heal that type of damage?"

The man nodded. "Yes, and more. But to heal her, I need you to let go and let me touch her."

Marco released Eduardo's hand. "Fine, but if you end up killing her, I'll kill you in return."

The young man merely shrugged, and placed his hands on Cam's forehead. Marco didn't like the sight of another man's hands on Cam, but if Eduardo could help her, he'd do whatever it took.

He squeezed Cam's hand and waited. But Eduardo didn't do anything. "Why aren't you healing her? The longer we wait, the greater the chance she could die."

Eduardo met his gaze, the other's man face calm beyond his years. "This isn't an easy task, and I had to prepare myself. I'm ready, but I need you to remove your ice staples and refrain from touching this woman while I do my magic."

He should just do as he said, but Marco didn't know this man, and sure as hell didn't trust him. "I've never heard of a first-born needing others to sever contact before they healed someone. What are you trying to pull?"

"You're here to find a Talent, aren't you?"

"What does that—"

"Well, I'm the Water Talent, and I can both heal and destroy, so let me do my job."

Diego grabbed Marco's shoulders. "Let him do his work, my friend. Eduardo is the best healer I've ever seen, and the longer you argue, the greater the chance your woman will die."

Eduardo added, "Please, trust me."

For some reason he couldn't explain, Marco felt compelled to trust this man. The only other time he'd felt that way had been with the leader of DEFEND, Neena Chatterjee.

Since there was so much he didn't know about the Talents, it was possible that this man shared her ability to induce trust.

He looked down at Cam's face and noticed she was paler than before. Something had to be wrong internally, and with the nearest healer who knew how far away, this man was the best chance Marco had to holding Cam in his arms again, alive.

Please let this work. He kissed Cam's hand, released it, and scooted back a few feet.

Eduardo nodded, and closed his eyes.

At first, nothing happened. Then water started flowing over Eduardo and onto Cam, until he'd covered her from head to foot. Marco was tempted to pull Cam out, but before he could act, the water froze, encasing Cam in an ice coffin.

Despite knowing all of the legends, despite his years of special training, Marco's first reaction was to get to Cam. But because he was an Elemental Water Master, he knew that elemental ice didn't have to be cold. Cam shouldn't freeze to death.

Still, his heart tightened as he stared at Cam's distorted form through the ice. He may not have known her for long, but he couldn't imagine anyone else he'd rather have at his side.

Cam was caring and kind, to a degree most people could never hope to match. First, she'd comforted the widow, Maria Vega, in front of a possible enemy, and then she'd checked out the abandoned car just to make sure it wouldn't harm someone in the future. Add these to her dedication to her teammates and her passion, and Cam became the only woman he would ever want.

He couldn't imagine a future without Camilla Melini.

Then it hit him—because he loved her.

Marco barely had time to digest his newfound feelings before the ice surrounding Cam started to crack. He glanced to Eduardo, who was now glowing a faint blue and swaying. Just as he started to slump over, the ice covering Cam shattered.

CHAPTER FORTY-ONE

Millie Ward looked across Victoria Harbour and couldn't help but stare at the buildings alight against the night sky. The mosaic of glass, steel, and stone of the massive skyscrapers had its own kind of beauty. She could understand why so many millions of people would visit each year despite Hong Kong being one of the most expensive cities in the world.

But Millie wasn't here to stare at pretty buildings. She singled out the tallest one, the ICC building, and studied it. That was the one they needed to break into to rescue Petra's friend.

She glanced at Petra, who was standing at her side. "Right. Since you've picked a bloody noticeable building to break into, I hope your contact comes through."

Petra never took her gaze from the structure. "If she doesn't, then we'll just have to try something on our own."

Millie usually relished a challenge, but this assignment had too many unknown variables for her liking. "I just hope that this man friend of yours is worth it."

Petra remained silent, and Millie went back to studying the buildings across the water. She'd learned on their travels here that Petra didn't like talking about Dr. William Evans. Apparently, everything Millie needed to know could be found in the assignment file.

But to her surprise, Petra finally answered her. "I hope so, too."

Before Millie could reply, Petra's phone rang and she answered it in a language that sounded like German. Since Millie didn't know more than a handful of phrases in that language, she watched Petra's face as she talked.

Her voice grew animated, and finally she turned off the phone. After a few seconds of silence, Millie said, "Right. So, what was that all about?"

Petra continued to stare across the harbor as she answered, "They've moved him. He's not here."

Bloody fantastic. "I reckon this changes things, am I right?"

Petra looked over to Millie and said, "Yes. We need to get a flight to Chengdu. He's inside a research facility in the mountains."

Millie stared at her sometimes friend. Something was wrong. She decided to drop her mercenary façade and ask, "Are you all right, Petra?"

Petra's face was like stone. "I will be once we rescue Will."

Millie sensed there was more; but she was a good enough judge of people to know Petra wasn't ready to tell her the whole truth. At least, not yet.

She slapped her hands together and rubbed them. "Right. Then let's hurry up and rescue this bloody man so I can return to a country that doesn't eat rice at every damn meal."

Petra cracked a smile. "Okay, then. Let's head to Chengdu."

~~*

Cam opened her eyes to an unfamiliar ceiling. She moved her head to scan the room—small, with just a cot and two chairs—before noticing the door ajar opposite from where she lay. There were two male voices talking in Spanish outside of her room, and while she couldn't understand what they were saying, she would recognize Marco's voice anywhere.

The soldier part of her wanted to let Marco carry on his conversation, but for once, she decided she wasn't going to follow that logic. She desperately wanted to see him again. "Marco."

The voices stopped, and Marco pushed open the door. His eyes were tender when they met hers, but in an instant he'd shut the door and was at her side with a stern expression. "It's about time you woke up."

She frowned. "I remember an explosion, but not much after that. What happened? Are Zalika and Jacek okay?"

Marco sat in the chair next to her cot, took her hand in his, and squeezed. "Yes, Zalika and Jacek are fine. They're busy outside, arguing. I'll tell you the rest once I know that you're okay. How're you feeling? Is there any soreness? How about twinges?"

She smiled. "You sound like an old mother hen."

He raised their clasped hands up against his chest. "Considering I had to extract a four-inch piece of metal out of your side—in the middle of a jungle, I might add—my questions are pretty logical."

Cam touched both of her sides with her free hand, but there was no pain, not even a slight twinge. "I would call you a liar except that I trust you. But to answer your question, I feel a little tired, but that's all. So tell me, what happened? How did I end up here, fully healed?"

Marco brushed his thumb against the back of her hand as he told her about Diego returning with Eduardo, and then about Eduardo healing her with his Talent powers. "So all of our clue-chasing worked? We found the Water Talent?"

He nodded. "Yes, and while it took some convincing, he's willing to ally with DEFEND."

"I sense a 'but'."

Marco shook his head. "Eduardo wants to stay hidden here, in the jungle. I was against it, but when Diego convinced him to move to a colony of sorts, deep in the Amazon rainforest, I agreed to it."

"What do you mean 'a colony of sorts'? Like a hippie commune?"

Marco chuckled. "No, not exactly. Apparently, the *Feiru* with latent abilities in the area have been banding together. Afraid that the AMT Oversight Committee would find out about them, they decided to move deep into the jungle. Many of the locals still believe in the *Encantado* myths, so if anyone gets too close to their colony, they break into song—*Encantado* are known for their musical abilities—and the locals go running. Considering they've lived in secret for nearly a year, they must be doing something right."

"So, that's it? Our mission is done?"

"Yes, *cariño,* once you're fit to travel, we're done."

"What does ka-reen-yo mean?"

Marco's gaze turned heavy, and she nearly stopped breathing. He cupped her cheek, and her body jolted awake, as if she hadn't just suffered a near death experience and a miraculous healing. Somehow, she found her voice again. "Marco?"

He leaned down and stopped an inch from her lips. "Honey, sweetie, dear, love—it means all of those things. But to me, it means that you're mine."

Cam expected to get angry at being claimed in such a fashion, but she realized quite the opposite. "*Cariño,* is that how you say it?"

"Yes."

She raised her free hand and threaded it through Marco's hair. "Good, because I want people to know that you're mine, too."

Marco growled and Cam pulled his head down to hers and kissed him.

~~*

Hearing Cam call him "*cariño*" snapped something inside of Marco, and when she pulled him down for a kiss, he devoured her mouth.

As her tongue twined with his, he moved to cover Cam on the cot. She parted her thighs to let him lay between them, but the cot shifted and he had to break the kiss to prevent from falling over. "Fucking hell."

Cam giggled, and his irritation melted at the sound—he wanted to hear it again.

But at the moment, he studied the cot, trying to figure out how he was going to make love to Cam on the wobbly contraption. He felt Cam dig her nails into his back. He looked up to see her grinning, and she asked, "What happened to your smooth way with the ladies?"

"Not even James Bond could be smooth on a wobbly cot."

Cam laughed again, and then she hooked her hands behind his neck. Her look turned mischievous. "There's more to life than missionary."

His cock was now pulsing at attention. He had a feeling this woman was going to keep surprising him in bed for years to come. "Are you sure you're well enough? I know Eduardo healed you, but you were this close to dying, and I don't want to hurt you."

"I told you, I'm fine." Cam moved her hands to his ass and squeezed. "Now, get naked so you can fuck me against the wall."

He leaned down and nuzzled her cheek before moving to bite her earlobe. "I thought we'd agreed that here, in the bedroom, I give the orders."

Cam's breath hitched. He moved so he could see her face. The desire and longing in her eyes told him that she was thinking of earlier, and she wanted to do it again.

He gave her a gentle kiss before he rose from the cot. She watched his every move, so he decided to tease her.

He lifted his shirt a few inches. "If you want to see what's underneath here, then I want you to take off your nightshirt."

Cam slowly inched the material up her body. First, she bared her toned belly. Then she exposed her ribcage. He held his breath until she finally showed him the undersides of her breasts. She stopped moving the shirt and started to rub it back and forth across her nipples. When she gave a soft cry, he growled. "Show me your lovely breasts. Now."

There was a mischievous glint in her eye. But she moved the material up over her breasts and left it there. He was about to give another order when she started to pluck at her nipples.

He let out a strangled sound. She might be following his orders, but she was doing it on her terms.

And he liked it.

~~*

Marco might be giving the orders, but Cam felt oddly empowered. Even from a few feet away, she could hear him suck in a breath as she continued to pinch and roll her nipples. She decided to push him further, and lifted one of her legs. Marco growled and she smiled. Going commando had its benefits in situations like these.

"Woman, stop playing with yourself. Lay your hands at your side, and look at me."

She reluctantly moved her hands to her side as she turned her head toward Marco. She tried looking at his face, but her eyes were drawn to the movements of his hand—he was slowly stroking his cock, which was now free of his jeans.

She imagined taking him in her mouth, sucking him deep, and wetness rushed between her legs.

"Camilla." She tore her gaze from his hand and looked up. "If you want my cock, then come kneel in front of me, and take it."

It didn't surprise her that he'd been able to read her. He was getting good at that.

She rose slowly from the cot and walked over to him. She gripped the base of his cock and squeezed before she knelt down and braced her hands on his muscled thighs.

Marco released his hand. She took his hard, long dick and lowered it in front of her mouth. There was already a bead of moisture, so she looked up at Marco's eyes and gave a flick with her tongue. Loving the salty taste, she gave another. Before she could torture him some more, he thrust a hand into her hair and gave a gentle tug. "Take it. Now."

She extended one of her claws and traced it down the underside of his cock, and then gently grabbed his balls as she took his cock into her mouth. Curious to see if the fierce side of him would come out to play, she stayed still, careful to breathe through her nose.

After a few seconds, his other hand grabbed her hair and forced her head back until only the tip was still inside her mouth. She looked up and used her tongue to tease his slit.

The cords of his neck were taut when he said, "I want to fuck your mouth, Camilla. If you'll let me, then release my balls and place your hands on my thighs."

She'd never done this before, but she barely resisted squirming. Marco was revealing a sexual side to her that Cam had never known existed.

She released his balls, relaxed her jaw, and placed her hands on his thighs. When she looked back up, he said, "Close your eyes."

She did, and he started to move. Gently at first, but his thrusts grew faster and she understood why he'd told her to hold on.

As he continued to fuck her mouth, she couldn't resist moving a hand between her thighs. She dipped her fingers, coated them with moisture, and started rubbing her clit. When she moaned around his dick, Marco stilled and then pulled out. She cried out at the loss of him and opened her eyes without a thought. She looked up and her heart skipped a beat at the fierce tenderness in his eyes.

He squatted down and cupped her face. "Now, it's my turn to take care of you, *cariño*." He kissed her and helped her to her feet. "Do you still trust me?"

She nodded without a thought, growing wet in anticipation of what he'd do next.

~~*

Marco gave Cam a searing kiss before he tugged her up and against his chest. He then placed his hands on her ass before giving her a quick slap and then lifting her. When she was high enough, she wrapped her legs around his waist, letting him know how drenched and ready she was for him.

Cam was turning out to be everything he'd hoped for in a woman. She had intelligence and a sexuality he would never get enough of. He planned to test her limits for as long as she'd have him.

He kissed her and hugged her tight, wanting to feel as much of her skin as possible. With her hot, wet core against his abdomen and her nipples pressing into his chest, he was done with the foreplay. It was taking everything he had not to come right now.

He maneuvered them to a wall. He braced Cam against it so he could move one of his hands from her ass to her core. With her pressed so tight against him, all he could do was rub a finger back and forth, but that was enough. Cam broke their kiss on a groan and growled. "Please, Marco. Don't make me wait any longer."

He was too far gone to reprimand her for speaking out. Instead, he leaned back a fraction, positioned his cock, and thrust up.

Cam moaned and he took her hips. Using the wall as leverage, he started to thrust upward over and over again, the force making her breasts bounce. He wanted to bite and tease her, but because he didn't want to give up his grip, he just watched them, promising to give them the attention they deserved later.

She gripped his shoulders. When she dug in with her claws, he looked back to her face and thrust harder. "So wet and tight, *cariño*. I'll never get enough of you."

From the glazed look in her eye, he knew she was close. "Touch yourself for me and let yourself go. I want to feel you squeezing my cock."

She moved one hand to behind his neck and the other between her thighs. As much as he wanted to watch her stroke herself, he kept his gaze on her face and said, "Are you close?"

"Yes."

He picked up his pace even more. "Then let go, Camilla. I'll catch you."

She let out a soft cry and he felt her start to spasm around him.

As she gripped and released his cock, his balls drew up even tighter. He was close.

Since he knew she had regular birth control shots, he thrust even harder. This was the first time he'd been inside her since realizing he loved her. He wanted to claim her, and claim her hard.

When Cam finally moved her other hand to his neck, leaned in, and nibbled his jaw, he gave a few more quick thrusts before he let go.

CHAPTER FORTY-TWO

Marco placed his forehead against Cam's, and tried to catch his breath.

While he'd realized he loved her back in the jungle, after this round of sex and him claiming her completely, his heart was near to bursting. But he didn't want to scare her away. If Cam rejected him, he would be lost. There was no way he could go back to hiding behind his playboy façade. That life was lonely.

After the taste of honesty he'd had with the woman in front of him, he didn't want it.

The woman in question tilted her head and kissed him before laying her cheek against his. "Mm, that was nice."

He hugged her close and slowly backed away from the wall. He kissed the side of her neck. "I take it you liked it, then? I wasn't too rough?"

Cam leaned back to look into his face and placed her hands on his chest. "If you want the truth, I've never done anything like that before."

He raised an eyebrow. "And?"

She smiled. "I rather liked it."

Marco nuzzled her cheek. "Does that mean I'm a gift to womankind after all?"

She slapped his chest. "Ego check, Alvarez, ego check."

He laughed. "Okay, so maybe a gift to Camilla-kind then?"

"A few more rounds like the one we just had, and I may agree with that."

She looped her arms behind his neck, and leaned her body against his. It took everything he had not to take her again right then and there. But while this particular mission was over, they had other responsibilities to take care of. His years of training and time with DEFEND were ingrained into his very being, and he couldn't ignore the need to discuss their next moves.

Still, he couldn't resist holding the woman he loved in his arms for a few more minutes. Marco pulled her close, her scent a comfort.

Cam let out a sigh as she released her legs and lowered them to the ground. "I wish we could stay like this all day, but we need to shower and start planning."

He nuzzled the top of her head. "I was thinking the same thing."

Cam chuckled. "What a pair we make. I suppose it's a good thing we're both soldiers at heart."

Marco hugged her tighter. "I wouldn't have it any other way."

She raised her head to look him in the eye. "While your words are pretty, your actions in the jungle—when you let me check that car for a bomb—will always mean more to me than you'll ever know."

He lifted his hand to trace her cheek. He was so close to telling her about his feelings, but he needed to be careful with Cam. She'd been hurt in the past, and he wasn't sure if she felt the same way.

Instead, he decided that Camilla Melini needed to get used to compliments, because he was going to be saying them to her for a long time. "You're smart, resourceful, kind, and unselfish, Camilla, and any man who can't see that is a fool."

~~*

Cam stared up at Marco, speechless. She instinctively knew that he wasn't telling her sweet nothings just to please her, but instead, he was telling her how he truly saw her.

Feelings she couldn't describe filled her chest, and Cam started to realize that anything she'd once felt for Richard Ekstrom paled in comparison to what she was starting to feel for this man in front of her.

Marco was handsome, yes, but not only did she respect his strength and intelligence, he'd opened up to her, telling her about his Elemental Master training and his cousin's death. By doing that, he'd allowed her to lower her own defenses and confide in him as well.

Just thinking about her life before Marco, she realized how lonely and isolated she'd been. Zalika and Jacek had helped, and maybe reuniting with her sister Kiarra would have eased her isolation a little more. But no matter how much she cared for them, Marco had filled a hole in her heart that she hadn't realized even existed.

If she were honest with herself, she loved him.

Love. Yes, just admitting it eased her heart a little. She'd already made a partial claim on him by calling him *cariño*, but that wasn't enough.

Cam had nearly died twice in just the last few days, reminding her that working for DEFEND was dangerous. She accepted that risk—her work was important—but just the thought of Marco dying without knowing her true feelings didn't sit well with her.

She needed to tell him.

"Camilla? Are you okay?"

She didn't know how long she'd been lost in her thoughts, but one thing was clear—she needed to tell him how she felt.

She moved one of her hands from his chest to stroke his cheek. Marco wasn't a hairy man, but she loved the feel of the slight stubble on his cheek. "I was just thinking about my life before I met you, Marco."

He grinned. "Bleak? Desolate? Not worth living?"

She slapped him on the chest. "Be serious for a second, Alvarez."

He put on a mock serious face, and Cam couldn't help but giggle. Before meeting Marco, she had *never* giggled.

That was just another reason she loved him.

She got herself under control and said, "The events of the past few weeks have made me realize how fleeting life can be. I believe in DEFEND's cause of freeing the first-borns, but this work is dangerous. Either one of us could go at any minute."

Marco's face was truly serious now. "Don't think like that, *cariño*. The two of us together are quite a force to be reckoned with."

"I know, but do you deny the danger?"

He shook his head. "No. Pulling that shrapnel out of your side was one of the scariest few minutes of my life."

"Right. That's why, before we go on another dangerous adventure, I want to tell you something."

Marco's face relaxed, and his eyes were tender. "You can tell me anything, Camilla."

The look in his eyes gave her the courage to say, "I don't expect for you to feel the same way, but I need to tell you that I, well, I love you."

Joy filled his face, and he smiled at her in a way that made her knees weak. "That's a relief, then. Because I love you too, and I'm quite possessive, in case you haven't noticed."

~~*

Marco had told Cam he loved her in a lighthearted way, but he meant it to his very soul.

When she slapped him playfully on the chest and she lost the battle to frown, he felt the need to kiss her.

He lowered his head and placed a tender kiss on her lips, but as he moved away, Cam growled and said, "You call that a kiss? I bet a teenage boy could kiss better than that."

He grabbed her hips and pulled her flush against his body. "Then let me show you how wrong you are."

He took her lips, biting her lower lip before she opened. He plunged his tongue into her mouth, and she started to battle him for control. He was lost in the warmth and unique taste that was Cam, but a small part of his mind was uneasy.

He needed to share the last big secret between them.

Reluctantly, he pulled away. He brushed Cam's hair behind her ear and said, "There's something else I need to tell you, Camilla. Something that I don't want to keep from you any longer."

This time she did frown. "Should I be worried?"

He smiled. "No. I didn't tell you before because I've never told anyone about it. This secret could cost the lives of hundreds of other Elemental Masters."

She cupped his cheek. "You can trust me. Tell me."

The trust in her eyes made her even more beautiful to him. It took everything he had not to kiss her. "You know that the EM training academies still exist despite the *Feiru* High Council's best attempts to squash them." Cam nodded, and he continued. "Well, I never told you what they do after they finish their training."

"I had wondered about that, actually."

"Of course you did, you brilliant woman."

She poked him in the chest. "Stop with the flattery and just tell me what they do already."

"Okay, okay. Just put the claws away."

Cam smiled. "Yes, funny man. Now, what do they do?"

"Well, most—not all—are assigned to various regions of the world to help stem natural disasters."

"What do you mean?"

Marco knew his statement was a lot to take in, so he decided to use one of his friends right here in Ecuador as an example. "There's a woman in Ecuador named Josselyn who is an Elemental Earth Master. We went through training together down in Colombia."

"A woman?"

He smiled at Cam's jealousy. "Just a friend, *cariño*. You have nothing to worry about."

Mollified, Cam asked, "Okay, so what does she do?"

"Well, let me explain. You may or may not know that Ecuador is prone to earthquakes, sometimes with a resulting tsunami. Joss is here to try to stop those earthquakes from killing thousands of people. In fact, she's the reason the 2010 earthquake here was minimal and didn't do any damage."

He watched amazement dawn on Cam's face. "She stopped an earthquake from happening?"

Marco chuckled. "Not quite. We all tease her for the small tremors that slipped past."

Cam blinked. "And there are others?" He nodded. "Then what about you? How did you end up working with DEFEND?"

He shrugged a shoulder. "Like with most things, it's thanks to Neena. She convinced my grandfather—he was an EM trainer when he was alive—to let me join DEFEND instead of being sent to Southeast Asia to help with tsunami prevention."

He stayed quiet, allowing it all to sink in. Cam eventually looked back up at him. "Thanks for telling me, Marco. I won't take this secret lightly."

"I trust you, Camilla."

He tried to kiss her, but Cam backed away and said, "A kiss could distract us, and we need to start planning our next job."

For once, he wished they could forget about their duties, but accepted that would never happen. "What job?"

She looked him dead in the eye and lifted her chin. "To help find the person who killed your cousin, of course."

He loved the fact that she remembered that. "Okay, we'll do that after we take a dip in the nearby lake."

"Lake?"

"There's no running water in this place. We need to get clean, and I plan to have a little fun doing it."

"Marco…"

"Shh, Camilla. Just think of it as multi-tasking. Women are supposed to be good at that."

"Are you really going to lump me together with all women?"

He smiled. "Of course not, but I live to tease you."

She shook her head. "And I still don't understand why, but that's one of the things I love about you."

"Then I'll just have to do it more often."

Cam opened her mouth, but Marco kissed her quiet. After all, it was his duty to warm her up before she had to swim in the cold lake.

And judging by her claws in his back, she seemed to agree with him.

EPILOGUE

Cartagena, Colombia

Cam couldn't stop staring at the colorful colonial buildings all around her. Marco had taken her to Old Town Cartagena for their meeting, and while she knew this wasn't a real representation of Colombia, she didn't care. The bright colors and style of the buildings reminded her of Merida, Mexico for a reason—they had both been major ports in the Spanish colonies.

In the five days since she'd been healed, Cam had spent nearly every waking moment with Marco. Neena and Aislinn had approved them working as a team—along with Zalika and Jacek—and they had been given two weeks to straighten things out before receiving their next assignment.

And while they hadn't heard anything yet from Jorge Salazar, she had finally accepted that Harry Watkins was now the Shadow-Shifter's responsibility.

Marco stopped in front of a restaurant with an open-air front, and he squeezed her hand. "This is it, are you ready?"

Cam nodded. "I'm supposed to be the nervous one, but somehow, I think you're worse than me."

"Yeah, well, it's been ten years since I last saw my parents."

"And that's why we're here. You think you've been protecting them by keeping your distance, but they need to decide for themselves which is greater—the risk or the reward when it comes to including you in their life."

Marco gave a half-smile. "You're too smart for your own good."

"And I'll never let you forget it."

He chuckled and tugged her forward. "Come on, there's no point in delaying the inevitable."

Marco spoke with the hostess, and she motioned for them to follow her. They wove through the restaurant, turned a corner, and were met with a table full of people, more than half of which look remarkably like the man at her side. "I thought you said that it was just your parents."

She looked up and saw Marco's stunned expression. "Marco, are you okay?"

"They brought my siblings, too."

Before Cam could reply, a woman she reckoned was Marco's mother rose from the table, rushed over, and kissed Marco on the cheek. As the woman started to chatter in Spanish, everyone else stood up and came over, surrounding them. Some of the Alvarez clan started hugging and kissing her, too. While she didn't understand much apart from her name, she nearly teared up at their acceptance—of both her and Marco.

When Marco finally got everyone quiet, he put a hand on her waist and pulled her close. "This is my girlfriend, Camilla Melini. She's still trying to learn Spanish, so if everyone could use English, that'd be great."

A young man in his late teens spoke up. "But English is for school."

Marco winked. "Then think of this as a bonus lesson."

One of the young women laughed. "We've missed you, brother."

Marco's voice cracked. "And I've missed you all, too."

He made the introductions, and then his mother took Cam's hand and pulled. "Come sit with me, Camilla. I want to know what my no-good son has been up to, and why he thought staying away from us was a good idea."

While Mrs. Alvarez's words were harsh, her tone was light. Cam smiled. "Call me Cam. And I'll tell you whatever you want as long as you tell me about Marco as a boy. I'm sure there's something I can use as blackmail later on."

Marco's mother smiled, and Cam knew where her man had gotten his heart-melting expressions. "Deal. Now, come on."

Cam followed, but she looked over her shoulder to see Marco surrounded by his siblings and other family members and knew that no threat was big enough to keep him away any longer.

No doubt his siblings would be shocked to learn of the world of the *Feiru*—they'd been raised human—but if they were anything like Marco, they'd handle it well. Certainly, one or all three of his siblings would want to help find their cousin's killer.

However, she wouldn't think about that right now. Marco deserved a few hours with his family, to enjoy himself.

Marco met her gaze with a brilliant smile. He mouthed the words, "Thank you, *cariño*. I love you."

Cam didn't care who was watching, and she blew him a kiss. Then she turned toward his mother and started interrogating her, hungry to know more about the man she'd once threatened to eviscerate, but now loved with all her heart.

~~*

Did you enjoy this story? Then please consider leaving a review. :)

Turn the page to learn about my newsletter and for an excerpt from *Shadow of Temptation*.

Dear Reader:

I hope you enjoyed Cam and Marco's story. While the next books will focus on Jorge and Sabrina and then Will and Petra, keep an eye out for Cam and Marco. They'll be back, along with a lot of the other characters in future books. I love it when authors show us how our favorite characters are doing later on, and I plan to do the same.

If you want to receive exclusive content (deleted scenes, short stories, etc.) and updates, you can sign up for my monthly newsletter at jessiedonovan.com. You can also find me on my Facebook author page.

Also, I need to ask you a favor. Word-of-mouth is crucial for any author to succeed. If you enjoyed this book, please consider leaving a review. Even if it's only a line or two, it would be a huge help!

Thank you for spending time with my characters. I hope you return to the world of the *Feiru* in *Frozen Desires*, and continue to follow the journey of Neena, DEFEND, and all of the rest. Make sure to turn the page for an excerpt.

With Gratitude,
Jessie Donovan

The story continues with Jorge and Sabrina...Excerpt from
Shadow of Temptation (AMT#2.5)

CHAPTER ONE

*"Deemed disbanded in 2004, the Federation League has re-formed
and is crawling its way back from obscurity. However, their aim
remains the same: to kill or harm anyone who has worked with or
for the Asylums for Magical Threats' prison system. Assassinations
and arson fires are their main tactics, but any unusual activity that
targets a* Feiru *(FEY-roo) should be investigated."*

—Case File on the Federation League, Mexico City *Feiru*
Liaison Office

Merida, Mexico

Sabrina Ono was about to crack. If she didn't find
somewhere private, and soon, she would blow the cover ID she'd
worked so hard to craft over the last two years.

And if she let that happen, all of the deaths, all of the
destruction, and all of the grief she had caused to innocent
humans and *Feiru* alike while undercover would have been for
nothing. Sabrina wasn't sure she could handle that amount of
guilt if she failed.

Come on, Ono. You can do this. She was this close to finishing
her current assignment. No matter what it took, she needed to
maintain her life of lies for a few more days.

Harry Watkins, her current team leader, came over to where
she was standing and scrutinized her face. "You look like you
want to say something, Ono."

She was careful to keep her emotions from her face and voice. "No, sir."

"Right. Then do the scouting I asked for. I want the layout, details, and your suggestions for the best ways to break in to the building by this evening. Once I receive your report, I'll send a follow-up task."

Sabrina nodded. "Is there anything else, sir?"

He studied her a second before waving his hand. "No, you're dismissed."

Careful to keep her face expressionless, Sabrina saluted Watkins, turned, and headed down the street toward the target she needed to scout.

Before she could do her job, she needed to find somewhere to get her shit together. If Watkins had anyone watching her, which was possible with this high-profile assignment, she couldn't show her fragile state or she would be replaced. Sabrina couldn't allow that to happen.

When she was about ten blocks away from where Watkins had dismissed her, she did everything she could to make sure no one was following her, and then she ducked into an abandoned alley. After turning down another side street, she squatted down behind a parked car, put her head in her hands, and focused on breathing in and out to calm her nerves.

She had harmed humans and *Feiru* alike as part of her cover ID over the last two years. Be it scouting a location, gathering intelligence, or helping to divert the attention of human authorities. She may not have pulled a trigger or detonated a bomb, but she was just as responsible as every other cog in the network. She had justified her actions because her end goal was to dismantle the Federation League. In the last few months, she'd finally pinpointed how to do it.

FROZEN DESIRES

If she could take down Harry Watkins, she believed the organization would start to crumble, creating a weakness her superiors from the *Feiru* Liaison office in Mexico City could use and pounce upon.

Watkins had been training Fed League members on how to select AMT-related targets, how to scout out locations, and finally, how to set successful arson fires without getting caught. But he was much more than just a mercenary paid to train a group of haphazard recruits. She was fairly confident he had a much bigger client bankrolling him, a client she wanted to identify.

Over the last few months, she'd studied the man's habits and even learned the names of some of his closest contacts. With a final push, Sabrina should be able to find out the information she needed to end this assignment. Yet because of Watkins's latest target, she was going to have to up her game and make her final play sooner than she had anticipated.

The reason? In less than a week, Watkins planned to set off a bomb at an elementary school during the day, while the children were still in class.

Sabrina felt tears prick her eyes and she took a deep breath. As the death tally rose, it became harder and harder to rationalize her actions. The death of an elderly *Feiru* woman and several young restaurant workers had shaken her up in recent weeks, and she knew the death of so many children would be her tipping point.

She rubbed her eyes and lifted her head from her hands. There was only one way for her to save the school and get the information she needed about Watkins. She would just have to take a few more risks and make her final move.

If done right, she should be able to stay in her undercover role for at least this week. However, once she foiled the plan to bomb the school, Watkins would quickly be on her ass and she would have to flee.

It wasn't a matter of "if" she could do it—she had to find a way to make it work.

With a last deep breath, Sabrina stood up. She would force herself to go through the motions for a little longer. She would scout the school and file her report, but then she needed to reach out and set up a secret meeting with her superior from the *Feiru* Liaison office. She only had five days to put her operation in place and execute it. She couldn't afford to wait another day.

Sabrina moved to the corner where the alley opened out onto the street and checked to make sure no one had followed her. The coast clear, she went back out on the main street and headed toward the nearby elementary school.

~~*

Once upon a time, Jorge Salazar had had friends, responsibilities, and even a woman he had wanted more than his own life. But then his latent ability had appeared nine months ago, and he'd learned that he was a Shadow-Shifter.

After that, his life had gone to hell.

Betrayal by the woman he loved? Check. Being kidnapped and tortured into working for a sociopath who called herself the Collector? Check.

Hell, about the only thing that hadn't happened to him was castration.

But thanks to some help from DEFEND—an activist group fighting to bring down the Asylums for Magical Threats' prison system for elemental magic users—he'd found a way to escape the Collector, at least for a little while.

The Collector woman had kidnapped his sister and had used her as leverage, making him do things that would haunt him until he died. But a few days ago, DEFEND had rescued his sister, also allowing him to escape. However, his sister's safety had come at a price—he had to agree to track down one of his old colleagues, a man named Harry Watkins, and stop the bastard from setting off any more arson fires.

While the Collector's people would only have noticed his absence a few hours ago, he didn't have much time to carry out his task. The Collector didn't like losing any of her assets, and anyone who tried to escape was hunted down and killed. To date, only two people had ever managed to escape her clutches and avoid death.

Jorge's odds didn't look good.

But he was determined to take care of Watkins before the Collector's soldiers found him. To do that, he needed information from the man in front of him, but his former colleague and friend was being less than helpful.

Jorge pressed his arm more firmly against the man's neck. "You owe me your life, Dylan. Tell me about the next fire, and I'll leave you alone. If you don't, then you'll find out firsthand why I was kicked out of the Fed League."

Dylan merely glared at him.

Jorge gave the man a shake before pinning him back up against the wall. "Don't push your luck. We might've been friends once, but I have a debt to pay, and you know how much importance I put on paying my debts in full. I need to know about Watkins's plans."

Dylan looked him dead in the eye and said nothing. After a long moment, he finally opened his mouth and said, "If you know

Watkins, then you know what he'll do to me if I tell you anything."

"Then I'd suggest you tell me and disappear. Changes are coming that you aren't going to like, and listening to my advice will save your ass for the second time in as many years."

Dylan scrutinized his face, and Jorge had to give him credit. The man was cool under pressure.

But Jorge had worked with the man for nearly a year before he'd left the Fed League, and he knew that Dylan only stayed because he had nowhere else to go.

Maybe a suggestion would prod him to reveal Watkins's next target. "Listen, soon Watkins won't be anyone's problem. Until I take care of him, go back to the US. Find a job, go to college, or, hell, live on a friend's couch for all I care. The Fed League is starting to crumble. Do you really want to be around when it does? The *Feiru* High Council isn't going to treat any of you lightly."

His old friend looked unimpressed. "Tell me why you were kicked out, and then I'll believe your message is serious."

"You wouldn't believe me if I told you."

Dylan managed to shrug a shoulder despite Jorge's grip. "Well, then, we're at an impasse because I'm not telling you anything. Despite everything we've gone through, you just vanished without a fucking word."

Jorge hadn't had a choice, but he didn't have time to explain the Collector and her methods. "Whether you believe me or not, contacting you would've endangered your life. And the longer you linger here with me now, the greater the chance you'll find out why I kept my distance."

"Do you know what they say happened to you?"

"I really couldn't give a flying fuck."

Dylan ignored him. "They say you switched sides, and were spying for the AMT Oversight Committee."

"And what makes you think that I didn't?"

"You hated the AMT for torturing your cousin and driving him insane. There's no way you would've helped those bastards."

This was taking too long. He wasn't about to stab his former friend, so Jorge decided to take a chance. "I would kill myself before I helped the AMT, you're right. But I didn't leave by choice. I was forced out. You know the rule about no Fed League member being allowed to have magic?" Dylan nodded. "Well, I sort of inherited some strange abilities, and they wanted me gone."

"Yeah, and I learned how to breath under water. Come on, Jorge, tell me the truth."

What did he have to lose? The Collector would find him sooner or later and kill him. He may as well reveal his powers to one of the few people he'd called a friend. "Fine, asshole. Have you ever heard of a Shadow-Shifter?"

Dylan shook his head. "No."

Considering the stories about his kind had been outlawed by the *Feiru* High Council decades ago, Dylan's answer didn't surprise him.

Jorge could only shift once every twenty-four hours, but he knew from overhearing conversations between Fed League members yesterday that Watkins wasn't due to strike for nearly a week. He could sacrifice one day of not being able to use his abilities if it meant he could find out enough information to help him come up with a plan.

He raised his free arm and said, "Well, they can do this."

He concentrated, relaxing the muscles in his free arm, and started to imagine each cell breaking down. The more he visualized the breakdown of his arm, the more transparent it became until there was a jolt of pain that flashed through his entire body, leaving his arm nothing but a dark, shadowy mist.

At first, Dylan said nothing. But when Jorge drew the shadowy mist tightly together in the shape of his arm and willed it solid, his friend finally said, "Holy shit, Jorge. We all know about elemental magic, but since when do superhero-type powers exist?"

He resisted a sigh and ignored his question. "Now that I've proven the reason I was kicked out, you're going to tell me everything you know about Watkins's upcoming target, and then get the fuck out of Mexico."

Dylan kept staring at his arm. At this rate, he wouldn't get any information. "Dylan, look at me." At first, his former friend didn't do anything. But after giving his old friend a shake, Dylan met his eyes and Jorge continued. "Tell me about the target."

"Well, the rumor is that Watkins is targeting an elementary school."

"I need more than a rumor."

"I do the science stuff, and help with making the bombs. Watkins doesn't tell me anything except how powerful he wants the explosive. I have to rely on rumors for what else is going on."

In the past, everyone who had worked on an assignment had known all the details. Things must have changed in the last nine months. "How confident are you of this rumor?"

Dylan shrugged a shoulder. "Pretty confident. The two people who let it slip have worked in the planning stages in the past with Watkins. I see no reason for them to lie to me."

Despite Dylan's stupidity in staying with the Fed League, he was a lousy liar. That was the reason he'd been assigned the task of bomb maker. Jorge decided he was telling the truth. "So, when is this all supposed to happen?"

"The current target date is five days from now. The bomb should go off in the mid-morning."

"And you didn't think twice about this?"

Dylan's face became serious. "You used to work with the Fed League too, Jorge. You know that if you don't do what they ask, they find a way to make you do it. Making a bomb for some faceless kids is better than seeing my friends tortured in front of me."

Usually the Fed League tortured family, but Dylan didn't have any; his friends meant everything to him.

Jorge had forgotten about that, and he had a split second feeling of guilt for abandoning one of his closest friends. But then he remembered the debt he still owed Aislinn and Neena—the two co-leaders of DEFEND—and he focused. "Which is why heeding my warning and getting the hell away from here is all the better. Maybe you can convince some of your friends to go back to the States with you."

"And what about you, Jorge? What're you going to do?"

"I'm going to stop Watkins, no matter the cost."

Dylan eyed him. "Well, if you make it out alive, you can find me in Houston under the alias Dylan Riker. If you buy me a few beers, maybe I'll forgive you for leaving me."

After his time with the Collector, Jorge had forgotten about friendship. He wanted to say he'd look his old friend up, but he wasn't about to give him false hope. "If I somehow make it out of this alive, I'll consider it. But I won't make any promises."

Dylan studied his face. "You may have ditched me without a word, but if you're in serious trouble, then just ask for my help, and you've got it."

Jorge released his friend and shook his head. "No. The best way you can help me is to give me the address of the next target and then get your ass out of here."

As Dylan stared at him, Jorge started to feel uncomfortable. But just as he was about to repeat his request, Dylan spoke up. "All right. But if I hear that you finish this alive and don't come see me, I'll kick your ass."

The corner of Jorge's mouth ticked up. "I would say that you don't stand a chance, but somehow I don't think that would make a difference."

Dylan grinned. "Good thing you realize that. Now, do you have something to write with or a phone to take notes? Here's the address."

As Jorge punched the address into his phone, it was almost as if the last nine months hadn't happened.

Almost.

==================

Shadow of Temptation

Available Now

For exclusive content and updates, sign up for my newsletter at:
http://www.jessiedonovan.com

Author's Note

Chichen Itza is a real place in Southern Mexico. I spent about six hours there, and if not for the heat, I would have stayed longer. I highly recommend you visit it someday. However, I did take a few artistic liberties with the place. While the observatory building is real, visitors can no longer go up the stairs to the main structure. When I started writing the story, I had read old accounts of people climbing to the top. Imagine my surprise when I saw it in person and noticed it was roped off! Also, I have no idea of the actual security of the place. There are security guards and lots of vendors hawking wares, but the rest is my invention. However, I did see some vendors sneaking in and out through the jungle rather than the main entrance, which is what inspired my characters to do the same.

Marco is from Colombia, so I had to rely on my brother-in-law's brother (who is Colombian and still lives in Colombia) to help me with the endearment of *"cariño"*. (Thanks Fernando!) Any mistakes in its usage, however, are entirely my own fault.

I owe a huge debt to my friend and critique partner, Jayelle Anderson. Not only did she whip the beginning of this book into shape, she has become a great friend who loves geeky stuff as much as I do. Thanks, dearie!

I'm also grateful for my editor, Virginia Cantrell of Hot Tree Editing. She went above and beyond when it came to pointing out the tiny inconsistencies I never would have spotted. Becky Johnson—the lady master of Hot Tree Editing—is also fabulous. A big thank you to Becky and her team of beta-readers for the final polish!

I also need to give a big thank you to Clarissa Yeo of Yocla Designs for giving me another beautiful cover.

And Wendy Lynn Clark proved yet again that she is an awesome beta-reader.

Lastly, I want to thank you, the reader. I have been blown away by the love for *Blaze of Secrets* and my crazy, unique world. I write for you all, and if you ever want to contact me, feel free. I love to hear your thoughts!

ABOUT THE AUTHOR

Jessie Donovan wrote her first story at age five, and after discovering *The Dragonriders of Pern* series by Anne McCaffrey in junior high, she realized people actually wanted to read stories like those floating around inside her head. From there on out, she was determined to tap into her over-active imagination and write a book someday.

After living abroad for five years and earning degrees in Japanese, Anthropology, and Secondary Education, she buckled down and finally wrote her first full-length book. While that story will never see the light of day, it laid the world-building groundwork of what would become her debut paranormal romance, *Blaze of Secrets*.

Jessie loves to interact with readers, and when not traipsing around some foreign country on a shoestring, can often be found on Facebook and Twitter. Check out her pages below:

http://www.facebook.com/JessieDonovanAuthor
http://www.twitter.com/jessiedauthor

And don't forget to sign-up for her newsletter to receive sneak peeks and inside information. You can sign-up on her website:

http:///www.jessiedonovan.com

19056464R00207

Printed in Poland
by Amazon Fulfillment
Poland Sp. z o.o., Wrocław